THE SUN ROSE IN PARIS

PORTRAITS IN BLUE-BOOK ONE

PENNY FIELDS–SCHNEIDER

PFS

COPYRIGHT

Love Books Set in Paris?

Sign up to Penny Fields-Schneider's newsletter and claim a list of all time favourite books set in Paris plus a link to her short story, *The Young Guitarist,* inspired by Picasso's famous painting, *The Old Guitarist.*

CONTENTS

PART I
BON VOYAGE!

CHAPTER 1

*S*electing his finest filbert, Jack carefully applied a touch of the palest orange to the lamp-post on the scene before him. Although minuscule, its impact was immediate. Glittering sunlight bounced off the iron post and Jack smiled with pleasure. Turning blank canvases into life-like scenes was his passion. Although he preferred scenes which included people, this painting had been more enjoyable than he'd anticipated. Requested by his mother ages ago, it was his gift to her and Dad for their silver wedding anniversary which was now only two weeks away. She'd specifically asked him to paint this spot on the Yarra River, the stretch between Chapel and River Streets. It had always been a family favourite. Jack had a lifetime's memories of rambling along the river's broad banks. Sunday picnics with family friends, games of cricket on the wide grassy verge, and more recently, the weekly walk to monitor the construction of the Church Street Bridge which now gave the residents of South Yarra direct access into Melbourne's city streets.

Jack had started the painting three months ago. However, the demands of his final school year, what with examinations, farewells, the annual graduates' dinner and the endless whirl of parties, had proved distracting, and the almost-completed canvas had been neglected. Two events prompted him to put the final embellishments into the scene.

Firstly, his mother's hint she would like to have the picture framed and hung on the dining room wall above the fireplace for the eve of her anniversary dinner to surprise his father. That meant it had to be delivered to the framer by the end of the week.

Secondly, and of greater consequence, was the present Jack had received at his birthday dinner, last Wednesday night. A thrill of excitement ran through him as he glanced at the wallet sitting on the mantelpiece for the hundredth time. The gift exceeded anything he could ever have imagined his parents giving him, and he wondered how his mother had kept it a secret.

The evening had begun like all his birthdays. As he liked—a quiet family dinner of roast chicken and baked potatoes followed by chocolate cream cake, which had been his favourite since he was a child. Throughout the main course, Jack had been conscious of a change in his mother's behaviour. Talkative and giggling after every sentence, she'd clearly been excited about something.

'Jack, you've grown up so much. And now you have finished school forever. Finally, a man,' she'd prattled, barely pausing. Her nervous chatter made sense when, towards the end of the meal, his father had cleared his throat as if to make an important announcement, and then changing his mind, he'd reached to the buffet to produce a large envelope which he passed across the table.

'Your mother and I thought you might enjoy this, Jack. Happy birthday, son.'

Intrigued, Jack looked from his father to his mother before slitting the envelope open under their watchful gaze. Their excitement was palpable as he slid out a black leather wallet which, on opening, revealed a shining grey folder, its cover grandiosely embossed with a stately emblem. The *Ormonde*.

Marian could contain herself no longer. 'Jack, the *Ormonde* is leaving for London on the eighteenth of January! We thought you would like an adventure now school is over. Meet Aunt Elizabeth and

Uncle Robert. They have always longed for you to visit them. It would be wonderful for you to see London!'

'Wow, thanks! Thank-you! Amazing,' he'd stuttered, barely comprehending the sudden change in direction his life was about to take.

To sail across the world was beyond imagining, and his first thoughts had been for the opportunities to paint the trip would provide. Increasingly, he enjoyed drawing scenes of daily events, and over the past few months, he'd gone down to the banks of the Yarra at every opportunity, sketchbook in hand, observing the gatherings—yacht crews training, families picnicking, couples walking along the broad banks, and with rapid flourishes, he'd brought them to life on his pages with charcoal or the small set of oils he had recently purchased. An activity under threat, as he was repeatedly reminded by his father.

'You may as well paint while you still can,' he'd said to Jack more than once, during Jack's final year of school. 'There won't be much time for dabbling once you start work.'

The two months ago, the pressure took another turn when his father came home with the news he'd landed Jack a cadetship at Goldsbrough and Mort, the place he'd worked for three decades. 'It will be a springboard for wonderful opportunities, Jack. Set you up for a secure future.'

Soon after, he'd encouraged Jack to join him at the office on Saturday mornings so he could meet the team and get a feel for the work. It had been awful.

Jack felt like a noose was dangling before his eyes, about to be slipped over his head and slowly tightened. He could not explain why his throat clenched and his breathing quickened every time he'd thought about a career at Goldsbrough Mort & Co. And there was no way work would interfere with his painting, surely?

Jack knew his mother sensed his apprehension about the job. He'd heard whispered conversations between his parents late in the evenings. One morning, he was about to enter the dining room for breakfast when he heard his mother tell William not to rush things: Jack would have plenty of time to go to the office after the New Year; they ought to let him have a good break beforehand. Silently, Jack had appreciated his mother's understanding, and suspected it was her concern for him that had prompted the ticket to London. She wouldn't have allowed him travel across the world unless driven by deeper concerns.

He was to leave at the end of January and return in mid-July: six months to see sights most Australian lads could only dream about: London Tower, Buckingham Palace, Big Ben. The very idea of the journey was fantastic. Like someone else's life. And now, he had so much to do!

Within forty-eight hours Jack discarded the remnants of his school year: exercise books, pencil cases, his school diary—most of it into the bin. He'd rid his wardrobe of all traces of blue shirts, ties, sport's gear and his dreaded blazer. And in between the cleaning and sorting, he worked on this painting. It was as though every loose end in his life was being tied up in preparation for The Big Trip.

While many of the boys at school might object to the thought of staying with elderly relatives, Jack did not mind. Aunt Elizabeth had been an invisible presence for his whole life. His mother regularly spoke of her sister. They'd been inseparable as young women, until Marian had met William, an Australian working in the London office of Goldsbrough Mort & Co; Australia's largest wool exporting business. She'd told Jack how his father had captivated her with his passion for wool clips and knowledge of shipping lines. How excited she been when he'd encouraged her to return with him to Australia; a land with wonderful weather, opportunity and prosperity.

Religiously, she and Elizabeth had exchanged monthly letters for over two decades, and like clockwork, a parcel wrapped in brown paper, tied with string and covered with stamps arrived for Jack's birthday. Always, they contained a hand knitted jumper, a book and a pound note. Under his mother's direction, Jack had dutifully responded to each with a neatly written thank-you letter and a photograph of himself wearing the jumper.

Jack was amazed his father had agreed to this trip. Always kind but nonetheless remote, William was preoccupied with the demands of his job, a dedication which had been rewarded by a meteoric rise through the ranks of Goldsbrough Mort & Co's finance department to reach the lofty height of Chief Investment Adviser. The accompanying wage rises meant he and Marian could afford this beautiful home in South Yarra. Fixated on work rather than pleasure, Jack had never known his father to have a day away from the office, much less consider an extended holiday.

As Jack had his entered senior school years he'd tried to make decisions about his future. His father had studied business finance at Melbourne University and suggested Jack might do the same, after all, he'd done well at mathematics. But Jack could think of nothing worse. However, with no clear direction, he'd been cornered when William announced the cadetship he'd organised.

To strive for power or success was not in Jack's nature, nor did he feel a flicker of excitement for any particular career. He wasn't drawn to pursue wealth, like those at school who bragged they'd be million-aires before they turned thirty, nor did he seek to join the military; be a hero like others, who were inspired by the legendary pursuits of the ANZACs in The Great War.

Jack's dreams for his future were simple and hardly the stuff of conversations, so he kept them to himself. Dreams about having a family of his own. Being a father. Living in a house filled with children who'd run to him, open-armed, when he arrived home each night; lifting them high onto his shoulders.

The interactions of families on trains or in the park had long fasci-nated Jack. He was intrigued by the sight of parents playing with their children, imagining what their lives must be like. He loved the sound of laughter when little children were being chased, or tickled, or teased. He felt moved to sketch scenes of families on the banks of the Yarra: fathers telling stories to children who listened with tilted heads, parents clutching the hands of their toddlers as they peered over the edge of the Yarra's bank to see the ducks hiding among the reeds. Perhaps his dreams were borne of being an only child, or maybe he longed for a relationship which had never existed between himself and his busy father?

As Jack returned his attention to the painting in front of him, he applied delicate touches of white against the soft sweeps of blue. Flashing sunlight now danced across the water's surface. Appraising the skiff he'd added to the lower right of the canvas, just like those who trained daily on the Yarra in readiness for a regatta, he imagined the bellowing call of the coxswain shouting—'Push for ten!'—urging the crew to row faster.

Jack's thoughts turned to large ships, ancient buildings and historical sites. He wondered how he was going to endure the long weeks ahead, awaiting the day of the *Ormonde*'s departure.

CHAPTER 2

*J*ack's pending trip flung Marian into a whirlwind of activities to prepare for her son's excursion 'home'.

'Home! What on earth do you mean, Mum?'

'Home of we British people. *She* is Australia's mother country.'

'Since when was Australia a baby? And if *she* is our mother, she needs to be more careful. What sort of mother leaves her child on the other side of the world?' Jack teased, feigning ignorance of Great Britain's colonising history that had claimed nations across the world. He was all too familiar with Anglophilic attitudes and the endless homage paid to the King and all things British, as though anything Australia had to offer was inferior to the cultured world of Great Britain. Like many of the boys at school, Jack was persuaded by the arguments of James Scullin, the leader of the Opposition Party, who believed it was time Australia became independent, rather than cling to the apron strings of a nation on the opposite side of the globe.

Notwithstanding his inability to identify with it as 'home', Jack was excited to be traveling across the world to visit England and fell in with Marian's preparations. She insisted he accompany her into the city, and dragged him up and down the streets, from Buckley and Nunn to Myer, Melbourne's largest department stores, not happy until she had purchased five new sets of trousers and matching shirts, socks and ties. Still not satisfied, she then led him to a menswear shop in Little Collins St and persuaded the salesman to wade through his storeroom's left-over winter stock, from which he returned bearing a woollen overcoat complete with a fur-lined collar and matching scarf.

'You have to be joking, Mum,' Jack laughed, when she insisted he try it on. She must be mad; Melbourne was in the midst of a heat wave, the daily temperature had exceeded one hundred degrees for three days in a row, for the past three days.

Marian was not to be dissuaded. 'Laugh you may, but you'll know you're alive when your nose turns blue and your ears are stinging,' she retorted, reminding him London would still be feeling the icy chill of the northern hemisphere winter during his visit.

∼

William had surprised Jack by arriving home from work one evening wrestling a large parcel wrapped in brown paper. Upon opening, it revealed a tan suitcase bearing shiny brass locks and a plate engraved 'J. W. Tomlinson' in ornate lettering. Swept up in the excitement of Jack's adventure, William had become unusually talkative, reminiscing about the crossings he had undertaken, first when he'd left London to the newly federated nation in 1901, and then making the return journey in 1904 for a twelve-month stint, where he'd been tasked to develop contacts for Goldsbrough Mort & Co and in addition, he'd met Marian.

'You'll have to be careful on the ship, son. There will be all types, and not all savoury. You need to stay within the first-class area. Pick-pockets and swindlers can appear in any shape and size and they don't necessarily look like they are hard up. Many a man with a suit and tie will try to take advantage of you, and... well... the young girls can be a bit... worldly and all.' William stumbled a little in his explanation, but Jack understood he was being warned to keep some distance between himself and the lower classes, particularly those of the female persua-sion who may take advantage of his youth and social position.

~

While the day of departure had seemed an eternity away on the eve of Jack's birthday, time quickly passed, what with purchases and packing, tidying and farewells.

His mother was determined Jack should have a bon voyage dinner on the eve of his departure, much to Jack's embarrassment.

'I'm only going for six months,' he argued. 'I'll be back before anyone even notices I've gone.'

'Rubbish,' she said. 'You have to have a party. It's not every day a young man heads off to the other side of the world. We'll invite Jimmy and Frank. And the Fitzgibbons' girls.' The former were class-mates and, more recently, study mates as they'd prepared for their matriculation exams. They had voted Jack's house to be the quietest location for serious study, with Marian's continuous supply of biscuits and cakes an added bonus. The truth was the three boys had spent more time playing gin rummy than studying; however, they'd all agreed their exam performance would be vastly improved by adopting a calm attitude, rather than jamming their brains with facts, figures and stress.

The Fitzgibbons' girls were sisters, and as the nearest neighbours they had befriended Jack when he first arrived on Copelen Street as a twelve-year-old. Their own home was enormous, a mansion, with a full-sized tennis court in the backyard. Sarah, who was just a couple of years younger than Jack, had occasionally asked him to join them for tennis games on weekends when she needed an extra player.

Really, though, Jack preferred his own company. While quite popular with the boys at Melbourne Grammar, often accepting birthday invitations or going to movies in the city, he did not overly seek entertainment, preferring to spend his weekends at home with his sketch-book and paintbrushes.

The dinner had been fun, Jack could not deny. His mother, always a little nervous about catering for guests, had enlisted Nina, the old Aboriginal woman who had helped with the housework three days a week for the past six years, to assist.

'How about roast beef, dumplings and then a nice pie, Master?'

This was her pet name for Jack, even though he hated it. Her ancient eyes sparkled as she teased him about his strong muscles and rapid growth; barely six years earlier he'd been a skinny little weed and now he was a sturdy rivergum! Jack laughed. Better to be described as a rivergum than a beanstalk, which was the description the boys at school gave his slender six-foot three-inch frame.

Nina's apple and rhubarb pies were second to none and in response to praise, she always said they ought to be good, she had been cooking them at the mission since she was a ten-year-old. Over the years, Jack had occasionally asked Nina about 'the mission', but she just shook her head. 'Too sad, Jack, too sad. Leave it be.' As a result, he knew very little about Nina other than she'd been separated from her own family as a young child and grew up at the Lake Tyers Mission in eastern Victoria; she lived with her husband, Dan, who was employed as a boilermaker with the railways; she always hummed quietly to herself as she worked; and she was quick with her broad smile and teasing words for him.

Following the lovely dinner, Jack and his friends played charades, laughing hysterically as they took turns to masquerade scenarios of Jack navigating London—lost at the railway station, a chance meeting with the king, and being arrested by a London 'bobby' for failing to hold his spoon with his pinkie extended. Finally, the night ended. Wishing him well, the girls insisted he send them postcards from London, which they knew he wouldn't, and demanded he bring back gifts from Harrods—expensive ones—or at the very least, a Harrods bag for them to show off.

It was after ten when they kissed Jack on the cheek, the boys shook hands, and at last, he turned in to bed, where he slept restlessly, rolling over every half hour to look at his bedside clock until eventually, darkness gave way to the shadowy forms of daybreak.

CHAPTER 3

Rising with the sun, Jack quickly dressed and then paced the house, waiting for his parents to rise. He was surprised at how his usual activities, like pouring a glass of water or collecting the milk bottles on the front porch, had a sense of finality, as if he were leaving home forever. His suitcase was packed and standing by the front door, and his only concern was to get to Port Melbourne as early as possible. Fortunately, Jack's parents were equally keen for an early start, hoping they'd be able to avoid the congested roads, and to park William's newly acquired Model T Ford within walking distance of the ship.

As they inched towards Station Pier, the gleaming white decks of the *Ormonde* rose into view, dwarfing the buildings surrounding the docks. The previous Sunday, Jack had accompanied his parents on a 'dry run' to the pier so his father could familiarise himself with the route through the city. Then, the roads around the port had been empty. Today it was an altogether different place. Thronging crowds; thousands of people forming lines like ants following a sugar trail, converged onto the pier from all directions. The atmosphere was that of a fair and the excitement, contagious. Shouting, laughing, jostling passengers of all shapes, sizes and nations swarmed towards the ship's embarkment office to have their tickets checked and collect boarding passes.

While waiting for William to park the car, Jack paced, impatient for the journey to begin, although on noticing his mother's quiet manner and her worried expression deepening as the time of the ship's departure grew closer, he attempted to look a little sorrowful for her benefit. Shouts, wolf whistles and hoo-roos drifted across the pier from above, and looking up, he saw people leaning over the ship's rails, waving and calling down.

'They are from Sydney; boarded two days earlier,' Marian told him, explaining how from Melbourne, the ship would collect passengers in Adelaide, then Fremantle, before finally departing Australian shores. Jack's heartbeat accelerated, his elation growing by the second. He looked across at the pier, an enormous double-storeyed structure running along the water's edge for as far as he could see. It was just the type of unusual architecture he loved to draw. A hiss of billowing smoke caught his attention and he watched as a train pulled in alongside the pier's upper level. Occupants spilled out and merged with the pedestrians pouring in from the car park, while on the lower level he could see the staff who serviced the ship rushing in all directions. Goods—food, drinks, linen and heavy cargo required for the six-week journey—were transported onto the ship via the lower storey. Fascinated by the growing crowd, Jack tried not to stare as couples bid emotional farewells and families anxiously regrouped straying children as they prepared for their journey, 'home'. Adding to the colourful environment was the clamour of foreign languages, the broken English of Greeks, Turks and Italians, a reminder of when his father took him to the fish market on the corner of Flinders and Spencer Street. Uniformed stewards in bright blue suits with small box-like caps and brass buttons were everywhere, calling out 'Make way' as they balanced trunks on their shoulders or stacked suitcases onto trolleys, which were skilfully manoeuvred up narrow gangways.

Finally, his father returned and they made their way through the crowds towards the first-class line and Marian grabbed Jack's arm, clinging to him tightly. It was obvious for as much as she tried to be excited for him, her nerves were on edge.

'Mum, it's not the *Titanic*. Stop worrying.' Jack guessed the tragedy of 1912 was at the forefront of her thoughts. Approaching the ship, it seemed to grow in size, and his own logic wondered at the capacity of the massive steel structure to stay afloat, but he refused to succumb to fear. Instead Jack focused on the prospect of traversing the enormous distance between Australia and England, of finally experiencing a real adventure.

~

Shuffling along the line, eventually he and his parents boarded the great ship, brochures and tickets in hand.

'It's like a floating hotel!' his mother exclaimed, relaxing visibly as she admired the ornate interior. 'Much bigger than the *Osterley*'. Jack knew she was referring to the liner she and William had embarked on as newly-weds, over two decades earlier. He suspected from his parents' linked arms, walking the decks of the *Ormonde* had transported them back into the past, to their own great adventure in 1907, when they had crossed the world to a fledgling nation, bursting with hopes and dreams for what their life might bring. He wondered if they were pleased with the results.

Together, they navigated the corridors, passing dining areas, games rooms and saloons as they followed the signs directing them to the first-class suites. Jack's cabin was located on the upper deck, a small room with a single bed and a neat little desk.

'I will be expecting a letter from every port stop,' Marian said, directing Jack's attention to the desk where the ship's stationery, fountain pen, ink and envelopes were neatly set out. She began reading aloud the instructions on how to send a telegram using the vessel's internal communication system, should he need to. However, William interjected.

'There'll be no need to be sending telegrams.' Though he did not say so, Jack knew hefty fees would be attached and, while not a penny-pinching man, William did not believe in wasting money.

'But what if Jack gets ill, William? We'd want to know!'

'Love, if Jack gets ill, the ship's surgeon can worry about him. And if he can't fix him, he will throw him overboard. I suspect then you might get your telegram.'

'William!'

'Mum! Dad's joking. I will be fine!' Jack smiled at his father, appreciating his humour. He always enjoyed the rare moments when William let it show.

The glistening waters of Port Phillip Bay were visible through the small round window. Peering out, Jack could see passengers relaxing, drinks in hand, reclining on the striped chairs scattered around the lower decks.

Leaving the room which would be his for the next six weeks, Jack and his parents wandered around the ship, impressed with the broad promenade, lounge area and smoking room of the B-Deck, which was reserved for the first-class passengers. The dining room was palatial—decorative-timber wall panels, carved and padded chairs, tables covered with white linen and set with silver cutlery, gold-embossed menus printed on small cards beside each dining setting. Turkish rugs lay scattered across the expansive parquet floor and gleaming brass light fittings added to the regal effect. They were amazed to see the installation of modern lifts and equally impressed with the grandly sweeping ornate iron staircases which permitted movement between the various levels.

Suddenly a loud bell chimed across the ship's decks and Jack shivered with excitement, knowing the sound heralded it was time for visitors to disembark. Time for his parents to leave! William again went through the business side of things, ensuring Jack had loose change for tipping porters, which he was to limit to three pence per day, and traveller's cheques to the tune of three pounds, to be rationed at a rate of two shillings per day on his stopovers. Once in England, one pound per week would be wired to the account set up with Barclay's in London, and Mr Jefferson, William's contact in England for his business dealings, would sort Jack out with a London passbook.

Again, Marian reminded Jack to send postcards from each stopover and Jack knew, beyond reassuring his mother he was well, the postcards would be passed around at morning teas amongst her church friends, and then pasted into a scrapbook. One which would be added to a continuing series, chronicling every detail of his life. The first, now yellow with age, opened with the newspaper clipping announcing his birth, and it's pages continued with an array of weights and measures, mile-stones—first smile, first words, first steps—locks of hair and even the first tooth Jack had lost as a five-year-old. The second scrapbook was dedicated to his primary school years and included lists of awards, friendships, birthday parties and school excursions. The third volume memorialised his senior schooling, and as Jack had grown less communicative about his daily life, his mother had relied on school reports and formal invitations to create it. Jack had no doubt a fresh new book would be started, possibly this very day, recording his Great London Adventure.

They finally arrived at the gangway, where friends and relatives bid final farewells before leaving the ship, under the watchful eyes of stewards.

'Bye, Mum,' Jack said, giving his mother a final hug, which predictably set loose the tears she had so carefully restrained for the past twenty minutes.

Frowning at her, William quietly shook Jack's hand with a gruff, 'All the best, son. Have a wonderful time. We'll look forward to your letters.'

Turning sharply, he led Marian down the gangway, where they melted into the thousands of people gathered on the dock. An overwhelming sense of being finally, truly and thrillingly alone swept over Jack as he anticipated the possibilities life might offer, over the coming months.

CHAPTER 4

*A*mbling, Jack watched the stewards and crew as they swept through the ship deck by deck, ensuring all visitors had disembarked and no stowaways were squirrelled away in linen closets, lavatories or guest bedrooms.

A sudden shudder ran through the ship, accompanied by a roar from the crowd, indicating the moorings had been released. The journey was beginning! Looking back at the shore, Jack already felt disassociated from the thousands of people thronging there, his parents amongst them, calling '*bon voyage!*', waving and throwing streamers towards the ship. However, compelled by ceremony, he joined the passengers gathered at the rails and waved as the land-bound crowd receded into the distance.

Soon, a subtle rocking sensation could be felt, and Jack knew they'd reached open waters. He watched the *Alivna*, the small pilot cutter returning to shore, having completed its job of transporting the *Ormonde* from the sheltered waters of Port Phillip Bay into the Tasman Sea. The massive ship was no longer an extension of all things *terra firma*, but rather an independent entity, solely responsible for the safe passage and comfort of over two thousand people as it chugged its way on the second leg of its twelve-thousand-mile journey.

~

Keen to explore the ship, Jack retraced the steps he and his parents had taken, revisiting dining rooms, decks and bars. Finding a quiet spot at the very front of C-Deck, Jack leaned against the rails. There, he was soon joined by dozens of shrieking gulls and a lone cormorant, none of which showed any fear of humans. Intrigued by the birds he could see, swooping into white-capped breakers, Jack searched the depths of the blue water with interest, spotting shadowy figures gliding below the shimmering surface.

Jack did not waste any time weighing up whether to venture into the lower decks, despite his father's warnings. While he was usually obedient to his parent's wishes, William's request he remain on the upper decks seemed unnecessarily fussy and Jack's conscience did not so much as prickle as he ventured down the iron stairs to wander around the perimeter of the lower level.

He found the second-class service, much like his own, though not quite so grandiose: tables in the dining room set with white tablecloths, silver candelabras, salt and pepper shakers providing ornamentation. Again, the buffet at the end of the room was loaded with petite cakes and iced biscuits for passengers to access, as they wished. Already, tables were starting to fill with excited couples and families relaxing into their new life at sea.

Continuing down the stairwell onto the third-class deck, Jack felt self-conscious. He could feel eyes upon him and, knowing his neat clothing stood out, resolved next time he ventured down he would abandon his tie. In fact, he might just leave off with the tie altogether, other than at dinner time.

Not only did clothing separate him, but Jack recognised a distinctive change in the atmosphere of the crowded third-class decks. Noisy laughter rang through the air; voices called to look at this and that; mothers roared in loud voices, 'Get back here at once!' and 'By golly, if I have to call you again, you'll get a thrashing!' to excited children racing around with new-found playmates, thrilled by the extraordinary change their lives had taken.

As always, Jack was intrigued by the relationships between parents and their children. He studied the face of a frantic mother, whose expression transformed from tearful anxiety to relief as she was reunited with a crying toddler she was sure had fallen overboard. Nodding 'hello' to a friendly looking young father who was holding a small girl tightly, Jack smiled at the white curls bobbing around each side of her face like elongated sausages, the bright green bow in her hair a match for the green smock she was wearing. The image was completed by a lady sitting off to the side, an adult reflection of the little girl, their matching outfits no doubt specially made for this important day of departure. The father pointed out the hungry seagulls swooping on to the tables, then offered a crust to entice the squawking birds closer, and Jack marvelled at his look of satisfaction. And then there was a fresh-faced couple clinging together, perhaps newlyweds on their honeymoon, and it seemed as though for them, the gently rocking ship held only themselves. A group of men, whose tanned faces and chambray shirts indicated they were rural workers, stood in a tight group at the end of the open deck. Ash spilled from the continuous burning of expertly rolled cigarettes, creating a swirling cloud of blue smoke around them. Their banter, punctuated by deep laughter, revealed an easy camaraderie had already developed between the men, and Jack suddenly felt alone and envious.

As much as he enjoyed the scenes around him, Jack felt uncomfortable on the third-class deck. Not the discomfort of feeling superior, as perhaps his father might have experienced. Rather, Jack felt like an outsider who did not belong, an uninvited guest at someone's party. As he was about to leave, the young father looked up and smiled. 'G'day, mate... Beautiful day.'

Jack nodded in agreement, unsure of himself; however, the man persisted.

'Hope it stays this way. It's going to be hard keeping this little possum indoors for six weeks if the weather turns on us.'

'Yes. I imagine it would be,' Jack replied, taking in the contented expression of the man holding the little girl in tanned, muscular arms,

Jack smiled. This was exactly the sort of sketch Jack loved, and he decided he would return, next time with charcoal and drawing paper, or perhaps his traveller's oils and the postcard-sized boards stored in a bulging canvas rucksack in his suitcase.

CHAPTER 5

*J*ack developed a comfortable routine over the next few days, rising early and heading to the dining room for porridge and toast before taking a walk around the various decks. Faithfully, he sent postcards at the Adelaide and Fremantle stopovers, knowing his mother would be waiting for their arrival, simultaneously thrilled and reassured to receive news of his journey.

Determined to experience all the ship's features, Jack settled into comfortable chairs in the quiet of the smoking room, where he glanced through the books in the ship's well-stocked library, joined in the shuttlecock tournaments on the upper deck and drank hot chocolate in each of the dining rooms. His favourite pastime, though, was to prop down on a step, small table or ledge with his sketchbook, his hand swiftly moving across crisp white sheets and bringing blank pages to life with the scenes around him: porters balancing drinks on silver trays on the first-class deck; couples leaning against the rails, staring into the distance; sailors busy at work.

As he'd anticipated, the lower-class decks were particularly rich for subject material. Most days he ventured down, sketchbook and charcoals in hand, increasingly feeling more relaxed amongst the noisy passengers. Quiet and inconspicuous, he'd set himself up to draw the children as they hovered playfully around him, their smiling mothers clustered on white deck chairs nearby to watch. He captured outlines of men as they stood together smoking or gathered around a table to play cards, clearly relishing the enforced break from employment and excitedly sharing their dreams of a bright future for themselves and their families.

Peter, the young father he'd met on the day of the ship's departure, was happy for Jack to sketch him and his little girl, Gretchen, as they sat at a small table feeding crumbs of bread to the seagulls. Chatting while he sketched, Jack learned they were travelling to Stockholm, where Peter's parents needed help to run their dairy.

The slow and friendly pace of life at sea suited Jack. He enjoyed chatting to the fellow travellers who stopped to watch him draw, admiring his techniques and returning to view the progress of his work. Numerous passengers offered payment, requesting he create charcoal sketches of their children or wishing to purchase one of the postcard-sized oils he'd set aside to dry. For some, it was to add to their own memorabilia; for others, perhaps because they respected his impressive talent. Jack, however, laughingly shook his head. He wasn't a professional artist. It was a hobby and he happily gave away the sketches, pleased to see them find homes where they would be appreciated.

When an ancient-looking lady sat on the settee to his left, the deep wrinkles layering her neck decked with strings of colourful beads, her unnaturally red coils of hair looped, pinned and topped with an enormous feathery hat, which looked like it descended from another century, Jack was immediately fascinated. His hand moved across his page, outlining her forehead, the vertical shaft deviating sharply at eye level, her nose an interesting projection with both a severe angle and exceptional length, as though an acute triangle had been planted onto the centre of her face.

'What on earth do you think you are doing, young man?'

Jack was so engrossed in the lines on his page he did not immediately realise the sharp voice was directed at him, until, glancing up, he saw two black orbs penetrating the heavy layers of skin-folds and piercing him.

Their intensity caused him to stammer. 'I'm sorry, ma'am... I didn't think you'd mind.' Jack quickly closed his book and put away his charcoal.

'Well, you were most certainly mistaken. I came here to sit in peace, not be gawped at by an idiot with nothing better to do than scribble the morning away.'

It was a lesson learned, following which Jack politely asked people if they would mind him sketching them or their children at play before proceeding with his drawings. Very few said 'no'.

CHAPTER 6

'You're very good, you know.' The cheerful exclamation came from above, interrupting Jack's focus as he created a misty horizon from his palette of grey-blue tones in the calm stillness of the early morning on his seventh day at sea. 'You must be a Meldrumite.'

The voice was unfamiliar and Jack looked up, into the inquisitive eyes of a young woman squinting over his shoulder at the painting in front of him. Her fair skin showed signs of sunburn, while her unruly curls floated above her shoulders, resisting her attempt to tame them with a bright green headband.

'No, no... just Jack,' he replied, wondering what on earth a Meldrumite was.

'Well, Just Jack,' she said, 'I am Just Margaret, and I am very pleased to meet you because you are pretty darned good! Is this your sketchbook? Do you mind if I have a look?' Not waiting for a reply, she sat herself beside him and started turning the pages of his well-worn drawing book. Her eyes widened as she looked at the many scenes he'd sketched over the last week.

'Which college did you go to? I'm sure I've never seen you before.'

'Melbourne Grammar,' replied Jack. 'Not many girls allowed there.' He grinned, reckoning she was at least five years older than he, so not chronologically likely to have crossed his path, and, given it was an all-male school, it was downright impossible she'd have attended.

'Not secondary school,' Margaret retorted, feigning exasperation. 'Bloody art college. There are not that many in Melbourne, and I have been to them all at one time or another—a fat lot of good it did me.'

'I've never been to art school,' Jack said with a shake of his head. 'I just draw for fun. Not serious-like.'

'No. No way,' Margaret exclaimed. 'You *are* an artist. You just don't know it yet. These sketches are remarkable. And this...' She waved at the oil he'd been working on. 'You're clearly born to paint.'

Jack laughed at Margaret's outraged expression as she spoke with such authority about his life. As well as passion, her voice betrayed an accent. British? Beyond the Fitzgibbons sisters, and his mother of course, he had little experience with females, especially outgoing older ones, but after the last few days of polite exchanges with various fellow travellers, it felt good to be having a real conversation of sorts.

'So, you paint, too?' Jack enquired.

'Well, it would depend on whom you are talking to,' Margaret said with a wry tone, reaching into the bag slung over her shoulder to retrieve a packet of cigarettes. Without pause, she waved one by way of offer across Jack's face, which he politely declined with a shake of his head, and she continued. 'I think I am okay. Not, however, according to anyone in Melbourne. That is why I am out of there. Too many men with bloody big egos running the show. They all say "paint like this, don't do that".' Margaret waved her hands to the right and left, emphasising opposing demands. 'Then they criticise everything you—tonally inaccurate, colour all wrong, subject not suitable, bloody waffle-waffle...' She trailed off; her expression so despondent Jack had to laugh.

'What is it to you, what they think?' he asked. 'If you like painting, just paint.'

'Well, Just Jack, it isn't so easy. Some of us would like to sell a painting or two. We like to eat. Pay the bills. And to sell paintings, one

26

needs a reputation. And to have a reputation, one needs to be noticed by The Powers That Be. And there lies the problem—the bloody Powers That Be are a collective bunch of idiots with egos so big, you couldn't jump over them even if you had a springboard to launch off.'

Again, Jack could not help laughing at the dramatic image Margaret had described and she looked at him, annoyed.

'It's easy for you, Jack, you're in the club. You are male. They would love you... God, they would love you. You are so raw. They would tell you to change this and adjust that, then they could call you their protégé. You would be fabulously successful and they would bask in the glory, claiming all credit. That is how it goes. Not so easy for me, however. I am a female. F-E-M-A-L-E, and in Australia's art world, there is no respect for women artists.'

Jack listened as he dabbed azure blue onto the board in front of him. He had never had such an entertaining conversation with an adult female, never been so close to a female who smoked and never heard a female use the word 'bloody' so liberally. Furthermore, he'd never had a serious political thought about anything, least of all painting, nor considered art as a means of an income. Not a job for real people. At least, not anyone he knew. Margaret had not finished with her complaints, however, and Jack listened with interest, attempting to adopt a serious expression as she continued.

'Really, what they don't comprehend is Melbourne is a complete backwater. Arguing about form versus function, tonal realism! Huh! And The Powers that Be are a bunch of cheats.'

'Cheats! Strong words,' Jack raised his eyebrows questioningly.

'No, Jack. Listen. They cut women out from any major art contest; Ethel Rix was the obvious winner of the Melbourne Library Art Prize, but the overlooked her instead awarding it to a man who hadn't even met the requirements of the contest, and now, they finally have a decent prize for portraits, but insist the subject must be "a distinguished person". Why, I ask? Who has access to "distinguished" persons? The hobnobs. That's who. I suppose you might know a few.'

'Hey! That's a bit of an assumption. Maybe I do. Maybe I don't. I certainly don't go around painting "distinguished people".'

'Well, anyway,' Margaret forged on, without apology, 'while the whole world has moved on, Australian critics reject modern art. Wouldn't know Cubism or Fauvism if they were bit on the bloody backside by them. Really, anyone who is serious about art will be in Paris.'

'Is that where you're going?' Jack was intrigued.

'Eventually. Sussex first to see my dotty family, followed by a couple of months in London. My cousin Freddie said he was sick to death of hearing me whine about going nowhere, unappreciated, starving and fed up. Told me if I thought I was so bloody good, to get over to London and prove myself. He has a couple of commissions he wants me to do. People's cats, I suppose. He's cat mad; has half a dozen himself. I'll be looking after them while he goes tripping all over England to visit clients, I expect. However, with free accommodation at his flea-ridden bedsit, free art supplies and cheap wine, the offer is too good to pass up; not that he seriously thought I would ever come. You'll have to meet him. He is fabulous. Lived in London for the last ten years and works at the New Burlington Gallery. Paints a bit himself, but not terribly well. More into hobnobbing with artists and sourcing paintings for filthy rich patrons. Organises exhibitions and so forth. More likely carries the paintings for the gallery owners and pins them to the bloody walls.' Margaret laughed with affectionate irreverence for her cousin before she drew back and inhaled deeply from her second cigarette, which she'd just lit off the first, mid-sentence.

Jack grinned back, not sure what to say, or indeed, what to take seriously from this outrageous woman who seemed determined to befriend him.

Together, they walked towards the stairs leading to the first-class deck.

'Ah... so you are up in first class? Would you like to do some painting together? I would love to join your "art class" later this afternoon, perhaps we could try for a sunset scene?'

'Oh, certainly. It would be nice to have someone to paint with.'

'I'm going to watch you, Just Jack, and pinch your tricks. You have no right to draw as well as you do... And you've not even been to art school, you say? Bloody ridiculous!'

Jack shook his head as if to reject Margaret's praise; but could not deny her words pleased him.

Jack's gift for reproduction was a great mystery to the Tomlinson family. He had vivid memories of his early days at Miss Bates' nursery school in East Toorak and of the enticing aroma of the newly opened pastels, the rainbow of coloured rods neatly laid out in little boxes, each wrapped in waxed paper. He'd loved the way they'd felt in his hands, smoothly gliding across crisp white sheets of paper. He'd enjoyed the blending of blues and greens to create glimmering water with colourful fish swimming in the ripples; reds and oranges erupting into dazzling balls of sunshine, high on tree-lined horizons. The compliments had started early and been frequent.

'Jack, how wonderful. Well done. Amazing!' He remembered seeing his first-grade teacher, Miss Tully, showed the school principal his drawings, and they would nod their heads and smile, clearly pleased with his efforts. The principal often applied his coveted purple stamp to the lower right corner of Jack's work—*Excellent Effort*. Over the years numerous teachers had spoken to Marian, advising her Jack's gift for drawing was extraordinary—a talent which should not be ignored.

At home, Jack would sit for hours, reproducing images from the picture books he was introduced to as a young reader, where he showed far more interest in the images than in the words. Often his mother had relayed the difficulty she'd had when Jack was small, trying to encourage him to read. How he'd only ever had eyes for the colour plates, studying every line, refusing to turn the pages until he had gleaned every nuance from the illustration. *'I could climb up that tree, Mummy,'* he would say, or, *'Is that boat going to catch a whale?'* For Marian it had been an ongoing battle to redirect Jack's attention to the written words, which he'd stumble over with cursory interest before returning his attention to the illustrations.

By fourth grade, Jack was borrowing books from the school library with pictures of cars, boats and motorcycles, which he reproduced with extraordinary flair. Quickly, he'd progressed to creating elaborate three-dimensional images—yachts on the river, their sails billowing in the breeze; streetscapes where cars motored along so life-like they appeared to be in motion—and his raw skill for portraiture emerged as he did drawings of anybody who would sit still for him.

As Jack progressed to secondary school, he was introduced to formal art lessons, further developing techniques to create foregrounds, mid-grounds and distance using aerial perspective—faraway hills fading into mauves while distant objects receded in size. His art teacher, quickly recognising he had a student of exceptional talent, worked tirelessly to develop it, although it had to be said, Jack was less interested in being developed and more interested in following his own musings with his pencils. He focussed on replicating, to perfection, objects around him. It became a game to his mates, who would say, 'Draw that car, Jack' or 'Draw Mr Davis.' They enjoyed seeing his pencil moving over the blank pages until objects and people would literally spring forth from nowhere. It was expected he would win first prize at the school art shows and top his high school classes in art prac- tice. Not so in art-theory, however, for Jack never had the slightest inclination to learn about long-dead artists or their works, and the drawing and colour exercises bored him witless.

Marian was always thrilled with Jack's progress, as she was with anything he did, and she'd beam with delight when he was praised or awarded prizes. She would have been very happy for Jack to select Art for his matriculation, but William had been adamant it was not a real- istic subject choice.

'He needs to be positioning himself for his future,' William had insisted. 'Science; mathematics; subjects which lead to real jobs. Lord knows, Goldsbrough Mort & Co could use someone with financial skills. Seems as if nobody knows how to add up a column of figures these days.'

As much as Jack loved any opportunity to paint, he had known to argue with his father was useless. Besides, he actually agreed; men needed good secure jobs to support their families, to buy houses, food, clothing and school fees and to meet medical expenses.

Hence, Jack's artistic skills were relegated to a pastime for a young man with many hours to occupy himself, much in the way another youth might play the piano or violin. A talent to be appreciated, even valued, but which was secondary to the pursuit of a serious career. Jack himself, a conservative by nature, accepted this view. He neither saw himself as an artist nor even remotely entertained the notion an adult male could support himself, much less a family, by drawing and painting.

CHAPTER 7

*J*ack and Margaret began each day by meeting on the second-class deck, gazing at the morning sunrise and discussing the merits of different subjects or which angle they should paint from.

Their chat continued over an omelette, followed by hot buttered toast and cups of tea, sometimes in the second-class dining room, sometimes in the first. Both agreed the food tasted exactly the same on either deck, although the table service in first class did make a nice addition, which Margaret thought she could get used to. During breakfast, they planned the day's painting expedition. To say they 'discussed' these plans would be an overstatement, as invariably Margaret presented an option and Jack, with an easy smile, would pick up his knapsack and follow along, enjoying the company of his fascinating new friend. He'd never experienced painting with a companion or been particularly strategic in planning his drawings. Usually he just drew what inspired him. As they painted Margaret chattered enthusiastically about light, backgrounds, focal points and perspective, and Jack nodded, set up next to her and draw whatever appealed to him. Often, she pointed out technical aspects of his drawings which she found interesting or questionable; however, more often than not, she'd shake her head in amazement.

'Jack, it's not fair. You are so bloody good. I know people who have painted for three decades who can't do what you do,' she complained, watching over his shoulder while he added the finest of details into a scene of the ship's smokestack breathing a misty grey film into the azure sky.

Passers-by cheerfully stepped around the familiar figures of the tall, fair-haired young man and the lively woman wielding pens and brushes across their canvases.

~

The *Ormonde's* stopovers, which allowed for restocking fresh supplies and the boarding of additional passengers, were a source of adventure. As the ship pulled into Colombo, Aden, Port Said, Naples and Toulon, Jack and Margaret hovered at the ready, knapsacks filled with their drawing materials. The ship stewards attending the disembarkation smiled at the enthusiasm of 'their young artists', quietly giving a nod as a signal for them to launch down the gangway the minute the ship was secured. Jack and Margaret were determined to gain the advantage of every minute on shore, keen to paint the exotic sights found in market squares and side alleys, even if only for a couple of hours. In the way of painters throughout the centuries, they repaid the stewards by discreetly slipping small rolled sketches into appreciative hands. Margaret laughingly said, 'Don't lose them. These will be worth a fortune one day!'

Margaret never stopped chatting with other passengers or inviting couples to pose, while her swift hand sketched loose portraits in ink, signing *MS* with a flourish and accepting tuppence for her works.

'Tuppence,' Jack said in amazement. 'I couldn't ask for money for my paintings.'

'Well, it's all very well for you, Just Jack—just *Rich* Jack, I might add!' she retorted. 'Some of us like to eat and *that* is *why* we sell our drawings.'

'I thought you painted because you liked it?' he asked teasingly.

'No, Jack. I love painting. I want to paint all day. I want to research latest trends and try new techniques.'

'So, why don't you?'

'Because, Just Jack, some of us must earn a living. Real artists have to paint people and cats. Take commissions. These are what put food on our tables, so we can get on with the real business of being an artist. As for you, Jack, every time you give away a drawing, you make it impossible for the rest of us.'

'Now hang on, that's a bit unfair,' Jack huffed.

'No, listen to me. You undermine the public's perception of the value of the work. Of. Art,' Margaret expounded, smacking her hand on the table to emphasise each word. 'And therefore, the livelihood of. All. Artists.' She continued her syncopated hand slapping. 'If people do not pay for your work, they can't possibly value it. If you hand your work out like a bunch of scribbles,'—slap—'it is how they will be received. Probably end up at the bottom of someone's rubbish bin. And if you give works away, then people will expect all'—slap—'artists'—slap—'should do the same.'

Jack argued he already had means, and it seemed unfair to ask people who'd saved money for their new life in England to part with it for a simple sketch. His comments outraged Margaret, and she convinced him it was a simple economic truism that his actions had implications for all artists. She wound up her monologue by saying, 'You may be bloody well-heeled, but most of us are starving.'

So, it was agreed; henceforth, Jack would charge tuppence for his drawings and five pence for his oils.

Over the next few days, as he worked alongside Margaret, not only did Jack's coin collection grow, but so too did his education about the sociocultural world of art, with a particular emphasis on its gender inequities. Together, happy hours of creativity was alternated between hours comparing the quality of iced tea and hot chocolate in every saloon and dining room, while Margaret chatted non-stop, sharing her views on practically everything. Feeling like an adult for the first time in his life, Jack attempted to appear sage, listening as she expounded her theories, nodding thoughtfully in agreement, even though the rapid pace of her tirades often left him confused. And although he found Margaret's view about the art world interesting, he wondered if it were a little biased.

She railed against the lack of opportunity for female artists and the endless criticisms they endured. The critics were not happy unless women painted pictures of "bloody flowers, or perhaps a portrait of someone sorting flowers or wearing flowery hats". Their paintings were perceived as *nice*, but deemed insignificant in terms of artistic or social value. And should any woman dare to paint in the way of the modern European artists, they were branded unfeminine. Even the bloody Mullah (whom Jack discovered was a reference to Margaret's old teacher—Max Meldrum, leader of the Meldrumites), had the nerve to publicly declare 'you could never take the work of a female artist seriously.' To this, Margaret looked aggrieved and Jack recognised her old master's comment had left a deep wound.

They sicken me, so caught up in their egotistical interpretations of "What is art?" and their endless fighting. The way they diminish the value of works by female artists. Too modern, too colourful, too plain, too masculine, blah, blah, blah. If we try to sell something to buy a loaf of bread to bloody well feed ourselves, we are criticised for being self-promoting. Honestly!'

∾

Jack pondered Margaret's words at length. He'd never considered paintings in terms of social value and had to admit he'd always thought flowers were the sort of thing a woman might paint. Not that he believed they had to. Jack just assumed women would like to paint those things. It was an opinion he wisely kept to himself.

Conversations about modern art intrigued him. He had to agree the art valued by his school masters, parents and even himself was largely traditional. Landscapes where a tree looked like a tree and portraits where the person was so lifelike, you felt you could touch them. Although for many of her woes, Margaret may well have been speaking a foreign language, Jack was rapidly learning about an art world far more complicated than he had ever imagined.

He also learned this was not Margaret's first trip to Europe. She had lived there as a young child, and returned in 1922.

'My friend, Norah Simpson...' Margaret looked at Jack enquiringly, then, with a disgusted shake of her head, continued, 'brought some amazing works back to Australia. Returned from Paris in 1920 raving about the artists there. Cezanne, van Gogh, Matisse and Picasso. Painters who were leading change. Cubism, Post-Impressionism, Surrealism.

'It was so inspiring! I was twenty then,' confirming Jack's guess Margaret was in her late twenties, 'studying at The National Gallery's Art School and desperate to know everything I could. It was so frustrating sitting at the feet of the Oh-So-Wonderfuls, hearing them prognosticate about utter nonsense and belittle anything remotely new and interesting. I knew then, I had to go and see for myself.'

Jack marvelled how Margaret, at his age, had so much drive and purpose—she knew what she wanted and was determined to get it. And in the summer of 1922, she'd left Melbourne Art School to work as an hospital assistant by day and a waitress by evening, where she'd saved every penny she could to purchase her passage back to London and then she'd gone to Paris.

~

Margaret's excitement at the prospect of returning to London was growing by the day and Jack felt it rubbing off on him. Suddenly, it seemed as though been living in a protected bubble all of his life, and now it had been burst. Jack had never thought there was any more to know about art than how to hold a brush or draw a line, which he already did better than anyone he knew. Seeing, mixing, shading and blending were his specialities. People, politics and theories were beyond him. Should such detail have been presented during lessons at school, Jack had, no doubt, been gazing out of the window or doodling in the margins of his books, awaiting the nod from the art master, granting permission for students to get out the pencils, ink and paints. He now wished he had paid more attention.

As the days at sea drew to a close, conversations across the ship turned to the future, and Margaret talked excitedly about the Who's Who of London.

'London is so alive, Jack, you won't believe it. Never stops. You must let me show you around. The galleries are amazing! I would so love Roger to see your work. He'll know what to do with you! Please say you will come and see me in Sussex. Ness knows the most amazing people. You must meet them.'

Margaret never stopped talking. Planning. Her enthusiasm was infectious, and to Jack's delight it was quite evident she viewed their friendship as something beyond a shipboard association. In fact, he had a strong feeling she'd chosen him as her personal disciple and it was her mission to lead him out of artistic wilderness into enlightenment. He didn't mind at all.

Happily, Jack accepted the contact details she scrawled on a piece of the ship's stationery, and promised he would make contact at the first opportunity.

CHAPTER 8

*T*he *Ormonde* had traversed the expansive waters of the Indian Ocean and Arabian Sea, through the Suez Canal and onto the sparkling turquoise Mediterranean. The sense of pending change was palpable as the ship deftly navigated the Strait of Gibraltar into the Atlantic Ocean and then journeyed northeast for the home run through the English Channel. Excitement was at its peak as passengers anticipated the end of the long voyage. For those travelling without children, the journey had been a wonderful time of rest and relaxation, reading, walking the decks, savouring endless cups of tea and afternoon drinks at the bar. However, for family groups the confined spaces of the ship had long lost their novelty, and increasingly, the frustrated voices of frazzled mothers remonstrating with whining children were heard throughout the ship.

Jack had mixed feelings about the voyage's end. He had loved the weeks at sea. The freedom to spend hours drawing and painting alongside Margaret. The meals they'd shared. The endless conversations about the art world. Or rather, of him listening as Margaret described its mysterious complexities. They had observed and painted waters in every variation imaginable. Their colours—Prussian and azure blues—responded to skies adorned with clouds of endlessly varied formation, from gentle puffs tossed about by breezes to streaks forming a blazing light show as the sun's rays scorched bands of fiery crimson trimmed with metallic silver and gold. Brilliant sunrises and shimmering sunsets; grey days with visibility of barely twenty foggy feet where he was chilled to the bone; sparkling days where the air was alive with birds swooping low, plunging into the deep waters or spiralling in lazy circles as they rode the thermals.

Nonetheless, it was hard not to get caught up with the collective excitement as, with increasing frequency, passengers spotted other vessels sharing the watery expanse. The large cargo ships, once only occasionally glimpsed on the horizon, the smoke from their chimney stacks drifting in the sky, now passed so close the occupants could wave their hands to each other in greeting. Then there were the fishing vessels dragging large nets in the water, surrounded by hundreds of seagulls hovering in the hope of scraps thrown towards them, and finally the yachts, whose occupants waved as vigorously as the passengers who stood gazing down from the ship's rails.

The English coastline emerged, first as a faint, indistinct smudge, then as a low grey streak across the horizon. Over mere hours its features clarified as the *Ormonde* moved east along the turbulent waters of the Channel towards the mouth of the mighty Thames. Passengers lined the deck as the *Ormonde* inched inland, tugboats guiding the massive ship along the deep channel. They watched silently, mesmerised by the lines of buildings, vehicles and then people, whose normal land-dwelling activities appeared strangely disconnected for the passengers who'd had more than six weeks confined to the ship. Finally, neat rows of boats moored against the banks of the river signalled they had arrived at the Tilbury Docks. Passengers collectively held their breath as the ship glided into position, then united in cheering and applause, showing their appreciation to the captain and his crew standing at attention on the bridge, who'd delivered them across the world in the safety and comfort that was the liner's hallmark. A flurry of activity followed as the time for farewells to newfound friends and preparations to disembark finally arrived.

Jack returned along the crowded walkways of the first-class deck to his room to collect his belongings. Grasping his suitcase, he glanced fondly at the tiny cabin which had been his home for over a month. These long weeks on the *Ormonde* had been life-changing. His first experience living beyond his parent's daily supervision. The time spent with a fellow artist, discussing painting, the world of art and its many conflicts, had been intoxicating to Jack, arousing a thirst for knowledge and, already, he was feeling the emptiness created by the absence of Margaret.

~

As instructed by the ship's crew earlier that morning, Jack waited at the exit point designated to first-class passengers, who would be the first to disembark. He had already said goodbye to Margaret over an hour earlier, immediately after they had shared a final lunch together, and Jack chuckled as he thought about their farewell.

'Bye, Just Jack, you darling boy,' she had said. 'Now, you make sure you don't lose my address, and come and see me as soon as possible. I have many people who need to meet you.' She had then thrown her arms around him, hugging him tightly, and suddenly went on tiptoe and kissed him square on the lips. Jack recalled her laughter–the wicked twinkle in her eye that had become increasingly familiar. He guessed she knew full well it was the first time a girl had ever kissed him. While not for one second intending to be flirtatious, Margaret clearly relished opportunities to open Jack's eyes to a world he had not imagined.

Walking down the gangway just after two pm, Jack could not help musing a very different person was alighting compared to the one who had boarded the *Ormonde* what seemed like a lifetime ago. Expanded. Free. An adult even, he considered wryly. Indeed, his mind now gleaned understandings that were once as utterly foreign as public displays of affection. His world had tilted on its axis so far, it now felt like an entirely different place—and he was irrefutably altered. The change had nothing to do with the mad bustle of London poised to engulf him, but instead, by time spent in the company of perhaps the most exciting person he had ever met. Margaret was like no one he'd encountered and yet it seemed he'd known her all his life. There had never been the slightest question of romance. She was more like a big sister, whatever that might be like. Bossy, challenging, argumentative, funny, teasing and kind.

For now, though, it was time to revert to life as the son of William and Marian Tomlinson, nephew of Aunt Elizabeth and Uncle Robert. Sit, drink cups of tea and eat sandwiches. Be led around the sights of London. Big Ben. The Tower. Somehow it didn't seem as exciting as it once had, in the absence of Margaret's indomitable presence, and Jack knew he was going to go through the motions of visiting relatives while counting down the hours until he would catch up with her again.

CHAPTER 9

*A*fter what felt like an endless wait on the deck while the ship was firmly moored, gangways fixed and maritime formalities between the captain and the ground staff completed, Jack was shunted off the ship, passed the public terminal, towards the first-class lounge, and was relieved to find it empty. His legs felt strange after the weeks on the ship and he was thankful for the opportunity to collapse into a huge padded chair. Looking around, he compared the grandeur of this room to the public terminal. Its high, ornate ceiling had a spectacular chandelier forming a cascading centrepiece. Draped windows provided a wonderful view of the dock, while its heavy glass doors were a buffer to the outdoor sounds and swirling gusts of wind. The door suddenly swung open.

'Oh, there you are... Jack?' a bright, lilting voice called across the room, a question mark lingering at the end of his name. The accent sounded surprisingly familiar, although a significantly stronger version of his own mother's.

Aunt Elizabeth was a trim woman with a friendly smile and a talkative manner; quite a contrast to Marian, who tended to be more reserved unless she was anxious or excited. Yet Jack immediately recognised similarities: warm blue eyes, a neat figure and her voice oozing with a gentle kindliness. Her husband, Uncle Robert, appeared equally pleasant. He stood quietly while Aunt Elizabeth fussed over Jack, rising on his toes every few minutes as though ready to launch into any action required, on command.

Seizing the opportunity created when Aunt Elizabeth paused for breath, he extended his hand to shake Jack's vigorously. 'How are you, me laddie?' he asked with his round eyes twinkling. Jack immediately felt cheered by their warm friendliness. 'You've had a big trip, son. Let's get you home, and you can tell us all about it.' Uncle Robert reached out a strong hand to take Jack's suitcase.

～

Aunt Elizabeth and Uncle Robert lived in Brixton, on the southside of the Thames, a distance they navigated with two trains. The first went into London, where they disembarked and crossed platforms to continue the journey home. The trip seemed all the quicker by their ceaseless chatter, the melodic rhythm of their southeast London accents weaving in tandem as they bombarded him with every interesting facet of the city they could think of. Jack smiled patiently and listened as his delightful relatives so eagerly shared with him the city they loved.

Arriving at the terrace house, where Uncle Robert had lifted Aunt Elizabeth over the threshold following their wedding breakfast over twenty-five years ago, Jack was fascinated by the rows of three-storey buildings attached to each other. Identical dark red brick, their fronts were lined with low wrought iron fences and matching balconies on each of the second and third floors. His aunt and uncle's house had a neat rose garden bordering the walkway, which led to a shiny green front door fitted with a polished brass letterbox and door-knob. Immediately, they gave Jack a tour, leading him up a narrow wooden stairway to the second floor. The main bedroom was set at the front of the house, its small balcony overlooking the busy street, curtains and bedspread in matching florals complemented by cush-ions and a padded chair in the corner. Jack recognised the same style of prints favoured by his own mother, and while his parents' bedroom was much larger, this was surprisingly similar in its furnishings.

Next, they showed Jack to his room on the third level, looking over the street and beyond. He could feel his aunt and uncle's enthusiasm as they tripped over each other's words, regularly weaving in and out of each other's sentences, and he recognised how much it meant to them both to welcome him into their home. He suspected visitors were quite rare, certainly the type who stayed overnight. He knew very little about these kindly relatives: Aunt Elizabeth was his mother's only sister and the one child they'd had, a little boy called Tommy, died as a five-year-old, succumbing to an outbreak of tuberculosis and breaking their hearts many years ago. Where the grief for a lost child could sometimes destroy a marriage, Uncle Robert and Aunt Elizabeth had, fortunately, found solace in each other and got on with life, although photographs on every surface revealed their abiding love for the smiling little boy. Looking at a photograph of Tommy on the dressing table in his room, Jack felt overwhelmed by the sadness of their loss, sure his aunt and uncle would have made the best of parents.

'Jack, what are we thinking? We haven't even offered you a cup of tea!' Aunt Elizabeth words broke into Jack's thoughts, and he followed as she led the way down the steep staircase to put the kettle on. The kitchen was warm and inviting thanks to the heat of the green enamelled stove, which she proudly explained was a recent instalment—one of the new gas, wood and coal combinations boasting an oven, hob *and* grill. Coal bricks were neatly arranged in a copper bucket beside it and, nearby, a stand held a brass-handled brush and a small shovel. Maintaining the floral theme, the room had a neat look and the carefully placed adornments suggested the thoughtfulness of a lady who loved her home. Teacups on the bench and cake set out on a crystal plate foretold his aunt's careful preparations before leaving to collect him from the docks, and again Jack appreciated their warm welcome.

Ushered into the parlour, a lovely light-filled room whose walls were decorated with wallpaper bearing rows of small lavender posies, Jack sat politely, with a china teacup balanced on his knees and a plate of boiled fruitcake settled on a side table in easy reach to his left. His aunt and uncle continued their incessant chatter, plying him with questions about his life. They asked about his parents, home and school. Their curiosity had no limits and Jack could not help but contrast their lives to that of his family as he awkwardly timed bites of the rich fruit cake between their questions, struggling to avoid speaking with his mouth full. Jack described the voyage: the ship, its size, meals, the storm at sea which had many passengers worrying they might meet the same fate as the *Titanic*.

He could not help but feel a bit sorry for them, as it was obvious they loved family and would have adored the opportunity to be part of an extended clan of kinfolk, with nieces and nephews to spoil.

Looking around the room, Jack again was conscious of the presence of the small child in the many photographs on display. An infant draped in a soft shawl, a toddler taking small steps between the hands of his parents, a four-year-old seated in a tin 'car' activated by pedals. He wondered if it was their memories of this little boy which held his aunt and uncle to this house.

At six o'clock on the dot, Aunt Elizabeth set the table, revealing the enticing aroma wafting from the oven throughout the house to be roast mutton and baked vegetables, served with neatly strung beans and carrots, freshly picked from their garden. An apple compote with thick clotted cream followed, washed down with yet his third 'nice cup of tea' since his arrival.

Jack's offers to assist with the washing up were refused. Instead, Aunt Elizabeth directed Uncle Robert to take him upstairs and show him how to extract hot water from the chip heater. 'Jack might like to have a bath tonight—in the morning the water could be frozen in the pipes, for they'd had a bit of a cold snap, even though it was spring.'

Fifteen minutes later, Uncle Robert paused before leaving Jack to settle for the night. 'How are you at whist, lad? Perhaps tomorrow night we may cut the deck and play a hand or two?'

He asked with such eagerness that Jack felt touched, and agreed he would love to play cards with them.

After setting his clothes on the Queen Anne oak chiffonier and his toiletries on the dresser, Jack looked at himself in the mirror. He scarcely recognised himself in the reflection. Who was this young man, twelve thousand miles from a home he could barely remember? Was he still Jack? The same Jack? Or was he now 'Just Jack', as Margaret had so often called him? Smiling wryly at his reflection, he could hear her voice. *'So, Just Jack, how about today we...'*

His suitcase now empty, Jack reached for his drawing book and flicked through the sketches he'd made on the ship. He gazed at the image of Margaret, completed only two days earlier when she'd insisted they draw pictures of each other before the end of their journey. She had dragged him all over the ship, seeking the best angle and background for the portraits. Claiming 'Me first,' Margaret had determined that the front of the ship on the port side, free of afternoon shadows, was the best place for her and, laughingly, she'd stood on tiptoes, her left hand extended, fingertips lightly touching the rail for balance lest the ship roll. Her right hand was tucked up behind her ear, pushing her hair up, her chin jutting out at a dramatic angle, doing her best to look glamorous. Chatting all the while, she held the pose for the twenty minutes it took Jack to run his charcoal over one of his largest drawing papers, usually reserved for easel work. On completion, Margaret bounced forward to inspect his progress; however, Jack held up his hand, halting her. 'Give me half an hour and then you can see it,' he said.

'Okay. I will find us hot chocolate,' she replied. By then, Jack was again lost in his work. On her return, with a mug of steaming chocolate in each hand, he stood aside to let Margaret see the drawing.

Margaret was quiet as she looked at the image of herself. 'Jack, you are amazing,' she finally said. 'No one should be able to produce a drawing like this in an hour. It's not just the likeness... it's the vitality. The movement. It is uncanny.'

He went to tear out the page from his book, to give to her. 'No, Jack, you keep it and turn it into an oil for me. That, I will keep,' she said firmly.

It seemed unbelievable that only this morning he had farewelled the woman who had brought so much energy into his life. Now, he had moved into yet another new world—a three-storey terrace house with two of the sweetest people he had ever met. If Margaret was becoming a quickly fading memory, the life he shared with his parents for the last eighteen years seemed aeons away.

∾

Over the next two weeks, Jack viewed the sights of London as a tourist. He was enthusiastically guided by Aunt Elizabeth and Uncle Robert, each determined to initiate him in the history, culture and quirkiness of London. They proved to be wonderful storytellers, knowledgeable and proud of their city's history, and shared an endless supply of tales to enliven their sightseeing expeditions. They had each taken two weeks leave to ensure Jack was settled, Uncle Robert from his job as station-master for British Railway and Aunt Elizabeth from her job as an admissions officer at Westminster Hospital. They had created an itinerary of interesting places to visit and eagerly consulted with Jack each evening to ensure he was agreeable to their plan for the following day, which of course, he was. His aunt and uncle had obviously put a lot of thought into his visit he realised, and no doubt saved carefully to ensure they could afford to do 'a bit of gadding about' as Aunt Elizabeth described their outings. Jack repeatedly offered to pay for train tickets or for their lunch in a cafe; but they always refused, telling him to save his pence for now, it was their treat. He couldn't help but notice although they were hardworking people with modest means compared to his own family, they oozed happiness and enthusiasm for life and extended enormous generosity of spirit towards everybody. Repeatedly, he witnessed their friendly dispositions–an appreciative thank-you to the bus drivers; and thoughtful comments to the shop assistants. 'Bet you've got a young sweetheart waiting for you' or 'Are you finished soon, love? You must be tired.' Furthermore, they were unfailingly polite and appreciative of the service of the most menial workers who, Jack reflected, were often treated as invisible back in Australia.

Jack found the colossal city of London fabulous, if not chaotic, with its enormous buildings, dashing motor vehicles, rattling trains and the red double-decker buses. Added to that were the bustling crowds who swarmed the streets with accents so varied that Jack could barely believe they were all British.

'Jack, me lad, we are an odd lot, we Londoners,' Uncle Robert said in an exaggerated cockney dialect. 'We can barely understand each other from east to west, let alone north to south.'

~

After day trips to the Tower Bridge, the Tower of London and Hyde Park, Jack itched to sketch some of the sites.

'Aunt Elizabeth, would it worry you if I took along my drawing-book? I'd love to sketch a scene or two along the way, and Mum would be thrilled to bits if I sent her some pictures of the sites.'

'No, Jack, not at all. I'd love to see what you can make of our London. You just do whatever you like.'

Each morning, Jack packed his small canvas satchel and slung it over his shoulder as they set out, and his aunt and uncle fondly watched as he sketched bridge crossings, Big Ben, Westminster Abbey and St Paul's Cathedral. In time, they developed an artist's eye themselves and debated potential sites of interest for his drawings.

'Robert, how about we take Jack to the Abingdon Gardens? He might like to sketch Westminster Hall.'

'No, love, Margaret Street will provide the best light—we could go there first and then walk in the gardens...'

'Jack, we must take you to Piccadilly Circus, the Shaftsbury Memorial Fountain is a must.'

And certainly, it was. Despite the chilly winter's day, the ornate bronze fountain was surrounded by tourists marvelling at its beautiful proportions. Jack's pencil flew over his page, drawing appreciative comments from onlookers. As Jack outlined the crowning feature of the fountain—the Angel of Christian Charity, poised in readiness to fly —Uncle Robert explained her mission.

'She's a fine creature, Jack. Off to rescue poor and disadvantaged souls. No doubt she's busy, for certainly there'll be no shortage of them,' he said sadly.

'Better than a photograph,' his aunt marvelled, looking at Jack's sketch.

~

Each day, they stopped for lunch at one of the quaint taverns positioned on every street corner and tucked in all manner of alleyways. Jack was fascinated by their names: The Pig and Truffle, Laughing Gravy, and The Mad Bishop and Bear. Today it was The Dancing Donkey and Jack wondered if the Londoners of old ever grew taller than five feet as he ducked his head yet again to enter the ancient doorway. He could barely see in the darkened interior, as he followed his aunt and uncle down stone steps so well-trod that each had worn concave. A legacy of thousands of customers over centuries, Jack realised, as his eyes adjusted to the dingy room where weak sunlight emitted through dusty leadlight windows.

Massive timber beams hundreds of years old supported the ceiling and the surface of the oak bar held a soft sheen, no doubt caused by generations of jacket sleeves–tweed, worsted and possibly even Australian wool–rubbing over the surface to create a luminous finish. Over the past fortnight, Jack had experienced service from all manner of bartenders, including the occasional Scotsman and Irishman, who all shared a jolly, chatty friendliness and were eager to investigate Jack's Australian background and the reason for his presence in London.

During the first few days, Uncle Robert had a shandy while Jack and Aunt Elizabeth each had a glass of lemonade, but today, that changed.

It was a Wednesday and Uncle Robert was feeling particularly pleased with himself, for he had won a small bet on the horses. Chuffed with his good fortune, he was in a triumphant mood.

'Hey, laddie, how about we share a pint? A little celebration,' he suggested to Jack.

'Do you think you should, dear?'

'It will be lovely for the Jack to try an English pint. What do you say, my lad?'

'Well,' Jack replied, 'I don't usually drink. Perhaps a small one.'

'A small one it is, then. What about you, my love?' he asked, oblivious to the worried expression on Aunt Elizabeth's face.

'No, I think I'm all right. Are you sure, Robert? Perhaps you should stay with a shandy?'

However, Uncle Robert was very sure and ordered two pots of stout, along with a shandy for Aunt Elizabeth, whose uneasy expression remained.

After quickly downing his first beer, Uncle Robert followed with a second, and then a third, ignoring Aunt Elizabeth's subtle hints of dissuasion.

Her concern increased as he returned to the bar for yet another round of drinks, the second for Jack and Elizabeth, the fourth for himself.

'So, Tommy, I mean Jack, have you ever seen a pub so fine as an English tavern?' Uncle Robert waved his hand around the room expansively, and Jack agreed. Certainly, the fire roaring in the grate, the heavy oak stools scattered around the room and the laughing patrons made for a wonderful atmosphere.

'A fine place for a father to bring his son at the end of a work day. Tommy would have loved it. What do you think?' His voice took on a waver and a tear trekked down his wrinkled cheek as he continued. 'Yes, a grand place. My boy should be here, with his daddy and his fine young cousin, Jack.'

Jack looked at his aunt, aghast at this sudden change in his uncle, whose jovial expression of five minutes ago had now been replaced with lines of deep sorrow.

'Oh, Jack,' said Aunt Elizabeth. 'We have a problem now. There will be no shifting him for a while yet. When he gets like this, it's as if he's in another world.'

Over the next hour, Uncle Robert rambled on about all things, not a lot of which made sense to Jack, other than the singular theme of his son, Tommy. In brighter moments, he patted Jack on his back with a fond expression in his eyes, referring to him as 'Tommy, me lad,' and in response to Aunt Elizabeth's small shake of her head, Jack did not correct him.

'I'm sorry, Jack. I didn't want you to see him like this. It's awful. Not the drinking—that's okay. Not even getting a bit tipsy. I can bear that. It's the sadness which is awful. Brings it all back. Our little Tommy going the way he did—and so suddenly. You think you'd get over it, but you never do.'

Jack searched his mind for an answer, but it was beyond his experience. He could only imagine; no, you would never get over it, and yes, it was awful and terribly sad. His heart ached for Aunt Elizabeth and Uncle Robert as he considered the loss of their little Tommy and he tried to imagine what it must be like to live with such sorrow.

∾

Towards the end of Jack's second week in London two particularly exciting events occurred in the one day. The first was when Jack and his aunt and uncle had stood outside Buckingham Palace to witness the changing of the palace guards. Buckingham Palace was enormous—an imposing rectangular building that lived up to its formidable status as the home of Britain's long linage of kings and queens.

'It's huge!' Jack said, amazed by the symmetrical beauty of the expansive building set back from the roadside and buffered from the public's gaze, firstly by an imposing wrought iron boundary fence and then yards of perfectly manicured green lawns. He was sure he could see movement in a third-storey window to the right of the entry and nudged his uncle, wondering if he too had noticed. Quite a crowd had gathered at the palace entrance, as was the practice on all but the very wettest of days, according to Aunt Elizabeth. Jack was fascinated by the set of guards positioned beside the gates, straight-backed and wearing ornate bright red jackets and towering bear skin hats which sat low on their foreheads and extended so high, he wondered how they remained in position. It was not just the resplendent uniforms of the guards that fascinated Jack, but also their stance. Stock still, they barely seemed to blink and he couldn't take his eyes off the young guard standing closest to them, who was utterly unmoved by the bantering and questions directed toward him from the tourists, nor to the endless clicking of the cameras pointed towards him.

A lady amongst them, her blue satin hat so fancy you could easily think she had come for afternoon tea at the palace, dominated the crowd. Sharing her abundant opinions in a loud voice, she was evidently the self-elected authority of royal comings and goings.

'We won't be seeing anyone today,' she announced, the tone of her posh voice suggesting she was used to commanding crowds. 'His Majesty and The Family are in Norfolk. Left last week for Sandringham Estate.'

Jack caught Uncle Robert's eye and almost laughed out loud at his wink.

'No, ma'am, I'm sure they're at home here. I heard they've delayed their departure,' his uncle announced, his voice deep, loud and all-knowing.

'That's not the information I received,' replied the Authority, huffing loudly.

'Yess-ee... just as I thought,' his uncle continued confidently when, seconds later, a sudden movement of the guards, the clang of a distant gate opening and the rhythmic clip-clop of hooves ringing against flag-stones preceded the vision of four beautiful horses. Ornately decorated with studded brow bands and matching breast plates, holding their heads aloft, as though they were above offering a sideways glance to mere commoners standing on the pavement.

The wrought-iron gates ceremoniously swung apart and an open carriage slowed as it passed through. Magnificently presented, its mirror-like lacquer reflected the sky and the grass and the people crowded at the gate, and its brass fittings gleamed in the sunlight. Right before them, almost close enough to touch, was Prince Albert, the young Duke of York, and his wife Lady Elizabeth, looking relaxed as they smiled at the group of onlookers. With a swift movement, Albert propped his little daughter up on the seat, where, leaning against him, the four-year-old princess sweetly waved to the ecstatic crowd.

'Hello, Princess Lilibet,' they called to her, thrilled by the chance glimpse of the child who looked like a doll in her white dress and pink ribbons.

Jack found himself waving and calling 'Hello, hello,' as enthusiastically as the people around him, strangers united in a moment of shared excitement. As the carriage faded into the distance, they smiled at each other in acknowledgement of their good luck. He could not wait to write to his mother, describing the moment, and decided he would reproduce the image of the carriage in a small postcard-sized oil for her.

'How did you know the prince and his family were home?' he later asked his uncle.

'He knew nothing of the sort, Jack. Just laying it on for the fun of it,' Aunt Elizabeth intervened. 'Our Robert here loves nothing more than to tease the hob-nobs! Can't help himself. All in fun, he says, but the day will come, no doubt, when he'll find himself on the wrong end of the argument.'

'Aw, Lizzie, you know I make you laugh!' Uncle Robert said, placing his arm around her waist and squeezing her tightly.

'Yes, I suppose you do,' she replied, and Jack smiled. It was nice to see them so happy together, he thought.

~

The second significant event of the day occurred later in the afternoon. They'd returned home early as a chilly breeze had picked up and ate lunch—cold lamb and pickle sandwiches, followed by Aunt Elizabeth's rolled jam sponge, washed down by their customary 'nice cup of tea'. A hand of whist had been dealt. The game was now a daily habit, the well-worn deck of Waddingtons a permanent fixture on the sideboard, ready to be shuffled at a moment's notice, alongside a small cup of well-worn farthings serving as the 'gambling kitty'.

The silence, laden with anticipation as a freshly dealt hand was being sorted into suits and runs, optimism and pessimism mutual table partners, was cut through by a sharp rat-tat-tat on the door.

'Oh... who could that be...?' Aunt Elizabeth rose to answer it and Jack and his uncle listened to the muffled exchange.

'Perhaps another hawker wanting to sell us a vacuum cleaner,' Uncle Robert suggested. 'They're a blessed nuisance, but then again, you have to feel sorry for them, the poor beggars! They're just trying to earn a few shillings to feed their families.'

When Aunt Elizabeth walked into the parlour followed by a windswept Margaret, stylishly dressed in a flapper coat and matching headband, Jack nearly fell off his seat. His conscience had been niggling, aware of his unfulfilled promise to catch up with her and occasionally he'd even looked at the slip of paper with the phone number she'd given him, but somehow Margaret had slipped into a past life—a life which had taken on dreamlike qualities. Here, ensconced in Uncle Robert's and Aunt Elizabeth's home, Jack's resolve to contact her had diminished, overtaken by the rhythm of the Brixton household and their busy schedule of tourist activities.

'Jack!' Margaret exclaimed, leaping forward and kissing him on the cheek. Jack tried to stifle the blush he knew was rising up his neck and staining his cheeks. Her exuberance, which he had grown used to in the anonymous environment of the ship, felt out of place in his relatives' small parlour, and he was conscious of his aunt and uncle watching with wide-eyed interest. 'So here you are, a regular card sharp, gambling your hard-earned pence away. What bad habits are your aunt and uncle teaching you?' she teased, looking at them.

Uncle Robert laughed back. 'Oh yes, me girl, and we've taught him too well for now we have to watch our ha'pennies, as he is a fast learner. He'll have the clothes off our backs before we know it—mark my words!'

A brief exchange established Jack had met Margaret on the *Ormonde* and today she had travelled up from Sussex on the morning train to catch up with her cousin, Freddie, and finalise her plans to cat-sit for him in the next couple of weeks.

'I was not going back to Charleston until I tracked you down, Jack. You were supposed to contact me... or did you forget?'

'Charleston?' asked Robert, and Jack could see his uncle's mind with its encyclopaedic knowledge of the British railway system working to locate the station's whereabouts.

'Sorry, Sussex—Charleston's the name of the house where my relatives lives. I've been there for the last couple of weeks.'

'Would you like to join us for a cuppa, love?'

'I would kill for a cup of tea... a real cuppa. There is nothing like tea out of a genuine London teapot, I always think,' Margaret replied to a beaming Aunt Elizabeth—who was clearly beside herself at the prospect of having not just one, but two young people in her parlour.

Jack watched with amusement as Margaret followed Aunt Elizabeth into the kitchen and assisted with the frenzied juggle of teapot, cake tins and crockery, talking all the while.

When they returned and settled the refreshed cups and replenished plates on the table, Uncle Robert insisted it was time for a re-deal, this time for four places, and the afternoon passed with much hilarity as young and old bantered back and forth over cards, tea and cake.

As the clock on the mantle chimed five, Margaret prepared to leave. She had a kiss for everyone and the broad smiles left on Aunt Elizabeth's and Uncle Robert's faces were priceless. Jack walked with her to the train station, where she would catch the 5:45 to London Bridge connecting to the 6:30 to Lewes Station, in Sussex.

'Sunday, Jack! You have got to come on down. Everyone is dying to meet the fabulous Jack Tomlinson, artist extraordinaire. I have told them all about you. Uncle Roger's going to be there, too. I want him to see your work. He is an important contact. Knows what is going on in the art world. Have you still got the address? Trains leave every hour to Lewes, and a taxi will take you to Charleston. They all know Ness' place.'

'Okay,' Jack promised. 'I'll be there.'

'Catch the 9:30. That will have you there at eleven. Don't be late!' were Margaret's final words as she dashed onto the train just as it began its slow, creaking slide out of the station. The last thing Jack saw was her waving hand and face at the window, mouthing 'You be there!'

When Jack returned to the terrace, he found his aunt and uncle sitting in the parlour, even though Aunt Elizabeth would normally be bustling around the kitchen, putting together a light supper. Unsuccessfully attempting to look occupied, it was obvious they were desperate to hear the expanded version of how the vivacious Margaret, who'd swooped into their dining room with such a whirlwind of energy, had entered his life.

'So, Jack. Are you going to tell us about the young lady?' Uncle Robert looked at him hopefully.

'Robert... really! That is Jack's business!'

'The young lady is Margaret,' Jack offered. 'Mad, isn't she?'

'Mad? She is delightful!'

'How ever did you meet her?'

Jack described the morning Margaret had introduced herself to him on the *Ormonde* while he was drawing and how they had spent time together painting as the ship had transported them across the world.

'Painting?' Uncle Robert ventured.

'Yes, painting. Sorry, not a romance, if that is what you thought,' Jack said, amused by their interest.

'She wants me to show my sketches to her uncle. He'd some bigwig in the art world. Her family are all artists. Margaret wants me to meet them this Sunday... she wants me to go down to Sussex.'

His aunt and uncle thoughtfully digested this new twist in their nephew's plans.

'Oh aye, Jack, she might be onto something... You are very good, you know,' Uncle Robert said. 'Me and Lizzie here, we think you have a real talent.'

Aunt Elizabeth nodded her agreement.

CHAPTER 10

*S*unday finally arrived and Jack was surprised by the fluttering in his chest as he prepared for the journey to Sussex. Repeatedly, he checked the time, combed his hair and restlessly walked around the house. His nervousness was contagious and it seemed the whole household was agitated by the anticipation of meeting 'Margaret's people' at Charleston. Up until that morning, Jack had only made a few short trips alone, so Uncle Robert went through the railway connections, drawing a map outlining the platforms he would have to navigate to make the journey.

'I don't mind coming in with you lad, and seeing you on to the Sussex connection. It would be a shame to miss it,' he offered.

'No, Uncle Robert. I will be fine, I'm sure. This map will get me there, without any problems.'

Jack inhaled deeply as he stepped out onto the street to walk the short distance to the Brixton and South Stockwell Station. He felt excited, as though he were embarking on a great adventure, and enjoyed the sense of freedom which came from being alone in a foreign country. A train soon arrived, already near full with people dressed for church or perhaps to visit their families for lunch. At each station there was an exchange of bodies as those gathering their handbags and children to disembark were replaced by an even greater number of passengers until, soon, only standing room remained. As he'd anticipated, switching platforms at London Bridge Station went without incident, and the carriage he boarded on the train out to Sussex seemed quiet compared to the noisy journey into London.

~

As the train rattled southward, Jack gazed out the windows. The fields of sheep, donkeys and cattle, stone barns, fences and rolling green hills reminded him of occasional trips his family had taken to Kyneton and Castlemaine to visit one or another of his father's more important clients. He arrived at Lewes far sooner than expected and flagged a taxi from the front of the station. The driver was an older man, familiar with the inhabitants of Charleston and not backwards in his effort to establish Jack's reason for visiting the isolated farmhouse.

'You don't sound like no Londoner I've ever heard,' he said as Jack settled into the seat beside him. The question in his voice suggested he was keen to extract as much gossip as possible, information which would no doubt be shared with the next passenger or at the local tavern.

'No, Australian. My first time here. It's wonderful.'

'Australian! And you'd be a friend of Miss Margaret's, I'm guessing. A wag, she is, mark my word!' One's private business was obviously common property down in these parts, Jack suspected, and was happy to add his contribution to the collective wealth of local news.

'Yes, Margaret's my friend. She invited me down here for the day.'

'Strange lot they are out there at Charleston. Prepare yourself. Nice strange, don't get me wrong. Artists... just see things differently to the rest of us. They're okay. Gives us all something to chew over, so for that we can be thankful. Bleeding dull, if it wasn't for them, I can tell you.'

After navigating narrow ribbons of hedge-lined tracks, the vehicle eventually turned into a long driveway lined by a raggedy hedge, the gaps providing glimpses of an unruly garden. The house itself was a large rectangular structure, three stories high, its windows, eaves and doorway looking like a coat of paint was long overdue. Three large windows faced down from the first storey and Jack could feel eyes upon him as he stepped out of the taxi.

His sharp knock on the door was louder than he'd intended, and the sound of muffled shouting, accompanied by running footsteps, echoed from within. Suddenly, the heavy-panelled door swung open and he was greeted with the mischievous grin of a girl, about ten years old, her impish face surrounded by straight fair hair cut to form a perfect horizontal line above her shoulders

'Hello,' she said breathlessly, grinning broadly and clearly pleased with herself for succeeding at opening the door ahead of the tall, grey-haired woman with a warm smile who appeared behind her.

'Hello to you,' Jack replied, adopting an exaggerated formal tone. 'Would this be the residence of the Bell family?'

'Yes! Yes, it is...' the child, suddenly shy, retreated into the hallway and the older woman stepped forward.

'Good morning. You must be Margaret's friend, Jack. We've heard so much about you. I'm Vanessa Bell, but please call me Ness. Do come in, if you're game.' Stepping forward, Ness took Jack's right arm and tucked her left into it companionably. 'Are you sure you're ready to join the menagerie?' She led him through a living room to a smaller sitting area aglow with afternoon sunshine where an assortment of people were gathered.

'Jack! When did you sneak in?' Margaret cried, leaping up to hug him and claiming his arm from Ness.

'Ding, ding, ding,' she called, stilling the chatter and creating an expectant silence as an array of faces turned towards her and, by proximity, towards Jack, making him squirm.

'Everyone,' Margaret announced, 'I would like you to meet my new best friend, Jack. And, furthermore, I would like to proclaim myself the sole discoverer of Jack's extraordinary talent, uncovered on C-Deck of the *Ormonde*, somewhere between second and third class on the passage from Australia to London. Languishing like a fiery uncut opal lost amongst shale...' Margaret was just warming up with her poetic monologue, but those in the room knew her well and laughed. Jack was convinced: Margaret loved nothing better than an audience to play to.

Ness stepped forward again. 'Welcome to Charleston, Jack,' she said. 'I am the mistress of Madhouse Manor, mother of the scoundrel who you met at the door, and related by blood, marriage, intimacy or association to everybody in this room.

'This is my... ex-husband... friend... Clive.' She waved towards a thin, slightly balding man on a reclining lounge in the corner, a newspaper spread open on his lap. 'My sister Virginia—you may have heard of her, she scribbles.' Ness laughed. The woman's long, thin face; small, clear eyes; fine, straight nose; high forehead and smooth skin gave her an ethereal other-worldly appearance. Although Virginia nodded at Jack, he felt she hadn't really see him until suddenly a strange expression rippled across her face, startling him. Was it fear? Had he frightened her? Within seconds, her face returned to a bland, bored expression and he wondered if he'd imagined the moment.

'Don't worry about her,' Ness said quietly, 'Today is a bad day.' More loudly she continued. 'This is Virginia's friend, Vita.' To the right of Virginia sat a striking lady with short-cropped hair and intense brown eyes wearing, of all things, trousers. She smiled at him and raised her hand in greeting.

'And here are my children. Julian, my eldest, although you would never know. Responsible, sensible, calm. Nothing like the rest of us, who abandoned all notions of respectability years ago.' Jack nodded towards the tall young man with sandy hair and bright, intelligent eyes who looked about the same age as himself. 'Quentin should be here, but he is out testing his fishing rod. Hopefully, he will catch us some dinner. My baby, Angelica—huh, better to be known as Devilica.' She smiled fondly at the girl whom Jack had met at the door, who was now leaning on a fragile-looking chair, swinging her legs and supporting the whole precarious operation with one arm gripping the edge of the doorframe.

'Oh, and here is Duncan, my... dearest friend and housemate... and our friend–Bunny, who's down from London for the weekend,' Ness said, turning to the doorway just as two particularly handsome men entered the room. Duncan was an extraordinary looking man, his features so fine he could only be described as beautiful. Full lips and large eyes, which were strangely swollen. Had he been crying? Jack wondered, surprised.

Bunny, clearly the younger, was very tall with an impressive physique. He glanced at Ness with a wary expression and, pausing in her introductions, she approached Duncan and lightly touched his face.

'Whatever have you two been up to?' she asked, and frowned at Bunny, but Duncan smiled reassuringly.

'All good, love, Bunny has been a darling. Everything is all sorted out now.' With that, he turned his attention to Jack. 'Well, hello. You must be the very Jack who Margaret has been raving about all week.' The sweetness of Duncan's voice affirmed the effeminacy Jack had detected when he'd first entered the room.

'So pleased to meet you.' Duncan stepped towards Jack and he stiffened, sensing he was about to be kissed by the man.

'Duncan, behave!' Ness laughed. To Jack's relief, Duncan fluttered his hands defensively and stepped back with a chuckle.

Margaret took over. 'So, Jack, you have just about met everyone. We are still waiting for Uncle Roger. I told him he must come. That he had to meet you. He's back and forth to Paris these days, so he can be hard to pin down. You did bring your sketch book and paintings, didn't you?'

Bunny and Duncan nodded expectantly, and Jack wished Margaret would stop drawing attention to him.

'Yes, but really, they are nothing special. Margaret just pounced on me because she wanted someone to boss around.'

'Stop being so modest, Jack. Your work is amazing.'

'We are all looking forward to seeing your work, Jack,' said Ness, and Clive agreed.

'Come, I'll show you around.' Margaret steered him through a side door through the dining room and into the lounge.

Looking around the room, it dawned upon Jack that Duncan and Vanessa were not just passionate about painting, but clearly nutty. He gazed in amazement at the abundance of works filling the space. A ridiculous number of paintings; portraits, flowers and still-lifes, as well as nudes—male nudes even, he noted with shock—filled every inch of space. Some were framed, others leaned against walls and rested on the mantelpieces, but what stunned Jack even more were the paintings that had been applied directly to almost every surface of the room. The walls, fireplace and even the furniture. It seemed no spot was spared the frenetic activity of their brushes.

'Art is all that matters to them, Jack. They paint every day. Sure, they work in the garden and make a few pounds selling flowers and vegetables. Vanessa has her own money which pays the rent and keeps things afloat. Really, it all works out very well.'

To Jack's eyes, the paintings seemed crude; unfinished works which looked nothing like reality and he viewed them with mixed feelings.

Margaret sensed his confusion. 'Jack, these are not in the tradition of Australian art. Ness and Duncan love the modern works. The abstracts, Post-Impressionism, Fauvism. Some artists use different techniques to portray the world as they see it.'

'They certainly are different!' Jack wondering how anyone could see the world so... primitively. His idea of a good painting was firmly grounded in how closely the finished image reflected the subject. Hair drawn so finely that every strand glistened; skin smooth and glowing, eyes bright and luminous and so lifelike, you'd swear you could see into the subject's very soul. Water shimmering in sunlight, pears and apples so real you'd feel you could reach into the frame and touch them. That was the art Jack understood.

～

The volume in the next room escalated with the sound of crockery and cutlery being extracted from the oak sideboard.

'Roger must have arrived,' Margaret exclaimed and steered him back to the dining room.

It had been transformed in the few minutes since he and Margaret had left it: the table's surface decorated in swirls of colours, lines and shapes, was now being laden with glasses, wine bottles, a platter of bread, cutlery and a pile of bowls, into which Ness was ladling thick stew.

Jack looked at the newcomer, who appeared to be responding to three conversations at once. Perhaps sixty years old, he had angular features and small wire glasses perched on his nose. His eyes were clear and direct, and his affection for the room's inhabitants evident by his broad smile and relaxed manner.

'Hey, love, I made it, like I promised,' Roger said, before hugging Margaret. Turning to Jack, he extended his hand.

'And this is Jack, I am guessing. Nice to meet you at last. Margaret has been singing your praises to anyone who'll listen.' He laughed and stepped back to make room for Jack at the table. Formalities, such as table settings and side plates, were absent. Everyone simply dragged up their chairs, grabbed a fork and bread roll and balanced bowls and wine glasses anywhere they could find a space.

Sitting back, Jack absorbed the lively atmosphere, watching 'Margaret's people' with interest. No doubt about it, he was in the company of some extraordinary characters. Virginia's 'scribblings' were soon revealed to be books of renown as she and Roger discussed the reception of her most recent novel titled *Orlando*. Apparently, there was some controversy surrounding the content and there was even a suggestion her book might be banned. Virginia didn't seem too worried at all. She just laughed, saying the greater the controversy, the better her books sold, so why should she care?

Jack was wondering what on earth Virginia could possibly have written to be banned when a comment from his left almost made him choke.

'Oh, so that's the secret,' Bunny exclaimed. 'I wonder how I might get some steamy copulation into my garden. *'Gardening for the Common Man* is doing okay, but a few more sales would be helpful.'

'The bees, Bunny. Imagine the queen and all of her workers meeting her every need,' Duncan suggested to Bunny with a lewd tone.

'*Bees?*' Ness asked.

'Yes, Ness, *bees*. I am quite fascinated by them these days, important little creatures that they are. The world needs to know more about them and I shall be the one to tell them.'

'Good on you, Bunny. You always were one for creating a buzz,' interjected Duncan.

'Tease you may, my love,' Bunny replied, 'but others take such things seriously.' He turned his attention to Angelica. 'How are you, my little sweetheart? No boyfriends yet?'

'No... I hate boys!'

'That's the way. And if anyone bothers you, let me know. I will beat them off with a sword. I've got one, you know. You are mine, and mine only. Don't you forget that! One day I will marry you, my little princess. So, you be sure to tell the boys you are taken.'

While Bunny's words generated an eruption of laughter from the adults, Angelica was not amused. 'I am not going to marry you! I'm not marrying anyone. Never.'

'Good for you, Angel!' said Ness.

'Sounds like you have been told, Bunny,' said Clive. 'I'd stay clear if I were you. She's a fiery one.'

Jack took in the atmosphere around the table with interest. Moments like these, with large groups of people gathered around a dinner table, had been few in his life and he enjoyed listening as banter ricocheted back and forth with the ease borne of years of familiarity and friendship.

Beyond his interest in the various conversations, Jack was ever observant of people's mannerisms. He noticed when a flash of sadness, or was it confusion, rippled across Virginia's face, following which Vita reached across to pat her shoulder as if to reassure her friend she was safe from whatever internal demon haunted her.

Vita's touch immediately drew a soft smile from Virginia. The brief gesture held so much tenderness that Jack felt embarrassed, as though he had oafishly stumbled upon a moment of extraordinary intimacy, and he looked away. And when Roger's arm slink around Ness' waist, giving her an affectionate squeeze as she leaned against him to fill his wine glass; Jack was surprised.

The rich hearty stew was followed by an amazing rhubarb pie and custard, accompanied by astonishing volumes of red wine and interesting chatter, when suddenly, Roger turned his attention to Jack.

'So, Jack. Margaret tells me you have a gift.' Roger's tone, while friendly, suggested he was yet to be convinced.

'No, no, not at all!' Jack refuted Margaret's comments. 'I just like drawing and stuff.'

'Drawing and stuff,' Roger repeated, shaking his head in amusement. 'Okay. Where are these doodlings? Come. Show me.' He tapped the table in front of him and Jack looked around, suddenly at a loss as to where he had placed his folio.

With Margaret's assistance, they found it in the front foyer, by an umbrella stand, where he'd unconsciously placed it on his arrival.

Returning to the dining room, the table had been cleared in preparation for the showing and Jack could not recall a time when he had felt so young, insignificant and unsophisticated as when he passed his drawing book and a wad of small oils across to Roger.

Funny. A few weeks ago, Jack knew nothing of the likes of Roger Fry and he was obliviously content with the works he created. He neither sought, nor worried about the opinions of others. People might like his work, or not. And usually they did, very much. Now, though, with a dry mouth and clenching hands, Jack felt as though some messianic judgement was being called down upon his skills; as though his future happiness lay in the balance of Roger's opinion.

Standing very still, he held his breath as Roger first looked at the oils, many of which had been painted *plein air* on the decks of the *Ormonde*, and some in recent days around London. No one said a word as Roger turned the pages of Jack's drawing book, scrutinising each sketch. Arriving at the page of Margaret's portrait, Roger studied it intensely, then rubbed his forehead, as though deep in thought.

'Margaret is right. You are very good. Remarkable, in fact,' he finally said. 'Few people have your instincts for line, shadow, atmosphere. You view an object and can faithfully reflect it in your drawing. But, more than that, the life you breathe into your subject is extraordinary.'

Pausing for a few seconds, he again looked at the page. 'What do we do with you next, though? That's what matters.'

Jack was not sure what Roger meant, or what he should say to this. *Well, possibly not much, as I will be leaving for home in June to take a position in my father's work-place,* did not seem quite the response Roger was seeking. He chose to say nothing and Roger continued.

'You see, Jack, we are living in interesting times with regards to the interpretation of art. Important art, that is.' Roger's words bore echoes of the distinctions between old and new styles of art which Margaret had so frequently made in their conversations on the *Ormonde* and when she'd taken him through London's National Gallery. 'The school of traditional thought is very dominant; those who insist we should continue developing the theories and practices passed to us from the masters of old. Certainly, we learn much from the likes of Constable and Vermeer and Da Vinci, who applied extraordinary skills to portray the world. Such work is utterly wonderful, and to be honest, you may well join the traditionalists, and you will please them, mark my words —your realism is very impressive.'

Jack nodded, not because he fully understood, but to demonstrate he was listening.

'Alternatively, there is the school of modernism. The Impression-ists and the Post-Impressionists. Eh, Clive?' Roger glanced back at Clive who was standing close, listening, as he viewed Jack's work over Roger's shoulder. 'It's Clive's theory, actually,' Roger said with a wry smile. 'His view that art—*significant* art—uses line and colour to arouse emotions. Where paintings are not merely the likeness of a subject—a beautiful woman, or a sunset, or a battle—but rather, should touch the emotions. Significant art stands or falls by its capacity to move people, to lift us above the mundane stream of life—take us beyond the world we know, into another place.'

Jack looked at Roger blankly. He barely understood a single word of what he'd said, and his sense of being utterly out of his depth amid these strange people deepened.

Looking at Jack, Roger laughed. 'Okay, let me show you what I mean.' He laid out Jack's drawings of the *Ormonde's* dining room—the wonderful interior, rugs, carved timbers, pressed metal ceiling—and set beside them the drawing of the Shaftesbury Memorial fountain at Piccadilly Circus. 'These are perfect reproductions; beautifully drawn. Wonderfully descriptive, accurate, detailed, informative. Galleries would be happy to exhibit them. People would buy these to hang on their walls. They are lovely. They will inform historians in years to come. But, are they really art? *Significant* art?'

Jack breathed deeply. He had no idea!

Roger paused and shuffled through the pages of Jack's drawing book, with increased fervour.

'Now. Look at this. And this.'

Roger laid out a painting Jack had created on the *Ormonde*: a sunset that had followed an afternoon storm; clouds visible in the distance, deep greys and blues pierced by golden fingers dancing on the quivering blue-grey of the ocean's surface.

'I look at this, Jack, and am transported to another world. The clouds call me to them. I feel them heaving and rolling; their turbulence threatens me. I'm drawn to them, disturbed by them. And see how the ocean swells in response? That is how significant lines and forms work on the emotions. Ask Clive—he's been talking about it forever!'

Roger looked at Clive who nodded, smiling. 'You've explained it well!'

'And see this…' Roger turned to the drawing of Margaret, with which Jack had been particularly pleased.

'Jack, if Margaret were the ugliest woman in the world, which thankfully she isn't, it would not change the outcome. Your lines are perfect. I am swept into them. I feel a sense of truth. A moment of honesty. Ecstasy. Transportation. *These* works *are* art.' Clive nodded again, agreeing with Roger's analysis.

Jack remained confused, yet glad to know at least some of his work qualified as art, in the eyes of these apparent experts. He knew his drawing of Margaret was one of his better ones and he looked forward to creating a painting from it. He imagined the sun reflecting off her face. Locks of her hair fluttering on the breeze. Jack was brought back into focus by Roger's words, '...you're not altogether there, but with the right teaching you could be extraordinary. So, you have decisions to make, and only you can make them.'

Jack was at a loss. He was not sure what was expected of him, but knew he should be responding in some way. He was deemed 'good' in the eyes of Roger Fry. *'Could be extraordinary.'*

'Thanks,' he mumbled, knowing he should be appreciative of Roger for taking the time to look at his work but instead feeling out of his depth; burdened by expectations placed upon him; when half-an-hour ago, there had been none.

'When I get home, I will do some research. There's bound to be a good teacher in Melbourne. Margaret might have some ideas.' He looked at her hopefully.

'Pah,' she uttered, shaking her head. 'Don't even get me started. A few of the artists who escaped to Europe are open-minded, but, by and large, in Melbourne modern art is ridiculed. If a painting's not a gumtree or a river, the Powers That Be believe it's a threat to society.'

Jack was puzzled. How could a painting be a threat to society? And how had the mere act of painting a picture taken on such proportions? And finally, what was wrong with gumtrees and rivers, anyway?

CHAPTER 11

'Who are these people?' Jack asked Margaret later in the afternoon as they walked along the hedged track towards the station where he would catch the 6pm Lewes to London. 'Not Ness, Virginia, Roger, Duncan, Clive or whoever, but *who* are they? Why does their opinion matter so much?'

'An interesting question, Jack. The papers have a nickname for them—the Bloomsburys, which they think is hilarious. It goes back to when they all lived in Gordon Square, decades ago. I'll take you there one day. They are thinkers. Artists and philosophers. Writers. Intellectuals who refuse to be dictated to by society's rules. They live according to their own values and couldn't give a damn what anyone thinks. Freedom—and honesty, of course—are the rules they live by.

'And art,' Jack added, stating the obvious.

'Art is the glue holding them together, I suppose. Their common heartbeat. To me, they are family. Ness and Virginia are cousins of sorts. Older cousins. Second cousins, really, as their father and my mother were related. I was only three when my mother died and I was sent to live with the Stephens; Ness and Virginia's home, in South Kensington. It was horrible.'

Jack nodded. 'It must have been awful to lose your parents so young and have to go and live with relatives.'

'Their father wasn't so bad, but those creepy stepbrothers—always so lewd! Ness and Ginny constantly complained about them, but nobody took any notice. They never came near me, though. Ness would have killed them if they had, I'm sure. And then, Uncle Leslie died. Ness was in her twenties by then. It was a terrible time. Aunt Caroline, Uncle Leslie's sister came to live with us, full of her Quakerism rules. Ness would have none of it. And poor Virginia! She was already sick, showing signs of her mental illness, and Ness was sure Aunt Caroline, with all of her religious nonsense, was going to push her right over the edge. It was all because of Aunt Caroline and her tyrannical rules that Ness took Virginia to live with their brother Julian, in Bloomsbury—hence they got the name 'Bloomsbury's'. Not that it helped me. But then Aunt Caroline died and I was sent to live with Aunt Mary, who was full of ridiculous ideas about how young ladies should behave, and forever asking me, "What would your parents think?" Ness used to come and get me all of the time. Take me out for the day, just to get me away from her.'

'Now I can see why Ness means so much to you,' Jack said.

'I can't imagine life without her. She knew how awful it was for me. And when I was fourteen, Aunt Mary got sick and I lived with Ness and Clive for five weeks! The best five weeks of my life, they were! That's when I really got to know Uncle Roger, Duncan and the rest of them. But of course she got well again and insisted I return to her. But then, the war started, and Aunt Mary said I had to go to Australia. She had a friend, Miss Stapleton, who offered to take me. I think Aunt Mary was just looking for an excuse to get rid of me, because all we ever did was argue. "You're just like Vanessa," she'd say, which I took as a compliment.'

'It must have been hard for you, leaving Ness and all, coming to Australia.'

'It was dreadful. I cried and cried. I begged Ness to have me, but she couldn't. She did say perhaps, after the war was over, I could come back and live with her; but who knew it last for years. She then suggested I should start painting; told me to

release my emotions, and promised Clive would send money for art lessons.'

'Was Miss Stapleton nice?' Jack could barely believe the many changes Margaret had to deal with as a young child.

'Nicer than Aunt Mary. But life was so bloody boring! Thank God, she died when I was sixteen. I tried to catch the next ship straight back to London, but the war was still raging, so Ness said I best stay in Melbourne. In a sense, I have been on my own ever since. Clive continued to send money so I could go to art school, and pay rent. Ness and Clive understand me. They always did.'

'At least you were safe in Australia, I suppose,' Jack added.

Margaret looked at him with a strange expression, her eyes glistening?

'Margaret. Are you okay? Did something happen?'

'No, Jack. It's okay. I was okay. I was safe. Sometimes pain and death come in different ways. We'll save that story for another day.'

Jack nodded, visualizing a sixteen-year-old Margaret, set free by the death of a fussy old aunt, wandering the streets of Melbourne with her canvas bag of paints.

'Ness and Duncan and all—they might be as mad as hatters, but at least they live their lives honestly. They refuse to tolerate rules and conventions just because somebody says they should. If they love someone, they are not ashamed to say so'.

Jack nodded, dubiously. 'But isn't their... behaviour a bit strange?' he asked. 'I mean, Duncan and Bunny? Isn't Duncan with Ness? I could barely keep up with who belonged to whom.'

'Sure, they're unconventional. Especially by Australian standards, and I must say, getting worse. Duncan's getting more effeminate every year. And the reappearance of Bunny! Who'd have thought! I didn't expect we'd ever see him again. He, Ness and Duncan—they were all close years ago. They lived together through the war years, in fact. But then there was a terrible row. It was when I was over here in 1922. Duncan drove us all mad, frothing with jealousy every time Bunny went anywhere. They would fight—threw punches and everything, and then Duncan kept threatening to do himself in. It was awful. In the end, Bunny had enough and left. Poor Ness. I don't know how she copes.'

'And so Duncan turned to Ness?' Jack asked, feeling like he was trying to put the pieces of a complicated jigsaw together.

'Well, no. Not really. Duncan has always been "with" Ness, I suppose. The truth is while *Bunny* is the big love of Duncan's life, *Duncan* is the big love of Ness' life, which is why she puts up with it all. If she made a fuss, she knows Duncan would go. And of course, they have Angelica, together. Duncan is Angelica's father... not that Angelica knows, so keep it to yourself! I daresay they'll tell her one day.'

Jack's head had started to hurt. This version of life was utterly foreign to him, and he wasn't sure if he felt fascinated or appalled. 'But I thought Ness was married to Clive!'

'Yes, Jack. True. But neither she nor Clive ever believed in monogamous marriages. In truth, Ness never believed in marriage at all. She always said she'd never be shackled to any man, but somehow Clive got to her. Asked her over and over until eventually she relented. However, he wanted other women, also. They came to an arrangement right from the start: an open marriage. As long as they were honest and didn't hurt anyone, they gave each other permission to be truly free and happy. So, Clive has always had his girlfriends, and Ness, well, she has had her own lovers. She was with Roger for quite a while. Then she broke his heart because she was, and still is, utterly besotted with Duncan. The best part about it is how they have all managed to stay great friends. Marvellous, really. I don't know why they don't just get one big bed and all roll around in it together. Then everyone might be happy!'

Jack could barely believe what he was hearing. Just the casual reference to beds and the obvious implications made him blush.

'Just joking, Jack,' Margaret added, seeing his shocked face as he tried to digest the complexity of the Bloomsbury's relationships. She changed the subject. 'Ness and Duncan, they're alright. It's Virginia who is getting madder. She's the one we need to worry about. I can see a big change in her since I was here last. Whispers are she is going the way of Aunt Laura, who was so ill she was placed in an institution. Hopefully, that won't happen to Virginia. At least she's got Vita to keep her sane.'

Jack, still stunned by Margaret's aspersions about Duncan and Bunny, did not know how to begin digesting this new insinuation about Virginia and Vita. He had never heard of such a thing. 'You're joking! Two women! But isn't Virginia married?'

'Well, yes, of course she is.' Margaret sighed, as though the explanations were starting to hurt her head. 'But sometimes a husband isn't enough. Really Jack, men have been with men, and women with women, for centuries. It is nothing new! Like I said, at least my cousins are honest. Not like so-called respectable people with their wars and addictions and secrets which are kept behind closed doors. At least "The Bloomsburys" speak out. You should have seen them during the war. It was bad enough they refused to enlist, but then there was conscription to dodge. They fought tooth and nail, and everybody was against them. At least they have the courage of their convictions.'

Eventually, the London train arrived and Jack boarded, relieved to find a carriage to himself. He leaned back into the seat and closed his eyes. The revelations of the day had been so bizarre he needed to still his mind, and try to make sense of it all. He was not sure if his aunt and uncle might not be right; perhaps these artists weren't his type, after all.

One thing Jack was pleased about was Margaret's news she was moving to London that week, as Freddie needed to go to Chester to set up a small gallery for a friend. This would be a preliminary visit; he would be moving back and forth between London and Chester over the next three months, and during this time Margaret would live in London and cat-sit for him. And not only would she keep Freddie's cat alive, but she intended to show Jack all over the city. He could not deny he was excited, sure that exploring London with Margaret would bring adventures beyond the conventional tourist experiences he'd enjoyed with his aunt and uncle.

CHAPTER 12

*A*unt Elizabeth and Uncle Robert were pleased when Jack told them Margaret was moving to London to stay in her cousin's apartment for a few weeks.

'That will be grand, Jack, really grand,' said Uncle Robert.

'Yes, we were wondering what you would do, once we'd gone back to work. Such a shame we have to! It has been lovely, playing the tourist with you. We've really enjoyed it.'

'It has been wonderful. I've enjoyed it, too,' said Jack, 'You've both been so good to me, taking time off work and everything.'

'It's nothing. The least we could do,' Aunt Elizabeth said. 'We have been looking forward to having you for such a long time. I can barely believe you are here sometimes, sitting in our lounge room, large as life.'

'Be sure you bring Margaret home for supper and a game of cards, son. We'd love to have her. That girl certainly is a cracker. She'd put a smile on anyone's face,' said Uncle Robert.

'Thanks, I will ask her. I know she would love to visit.'

Over the next couple of days, Jack enjoyed the quietness of the house, happy to relax in his own company, but when he heard a knock on the door on

Wednesday afternoon, he was excited.

Margaret swept into the dining room talking non-stop, full of instructions about the things they needed to do, outlining the various galleries Jack must see, the people he had to meet and the interesting sights she planned to show him. He noticed the opportunity for choice, the question of 'would you like to do that, Jack, dear?' which had always underpinned his aunt and uncle's planning was conspicuously absent with Margaret.

'Tomorrow, we will visit The National Gallery,' she told him. 'I have to go there whenever I am in London. To stand before a Rembrandt and marvel at his skin tones, so translucent they almost glow, and the Turners, Jack—you will love them!

They talked through the afternoon, Margaret updating him on the latest gossip in Ness' household in Surrey, until the clock chimed its hourly chorus for the third time. Margaret glanced up, as though it was the first time she'd heard the chiming bells.

'Oh gosh, is it that late? I had better go. I didn't realise it had gone five. I am supposed to be at the station at five-thirty. It's Freddie's last night before he leaves for Chester, and he's meeting friends for dinner. Wants me to join them. Should be fun—Freddie's friends are always interesting!'

⁓

The next morning, as Jack joined the crowds exiting the train at London Station, he caught sight of Margaret waving a red scarf at the top of the ramp.

'Jack! You made it!'

'Hey, of course I made it. I have been navigating the myriad of railway tracks zig-zagging across London with the best, these last weeks. There is nothing I don't know about the art of buying a ticket and boarding a train without getting lost!'

'Well, good on you... but listen. Change of plans. We are going to take a quick walking tour before we go to the gallery. I need to see Freddie...'

'Walking? I don't do walking. I do ships and trains, but walking is not my thing at all...'

'You'll be walking whether you bloody-well like it or not, so stop whinging and get hopping,' said Margaret as she slipped a hand onto his elbow. 'Freddie should still be at the gallery—The New Burlington. I want to catch him before he leaves for Chester... Hurry up.'

'Ouch... you're dragging me!'

'Come on, it's not far. Mayfair.'

'I know Mayfair... it's where the fountain is... I sketched it... the one with the angel...'

'The Shaftsbury Memorial Fountain? No, that's Piccadilly Circus. It's on the way, we'll pass it in a minute...see, down there...the crowd's already gathering. Let's stop by on the way back.'

'I'm sure I've been to Mayfair, too.'

'Twice won't kill you. Watch the dog shit.' Margaret veered to the right.

'No, I'm good. I love seeing places twice. Three times if necessary. How was your dinner last night? You must have had a late one.'

'And why would you say that?'

'Because you're... tetchy.' Jack laughed again.

'Well, let's just say Freddie and his mates don't mind a wine or two. God, my head hurts! It was fun, though. We went to a jazz bar...music was amazing... Bond St... Here we are, down here. Wait! Stop, look in here! This was where the Grafton Gallery used to be. Looks like it has closed. Ness used to bring me here all of the time!'

Jack peered through the dusty windows of the large, empty room.

'This, my friend, is a piece of history. The place where Roger fell from grace.'

'Roger? Fry?'

'What other Roger do we know?'

'Whatever happened?'

'Let me think... it was years ago now, way back when I was a child. I do remember it, though. Vanessa and Clive—everyone, really —were in such a tizz. In those days, Roger, Clive and Ness ran a gallery in Gordon Square. It's near Freddie's apartment. The Omega Workshop... the place where Ness used to take me on Saturday afternoons. Probably where I got my love for art.'

'But how did Roger ruin his reputation?'

'Wait a minute, I'm getting to it. Roger was...is again, luckily... enormously influential, you know. In those days he was the absolute expert on art history. Lectured at university. Wrote articles. His knowledge of the old masters is phenomenal. But then he committed the crime of becoming fascinated with the modernists in Paris. He was fixated on bringing them to London. And he did.' Margaret pointed through the window, into the darkened interior of the building before them. 'He brought Gauguins, Matisses, Picassos and van Goghs to this very place. And everybody hated it. What an uproar! The critics said he'd gone mad. His name was mud. Now, of course, he is considered a genius. "The man who changed the way the world views modern art." Just the sort of rubbish that goes on in Australia. One minute someone's work is scorned; the next minute, everybody thinks it's wonderful—usually following the person's death after they've lived a life of poverty. I get so sick of all the bloody carrying on. I'm glad Roger has been recognised for how brilliant he is, while he is still breathing!

'I wonder why the Grafton closed....?' Margaret turned away and they continued their walk. 'Here it is...The New Burlington Gallery. Roger's tangled up with the Burlington's, too of course... I swear that man is everywhere!'

Jack followed Margaret through a glass door which opened into a surprisingly light large space, with pristine white walls and artworks hanging in parallel lines along each side of the long, thin room. As they'd stepped through the doorway a bell tinkled, and a man with a shock of long red hair looked up from where he was working.

'Freddie! You left before I'd even woken,' Margaret chided him.

'Sleeping Beauty needed her sleep!' Freddie looked at Jack. 'The truth is I wasn't game to stir her. Margaret's claws are far sharper than

Michelangelo's I fear.' He turned to Margaret with sympathy. 'Especially after such a big night, my dear. How's the head?'

'Michelangelo?' Jack asked.

'The cat,' Margaret replied. 'He's a monster. A huge beast of a Burmese, who stares at me with evil in his eyes. I am going to have nightmares stuck in the apartment alone with him, I swear.'

'It's all in your imagination, my dear. He just wants to snuggle.'

'Well, I will feed him, but he'll have to wait for you to come home if he's looking for a bloody snuggle session.'

'You'll get along fine, I'm sure. In no time at all, you'll be best of friends, and when I come home, he won't even want to know me.' Freddie turned his attention to Jack. 'I'm being rude. Welcome to London, Jack. Margaret tells me you are quite the artist,' he said, offering a firm handshake.

'Margaret says far too much, sometimes. She is very easily impressed, it would appear.'

'I don't know...she shows quite a good eye for quality art. You must be good! Have a look around here. There are quite a few new artists on display. Perhaps one day we might have some of your paintings on our walls?'

'You certainly will, Freddy. Wait until you see his work. Even Roger thinks he's amazing!'

'Margaret! He thinks I'm good, okay. Not amazing. Just good. Let's not get carried away. He says I'm not "there" yet... wherever "there" is.' Freddie laughed.

'You've got me interested, Jack. If Roger says you're "good", then certainly that means something.'

While Jack digested the compliment, Freddie turned to Margaret. 'I will be heading up to Chester at about two pm. First, I need to tidy up a few things here. I left a note on the bench with all the routines—rubbish, milk, cat feeding schedule, all that sort of thing. Did you see it?'

Margaret nodded. 'I did. Thanks, Freddie. You've thought of everything.'

'I also left a phone number for you to contact me if there's an emergency, and you'll find ten pounds on the dresser. That should get you whatever you need to buy. The cellar is stocked, as is the fridge, so all in all, you should have a lovely time living the life of a Londoner for the next couple of months. I will pop back every so often, just to see how you are going, and to restock, but I'm sure you'll be fine.'

'This is nice, Freddie.' Margaret waved towards the interior.

'Yes, the new look. We are very modern here at The Burlington. White is the word in galleries now. White on white on white. Not everybody's thing, but we like it.'

'Mmm... it does seem to show off the paintings better... Everything's not jammed together like they usually are. Just a single row of paintings—interesting. I think I do like it. What about you, Jack?'

Jack felt self-conscious. Now he was being asked to be an art critic. In truth, he wondered at the gallery's small number of paintings. Fifty at most, all spaced at head-height along the walls. Wouldn't people get sick of seeing the same pictures over and over?

'I think so...yes, it's helps to see each work for itself, rather than have paintings crowded on top of each other. It doesn't allow for many paintings, though.'

'You are quite right, Jack. But luckily, we have excellent storage space here: a couple of hundred paintings tucked away, ready to produce at a moment's notice. See, the catalogue is here, so people can ask if they want something in particular. We can change the exhibition every month. Or just show off a single artist or two. By doing this we create a point of interest and encourage people to return often.'

'I love it,' said Margaret. 'I wonder what they'd think of this in Melbourne. Probably have conniptions, the old stalwarts. How they hate change!'

Jack followed her along the perimeter of the room. The exhibition was called 'New Burlington Gallery's First Exhibition of the Young Painters' Society' and amongst the paintings, Margaret was thrilled to spot one of Ness', titled *Still Life with Eggs*. Although Jack did not mind it, he could not help thinking it was a strange subject for a painting. Who would ever put a painting of eggs on a wall? He decided not to question Margaret on Ness' choice—besides, thinking about some of the images on the walls of Charleston, this painting was not so unusual after all. And besides some of the other paintings in the exhibition, Ness' painting was very good. There was no denying much of modern art confused Jack, but he did find some works—Augustus John's portraits and James Boswell's colourful paintings of city life —interesting.

After farewelling Freddie, with Margaret promising to telephone at the first sign of any problems, Jack and Margaret began their return journey to London, agreeing they would find a bite to eat on their way to The National Gallery.

'Let's walk around the block, Jack. Cork Street is full of galleries. We won't stop, but we may just as well walk along there as go back the way we came. It's definitely worth seeing. I hope it hasn't changed too much!'

Walking, talking and peering through gallery windows, they made their way back to Piccadilly Circus, where the crowd was even larger than when they'd passed by a couple of hours earlier. The day was surprisingly pleasant if they avoided the wind, and Jack was pleased with himself when he spotted a couple of seats inside a small tearoom which looked directly towards the Shaftsbury Fountain, its Angel of Mercy protruding above the heads of the tourists jostling for position to take photographs.

'I say we have strawberry shortcake and lemonade,' said Margaret.

'But what about lunch? Sandwiches or something?' Jack put forth.

'Puh! Always so sensible, Jack. Strawberry shortcake *is* lunch. That's what I'm having, anyway.'

Just then a waitress appeared. Jack ordered a pork pie and a glass of lemonade and, as she'd said, Margaret had her shortcake, much to his amusement.

~

By mid-afternoon, they were wandering the halls of The National Gallery, and Jack listened carefully to Margaret as she described the layout of its broad corridors and how the paintings, drawings and lith-

THE SUN ROSE IN PARIS

ographs were separated into the various movements throughout the centuries.

He found the works of bygone eras fascinating; the Dutch masters with their earthy realism and the Italian Renaissance artists with their religious and mythological images. Looking upon the works of Caravaggio, Rembrandt and Vermeer, Jack felt humbled. These paintings, astonishingly beautiful in their detail, left him speechless. Standing in their presence, he imagined the masterful hands which had first sketched an outline onto the board, mixed powdery grounds with oils to create the vibrant array of colours, and then painstakingly applied them with mind-boggling precision to create these wonderful works. The skin tones of the subjects were luminous; ethereal, beyond perfection. The details of lace and the textures of fabrics—velvets and satin—sublime. Jack could not even begin to imagine the skill required to create such astonishing effects.

'Now you know why I come.' Margaret's voice broke through his musings, echoing the reverence for the works Jack felt. He nodded his agreement.

'They are extraordinary. You can't imagine anyone painting like this, anymore.'

Reluctantly leaving the traditional works, Margaret led Jack through the corridors to the modern paintings. *Impressionism and Post-Impressionism*, Jack read. Margaret pointed out the latter description.

'You know, it was Roger who first used the term *Post Impressionism*; he used it in the title of the exhibition which brought so much criticism upon him: "Manet and the Post-Impressionists".'

'*Post*-Impressionism? Roger? Fry?'

Again, Margaret gave the reply, 'How many Rogers do we know?'

'Yes, but to think he named a whole art movement! That's pretty amazing, don't you think?'

'Jack, the man's a genius. I keep telling you!'

And Roger was the man who thought Jack had promise! Jack felt a flicker of gratification that made his pulse quicken. Roger, namer of art movements, thought he was good. That he could be exceptional! If only. How he wished he could paint like... well, not like these moderns, so much, but certainly like the masters they'd just seen!

~

After they'd gazed at walls of art for almost two hours, Jack's mind started to numb and the paintings began to blur. He remained unconvinced of the significance Margaret attached to the modern works, but conceded that perhaps his eye lacked sophistication. Some paintings, he was sure, were downright ridiculous—something he would have drawn as a three-year-old—and arriving at Matisse's *The Yellow Curtain*, Jack could not stop laughing, yet again drawing the attention of the stern-faced attendants, who'd shushed him and Margaret more than once, when their laughter and debates about the merits of the works exceeded the gallery's tolerance for noise.

'You are trying to tell me this is an *important* painting,' he said, 'That they paid five hundred pounds for it! Well, what on earth are we standing here for? I am going home to paint like a three-year-old. I'll be a rich man in no time!'

Margaret playfully punched him in the arm. 'I waste my time on you, Jack Tomlinson. Go back to Australia, and paint your gum trees!'

CHAPTER 13

*D*aily, Jack met with Margaret and he found himself learning about a side to London he'd never have found with his Aunt and Uncle. Margaret always started with a plan—a gallery, a park or a visit to some of the famous London sites, always armed with their sketchbooks, ever ready for a spot of drawing. Aunt Elizabeth relished the opportunity to contribute to their jaunts by insisting Jack carry a small bag packed with homemade sausage rolls or pork pies, packaged with a tiny jar of mustard, a pair of scotch eggs or a punnet of strawberries and something sweet to follow—two large slabs of her fruit cake or some jam tarts.

'You might like to buy some ginger beer,' Aunt Elizabeth suggested.

'Or perhaps a cider at the tavern,' Uncle Robert added with a wink.

In the end, it was neither ginger beer nor cider that was their beverage of choice, but rather the aromatic cups of tea which they bought at the Kardomah Cafes dotted around London, always lively with the music of jazz quartets attracting crowds of younger people. Jack and Margaret's accents drew the attention of adventurous Londoners who were fascinated to learn about Australia, and keen to find out about the opportunities it offered, what with gold, land, freedom and equality purportedly attainable for the working classes.

'You should definitely come. Gold lines the pavement—you will be rich in no time at all!' Margaret offered.

'Sunshine and beaches with white sand and clear blue water!' Jack joined in the fun of spruiking the appeal of Australia to the appreciative audience.

'Oh, luv... I do feel we should consider emigrating; what do you reckon?' The man's eyes were bright with enthusiasm. 'It would be a real adventure. Might give us a chance to own a house or something. Not much future for us here...'

Jack liked the young fellow, and hoped he would come... that his dreams might come true, and he wouldn't be disappointed.

The days were fun and carefree, exploring London, stopping at a moment's notice to view its amazing sights and embrace experiences as they arose, with time being of little consequence to either of them. One afternoon, walking along the streets of Soho, they were surprised when a heavy shadow swept over them. Awestruck, they stopped in their tracks, along with the pedestrians around them, watching as an enormous airship drifted across the sky.

'Give 'em a wave, all the grand dames and their fine gentlemen up there fine-dining and foxtrotting their way across the heavens,' an old man encouraged them, spittle flying through gummy jaws towards Jack as he shielded his eyes and looked to the sky.

'No. Surely not,' Jack said.

''Tis true. God's honour! They've got deck chairs and silver service and everythin'. Waiters even, attendin' to 'em, and a brass band fer intertainment. B'fore long they'll be a whole fleet of 'em driftin' from India to America to O'stralia and back agin.'

'It looks enormous.' Jack had never seen anything like it.

''Tis 'inormous. Seven hundred and seventy-seven foot 'tis o'er two football fiel's long. Full of 'ydrogen. Wouldn't get me up there. If she goes off, ther'll be a bang—mark me words!'

With surprising speed, the airship moved out of sight and they continued their walk. However, the cry of a man in a blue striped apron captured Jack's attention as he lured customers with calls of 'All jelly, lovely grub—all large lumps!'

'Wow, Margaret. We've got to try these.'

'Eels—jellied eels! I couldn't, Jack. I feel nauseous just thinking about them!'

'Yes, you could! You're the one who's always game for anything.'

'Don't be shy, love... they're all fresh. Lots of lumps. Made 'em this morning, we did, me and the missus' encouraged the vendor when he spied Jack and Margaret hovering near his table.

'We'll have two cups, thanks. Come on, Margaret. Like the man says—don't be shy.' Spooning a mouthful of the grey-jelly into his mouth, Jack was surprised at how sweet it tasted. He watched expectantly as Margaret cautiously placed the tiniest of spoonfuls into her mouth.

'I suppose it's okay, but next time, it'll be fish and chips, thanks!' Margaret retorted.

～

'Come on, Jack, I'll take you to a café you will love,' Margaret said one afternoon. They'd spent a few hours in Hyde Park painting, as it had been a particularly fine day, but both agreed they'd had enough fresh air and sunshine. She led him into Regent St, towards a building with the words 'Café Royal' blazoned across its façade in bold blue letters. Entering, Jack gazed around the crowded room, where gilt caryatids, plush red banquettes and marble tables seemed extraordinarily excessive in the cold light of day. It was three pm and almost every seat was taken. Looking around, Jack thought if Margaret's relatives were odd, here, eccentricity was multiplied tenfold. He felt like a gawking sightseer who didn't belong there at all.

Stylish young women, dressed in all manner of getups—headbands, feathers, berets, dark red lipstick—chattered loudly.

'Would-be models,' Margaret said. 'They come here hoping some artist might spot them.'

'What on earth is that smell?' Jack sniffed the smoke-infused air curiously.

'Opium, Jack. Haven't you ever smelt opium before? You are just a baby, I suppose. Try not to look so shocked.'

Jack relaxed his expression as best he could, but doubted he could fool anyone that he belonged here.

'Everyone who is anyone comes here,' Margaret informed him. 'Movie stars and politicians, writers and artists. It's the place to be seen. The Café Royal serves marvellous afternoon tea and the best wine in all of London.'

As they stood looking around, a group of young people entered the room, jostling rudely as they moved between the tables, bumping into people and causing drinks to spill. They laughed hysterically, repeatedly saying, 'Sorry, darling, sorry!' Jack his cheeks burn as a woman ran straight into his arms. Margaret pulled him aside, muttering, 'Bright young things... Bright young idiots!'

'Who on earth are *they*?'

'Idle youth, Jack, with far too much family wealth for their own good. They are impossible. All they do is sit around all day, spending their daddy's money. Bored. Wasting their time doing nothing but making trouble. Always in the newspapers for their ridiculously bad behaviour. They hang around the artists and writers just to annoy their parents. Mind you, should they latch onto an artist, it can have its advantages. They think nothing of spending hundreds of pounds on a whim. They make a fuss over some new fad and, suddenly, a nobody painter becomes the latest fashion. Their money certainly can stand between an artist and starvation, that's for sure, so I suppose they're good for something.'

Moving deeper into the room, Margaret led Jack to a table where half a dozen people were seated.

'Well, well, well. Margaret, lovey! Freddie told me you were in town. How are you, dear? So nice of you to come back to London to see us all again. How is the land of the convicts doing?' An older man with thinning hair, a clipped moustache and a blue striped suit stood up to hug Margaret before making room for two more at the table. She

responded with a general greeting to the group, including an introduction of 'Jack, from Australia, a brilliant artist found floating around the
Indian Ocean. Jetsam of amazing talent.'

Jack wished he could have vanished into the floor, but he needn't
have worried; they were a friendly group.

'Hi, Jack! Welcome!' came calls across the table. Margaret turned
her attention back to the man who stood stroking his moustache as he
watched her fondly, amusement in his eyes.

'Jack, this is John. John Maynard Keynes. He's an old friend of
Vanessa and Clive's. I've known him since... forever, really.'

'Margaret! You make me feel ancient!'

'Sorry, John, but I can't help it if I still remember sitting on your
lap at the Omega, listening to you drone on about the threat of
Germany and the impact a war would have on world finances and
whatever. I hope your conversation is a whole lot more interesting
these days!'

'Well, young lady, speaking of interesting—I'll never forget seeing
you dancing on my dining room table at Gordon Square. And that was
only... what... ten years ago? Eight? You had every poor man in the
room's blood rushing to all of the wrong places, bedazzled by your
beauty. Your poor Aunt Caroline would have been rolling in her grave
if she'd seen you.'

'Well, I hope she did, the old witch. She made all of our lives
miserable. I blame her for half of Virginia's troubles.'

John turned to Jack. 'It was the night of Margaret's birthday...
What, you were twenty-two or thereabouts'—he glanced at Margaret
questioningly before continuing—'and Ness was determined to give
her a homecoming and birthday, combined. What a night! Those were
the days when we Bloomsburys really turned it on. Gosh, we had some
parties.'

'Don't remind me, John! Mind you, I can't say I remember a whole
lot about that night myself, which is probably a good thing.'

Jack imagined Margaret dancing wildly on a table. It wasn't hard to
envisage at all.

'How are they doing down there in Sussex, Margaret? I haven't seen Ness in ages. I see Virginia and Leonard here occasionally, or sometimes she pops in with Vita, but I haven't seen her for a while now. Is she well?'

'Oh, you know, John, Virginia always has her ups and downs. I think she's okay. She's pretty pleased with her latest book, even though there's talk it will be banned.'

Jack slid his chair back as the lady beside him leant forward and spoke to Margaret, declaring any suggestion of banning Virginia's book, *Orlando*, was an outrage. Her comment ignited a debate across the table on the rights and motives of censors to restrict public access to literature. A call for action ensued, with a discussion on letters to be written or which should be written or were going to be written in protest at the "attacks on artists' and writers' liberty and freedom of expression".

Jack listened, intrigued, as the conversation evolved into a debate around whether The National Gallery was progressive or whether it just reinforced traditional conceptions of art. There was nothing overly traditional about many of the paintings he'd seen there, he thought to himself.

Yet again Jack was surprised by the depths of feeling people held when it came to art, and he thought everybody seemed terribly heated up about nothing. What did it matter if some people liked a painting and others didn't?

'Why does it all matter?' he turned aside to ask Margaret. 'Surely if a painting is good, it is valued.'

'Yes, Jack, that is true. The problem is in the definition of *good,*' a man sitting near him replied. 'What matters is the role both art and writing plays in both recording history and challenging social values. If it's all just nice stories and pretty pictures, well, what's the use? None of this is new. Books and art have always recorded history. People's lives and beliefs. The biblical scenes. The battles. Prominent people.'

Jack had to agree, painting like writing did have a role in recording history.

'The problem we have today is the people in charge of the big institutions think they have the right to decide what the public should see.

Or read, for that matter. And they ridicule or ban anything they disagree with.'

The conversation continued and listening, Jack was conscious of a parallel universe, of individuals who were inspired by very different values and social expectations to those he had understood all of his life. To the people here, painting was more than just a thing a person did in one's spare time. They lived and breathed art. And not just painting, but poetry and literature too, as though such things were life and death to them. Jack watched the men and women around him, animated and serious, waving cigarettes, neglecting the ash they spilled across the table-cloth to merge with splashes of red wine as they tossed their opinions around. Listening, he felt utterly ignorant and naive.

~

Increasingly, Jack was aware of the change he went through as he returned to Aunt Elizabeth and Uncle Robert's home each afternoon moving between a bohemian artist world and that of conservative nephew. Naturally they were curious about his day, and he sensed their puzzlement for why he and Margaret passed so much time in galleries and cafes. If Jack found it difficult to elaborate on their gallery visits, it was nigh impossible for him to describe the characters he had been meeting up with at the Kardomah Cafes or the Café Royal, to which they returned frequently. He knew they would be horrified by the clientele of such places, where different moral codes dictated relationships, women swore and smoked at will and there was endless philosophical conversations that disdained authority, opposed war, disregarded marriage and ridiculed the entrapment of workers in meaningless jobs to increase the wealth of the *bourgeois*. Then there was the alcohol which lubricated the flow of conversations, which, despite his father's stern warning, Jack was finding he quite enjoyed.

~

Margaret had been in London for three weeks when she told Jack she was going to Sussex on Friday evening.

'You need to come to Charleston, too' she told him. 'Roger will be there. He's just back from Paris and he wants to speak with you.'

Jack was intrigued. What on earth could Roger Fry, want to say to him? He agreed, like last time, he would catch the Sunday morning train to Lewes.

∾

The same taxi driver as on his previous visit transported Jack to Charleston, this time greeting him as if he were an old friend.

'You'll be coming to see Miss Margaret again?' he asked as Jack climbed in beside him, and during the drive out, he quizzed Jack on Australia. Once he'd had a mind to settle there, he told Jack. Australia or America, he'd thought, for he'd heard stories of gold strikes and acres of land for the taking. Those were the days when he was young and working in the pits at the Wigan Colliery, racking his brains for any escape from the tedious, backbreaking work which turned the eyes and clogged the lungs. But then he'd married Bessie and they'd moved down here to Sussex and he'd found the sweet life of a dairy farmer suited him well. He drove the taxi between milking's; just bringing in a little extra to help keep the cream on the jam, he told Jack.

Soon Jack was standing at Charleston's front door, noticing the house seemed much quieter than on his previous visit. Like last time, it was Angelica who answered to his knock.

'Welcome, Jack. Would you please come in?' she asked formally, as if she'd been practising the greeting all morning.

With an exaggerated flourish, Jack removed an invisible hat from his head, sweeping low before the delighted Angelica. 'Very honoured, m'lady. Can I trouble you to escort me? I fear I might get lost in this grand palace.'

Taking him by the right hand, Angelica led Jack through the house to the same room as on his previous visit. Again, Clive was seated in the corner reading quietly. This time, a fair-haired woman leaned against the arm of his chair, reading over his shoulder.

'Oh, hello there, Jack.' To the lady at his side, Clive added, 'This is Jack, Mary. The young fellow I was telling you about. Margaret's Australian friend with so much talent! Jack, this is my girlfriend, Mary.'

Jack reached out and shook her hand, hoping to conceal his amazement. Ness Bell's ex-husband and his... girlfriend? Over the past weeks, Jack had spent many tortured minutes trying to fathom the complex web of Bloomsbury relationships. It baffled him to understand how Clive was able to remain on friendly terms with Ness and claim Angelica as his own child when his ex-wife openly shared the house with Duncan, Angelica's true father. And then there was Duncan and Bunny and their homosexual relationship? And now, here was Clive, happily visiting with a girlfriend! Jack was at an utter loss to understand the morality of these people.

'Jack, good to see you.' Ness wiped flour from her hands as she approached him and took his hand between her own. 'You'd better brace yourself because your life is being rearranged, even as we speak,' she warned. 'Honestly, put Margaret and Roger together and anything can happen. I swear that girl has him twisted around her little finger. Nonetheless, it is a wonderful opportunity. They've just gone down to the river, but should be back any minute and will fill you in, and after that...' She looked up as voices could be heard approaching, 'you and I must talk.'

Jack did not know whether to be intrigued or gobsmacked. His life was being rearranged? Roger had made plans for him? Whatever next?

Margaret and Roger both entered the room, Margaret, as usual, talking excitedly. She stopped mid-sentence when she saw him.

'Jack,' she cried breathlessly, 'wait until you hear what Roger has organised. It is so thrilling. You are going to art school in Paris! It's all arranged!'

With wide eyes, Jack looked from Margaret back to Ness, but her face was inscrutable. For now, at least, she was withholding her thoughts on this portentous issue. Jack marvelled how Margaret truly believed he was free to live spontaneously, without any regard for his responsibilities and obligations that awaited him in Australia. Nor was she alone. Over recent weeks, he had been repeatedly amazed by the way people she'd introduced him to spoke of skipping down to Paris for a month, or spending a summer in a little coastal village in Spain, or popping over to Rome on a sketching tour, as though it was of no more consequence than taking a walk on a Sunday afternoon. These people were unbelievable. And now, apparently, he was to be drawn into some crazy arrangement.

'Slow down, love, slow down,' laughed Roger as Jack's face revealed the apprehension suddenly overwhelming him. 'Jack thinks you are quite mad and he may well be right. We need to explain things. See what Jack wants to do. He does have his own mind, you know.'

Jack wasn't so confident that he did have his own mind. His immediate thoughts were of his parents; of what would they think, and he was fairly sure he knew. He could hear his father, who would be flabbergasted at the idea of Jack taking off on some Parisian jaunt with a bunch of artists: 'Jack, this is the most foolish nonsense I've ever heard. Don't be so bloody ridiculous. Get yourself home immediately.' Equally, he could see his mother nodding and agreeing with her husband, even as his swearing would cause a frown to furrow her forehead.

What Jack did not know, was how to say, 'Thank you very much for your time and interest, but I don't think Mother and Father would like it.'

There was nothing for it but to listen, while simultaneously his mind summoned its internal voice of reason to find a counter-argument to Roger's proposal.

'Jack, I have a friend in Montparnasse, an Australian artist. Hilda Rix. Quite well known in Australia, you may have heard of her?'

No, Jack hadn't, although he felt vague stirrings that Margaret had mentioned her at some time.

'She's lived abroad for years now—has contacts everywhere. Keeps an apartment on the Passage Dantzig and would be very pleased for you to stay there. Thankful, really. She is just about to leave for

Morocco and doesn't want to leave her studio empty. It would be bit of a hike into the Julian for you, but not impossible. The railway is very good in France. How does that sound?' Without waiting for a reply, Roger continued, 'So, that's your accommodation sorted. Now for your art classes.'

Jack listened incredulously as Roger went on. 'I'm thinking we should connect you to Lucien Simon. He's doing a stint at the *Académie Julian* this year and is just the right teacher for you. He has a brilliant execution of colour and detail and combines traditional techniques with modern expression. He loves to encourage young artists and will know exactly where to take you. Three months with him will develop your technique nicely. After that, I am thinking... but let's not get too far ahead of ourselves.'

Jack's amazement grew with each sentence, as Roger not only had a suggestion, but rather had organised a full-blown plan for his life—at least for the next three months. He was speechless. All eyes rested on him expectantly, waiting for gasps of appreciation, no doubt, but Jack was at a total loss. He was meant to be leaving for home in June—how could he possibly go to Paris for three months? Not to say the idea did not excite him, but it sounded like an outrageously impossible dream. Somebody else's life. One to which his parents would never agree.

'I'll have to think about it,' stammered Jack. 'It's so sudden.' And then it was out. 'I really don't know what my parents will say.' He did, actually. 'I will write to them and see what they think.' That should buy him some time.

'Jack, really! Writing letters will take months and we don't have that long. Classes start in mid-May. We need to get you down there and set up.' Margaret's face lit up with another bright idea. 'How about if Roger writes a telegram to your parents? Tells them he has spotted your talent and wants to ensure you access the best teachers in Paris. They wouldn't refuse his recommendation. Roger's one of the finest art critics in the world. They've probably heard of him.'

Roger nodded in agreement.

Jack thought, yes, they could very likely refuse him, and no, they would not likely have heard of Roger Fry, regardless of how famous he was. However, it was an option with some possibilities. Worse, though for Jack was how he must seem like such a child. All this talk about his parents and what they would think. What was he? Still a schoolboy?

'Excuse me, Margaret and Roger, but it is time for us to talk. Me and Jack, that is,' Ness intervened and, with a flick of her wrist, she beckoned Jack to follow her.

'Ness, no, it is a wonderful opportunity for Jack!' Margaret exclaimed.

'Yes, but let's be sure he has his eyes wide open before he goes and gets swallowed up in the madness of the Parisian art world. Come on, Jack.'

CHAPTER 14

*T*here was nothing to it but for Margaret and Roger to stand quietly and watch as Ness led Jack into the cluttered lounge room. It permitted him a closer look at the paintings covering the walls, the mismatched furniture and the fireplace.

As he sat down, Jack could feel Ness' keen eyes upon him as he took in the surroundings.

'We really are quite mad, aren't we?' she said, her soft grey eyes crinkling with amusement.

'No, not at all,' Jack stammered, not wanting to appear as if he was passing judgement on the surroundings—which, undoubtedly, were the workings of eccentrics.

'Well, most of the world thinks we're crazy, and we probably are. And that is the truth, Jack. Artists are a crazy lot of misfits. Real artists. The ones who are passionate about their work. Are you passionate about your art?'

Jack reacted to this question with a jolt. 'I suppose I am,' he replied thoughtfully. 'I mean, drawing and painting is what I like to do best. I see things, people, cars, buildings, and I want to draw them. I'd draw all day if I could.'

'Well, how do your parents see it? Do they see your future as an artist?'

'Heavens, no!' Jack responded without a second thought. 'Mum is very pleased with my paintings, of course. She likes to show them to her friends. Dad doesn't take much notice. He thinks it's something to fill in time until I leave school and get a real job, I suppose. No, they would never see my future as an artist. No one is an artist in Australia —unless they are really famous!' Jack thought of his parents' Streeton, hanging on their lounge-room wall.

'Well, Jack, that is it. Lots of people are artists. Even in Australia. And we artists know many other people who are artists, so for us the artistic lifestyle is quite normal. It's the people like your parents, those who are not artists, who do not know artists. They may know people who paint, but they don't really understand the passion which burns within them. It can be very difficult, really.'

Jack nodded, not knowing if he was expected to respond.

'You've just finished school, haven't you? Just turned eighteen? I expect you have a job lined up for your return to Australia?'

'I have a traineeship organised with Goldsbrough Mort & Co. It's where my father works,' Jack replied. 'Starting in July.'

Vanessa's eyebrows rose at this information. 'And your parents will be expecting you to work hard? Save up to buy a house? Get married? Work and provide for a family?'

Of course, Jack thought, nodding his agreement, although it sounded strange to have it said out loud. Without doubt, his parents had a very clear view of his future. Like his father, a job in the financial world. It had always seemed logical. Mind you, if he had said he wanted to go to university to study law or engineering, they would have agreed. But be an artist? They would never consider painting pictures as a career. Jack would not have thought of it, himself.

But then again, Roger was only suggesting he go to Paris for a few months. He would be home in August; then he could take up his cadet-ship with Goldsbrough Mort & Co.

Ness seemed determined to ensure Jack did not rush headlong into the opportunity being presented, without serious consideration.

'That is why it's important you think very carefully about Roger's plans. It is all very well for the likes of us, here in England. We've made a lifestyle of rebuffing society. For the Stephens—that is, Virginia and I, and Margaret too, I suppose—wayward thinking is in our genes. Father was an intellectual and most certainly a freethinker. He did a bit of everything. He was a clergyman, until church dogma got too much for him, then a journalist and then an editor. He even took to climbing mountains, for heaven's sake! But most of all, he was a philosopher, who taught us to question rather than blindly follow others. Mother, well, she died when we were very young, but she used to model for artists. Perhaps that's where Virginia and I get our creative inclinations from. Our parents understood how the boundaries set by society aren't for everyone. Billy-goat and I—sorry, that has always been my name for Virginia—we have never felt the need to please others, so we are not so bothered when they ridicule us. Plus, Father died before we really threw ourselves into art, so we never had to deal with his reactions. Could you cope with going against your parents' wishes, Jack?'

'But I would only be gone for a few months. I would be home by August.' Jack wasn't sure if he was telling Ness or asking her.

'This is the trouble. I'm only saying this because I know Paris. The seduction of a bohemian lifestyle, where people do as they please and shun all the rules—it's intoxicating. You will be forever changed if you go there.'

For Jack, Ness' warning roused a sense of excitement rather than caution. 'You make it sound so thrilling,' he ventured.

'It is thrilling, of course. That's the trouble. The thing is, Jack, for as exciting as bohemia is, being odd is not always easy. Look what art did too poor van Gogh and Modigliani. And if art doesn't kill you, it can certainly send you mad. I look at Virginia and her breakdowns and wonder how much her world of writing contributes to them. All of the controversies about her, the newspapers love to sensationalise. She says she doesn't care, but of course she does.'

Jack nodded, thinking of the strange expressions which crossed

Virginia's face. However, Ness' intensity began to make him uncomfortable. Surely not all artists were misunderstood.

'We have some well-known artists in Australia. They seem to be respected,' Jack said, again thinking of Arthur Streeton.

'Well, of course. The traditionalists, the men, have an easier road. They have a respectability about them we modernists are yet to receive. It is they who get the commissions and recognition, while the rest of us are left out in the cold, clinging to each other for reassurance. And even though we say we look after each other, and sprout on about rejecting the social order, life still has a way of biting us.'

As Ness spoke, her gaze fixed on the male nudes springing forth like Adonises on each side of the fireplace and Jack was sure she was referring to herself. Her marriage to Clive. Her love for Duncan. His obsession with Bunny. What a mess!

'So, Jack. What's the verdict? Do you think you want to join the mayhem of the art world?'

Jack nodded, and he was suddenly sure he did want to go to Paris and have art lessons more than anything in the world, despite Ness' caution. 'Yes... I think I do. I am pretty sure I'll be all right. Three months. I'll never get a chance like this again. But thank you for your warnings. I'll be careful.'

'It is a wonderful opportunity, of that there's no question. You seem to have a level head, which you will need. Stay away from the opium, the absinthe *and* the women!'

Jack grinned. 'Spoken just like my father!'

'And would you like Roger to contact your parents?'

He shook his head vehemently. 'No. I will send them a telegram myself. Immediately.' His words rang clear, resonating with a full-fledged manly conviction he did not necessarily feel.

'I'll explain how I've been given an opportunity which is too good to refuse. They'll understand,' he lied. Besides, he thought, by the time they received his message and replied, no doubt insisting he come home immediately, he'd be well and truly ensconced in Montparnasse, attending art school at the *Académie Julian*.

~

On the return journey to Brixton, Jack's mind spun with the extraordinary twist his life had taken within the space of a few short hours. Surges of nervous tension churned through him. Paris! Art school! It was too much to absorb. Over the last few weeks, he couldn't deny he'd been increasingly intrigued by the views of artists he'd heard espousing the social and political ramifications of their works and whilst he didn't always agree with their ideas, he'd found their passion exciting. Furthermore, he'd loved visiting galleries—the centuries old paintings he'd seen had triggered a burning desire within him to test his own skills. And now, thanks to Margaret and to Roger Fry, he was going to Paris!

Needless to say, Aunt Elizabeth and Uncle Robert were alarmed at Jack's sudden decision to defer his trip home and instead, travel to Paris to study art at the *Académie Julian*.

'But Jack, do you think it is safe?' Uncle Robert asked. 'I mean Paris? You can't always trust foreigners, you know. Are you sure these artists are... savoury? Not Margaret, of course. She is a charming girl, but... artists... they're bohemians really. That's what they call them, you know. They don't seem to have jobs. And their morals can be a little loose, if you know what I mean. Nice people tend to be a bit wary. You can't trust everybody these days.'

Indeed, amid the warmth of the dining room, sipping tea and eating fruit-cake from Aunt Elizabeth's best china set upon her lace table-cloth, surrounded by the solid oak mantlepiece laden with photographs of Tommy, and the crystal vases filled with Uncle Robert's violas, Jack was suddenly filled with doubts. It was as if the room's countenance, the very wallpaper with its reassuring, repetitions of floral bouquets was urging him to stay put in a world which was solid and honest and uncomplicated. All at once, the very idea of Paris seemed irresponsible and reckless. But Roger's plans had taken a hold of him, and Jack knew, more than anything, he had to go to.

Nonetheless, Jack was sorry for the quandary he had placed Aunt Elizabeth in. Her world was firmly grounded in the British Isles and, apart from a honeymoon in Glasgow over twenty-five years ago, with occasional return visits, she and Uncle Robert had rarely ventured outside the greater London area. To them, the French were a foreign species, to be regarded with suspicion. Even worse, Jack knew she and Uncle Robert felt accountable to his parents whilst he was on his visit to London, and therefore responsible for his wayward decision, as if they personally, had led him astray. Obviously, they did not feel the right to forbid him, but they no doubt felt it was their duty to dissuade him from this mad plan to head off to art school at the recommendation of a bunch of strangers.

'What do you think your parents will say?' Uncle Robert asked.

~

What would his parents say? Jack mused, wryly, imagining their shock. However, now the opportunity to go to Paris was on offer, he knew without a doubt he had to go, no matter how upset his parents would be. Deciding the best course of action was to send a letter to his parents explaining the change of plans, Jack kept it brief, light on detail and matter of fact.

Dear Mother and Father,

I hope this letter finds you well. I have wonderful news which I know will be as much a surprise for you, as it has been for me. I have been offered a marvellous opportunity to study painting with an art teacher of exceptional talent at the Académie Julian (Montparnasse, Paris)—Mr Lucien Simon. He is a friend of Mr Roger Fry, one of England's most respected art critics, whom I met through Margaret, the lady I met on the ship, who was very taken with my drawings. You may have heard of him. Mr Fry believes I am quite talented—who would have imagined?—and thinks I could even have paintings in galleries and sell them!

Mr Fry has organised some accommodation with a respected Australian artist, Mrs Rix, who lives near the Académie Julian. My savings should cover my expenses initially, so money will not be a problem, and I am sure I could pick up a job or maybe even sell sketches to tourists.

I know this is all a bit sudden, but I am sure you agree it is an opportunity which is too good to miss. I will write each week and let you know how it is all going.

With Love,

Your son, Jack

Jack was under no illusions about the forced cheery tone he had adopted in this letter. He may as well have said he was flying to Mars on a saucer accompanied by little green men, for his parents' reaction would be the same. Nothing about the idea of going to Paris was going to make sense to them. His contrived emphasis on 'Mr this' and 'Mrs that'—a bid to create an aura of respectability—sounded as unconvincing to him as it no doubt would to them. However, at present he was twelve thousand miles from home, on the opposite side of the earth. Really, what could his parents do? And surely everything would turn out fine in the end, Jack reasoned.

His parents response arrived barely a week before he was due to leave for Paris: a telegram, so long it must have cost them a fortune.

DEAR JACK,

YOUR CHANGE OF PLANS IS VERY SUDDEN AND A BIT OF A SHOCK STOP WE WERE SO LOOKING FORWARD TO HAVING YOU HOME IN JULY AND MISS YOU VERY MUCH STOP WE HAVE CONSIDERED THIS OPPORTUNITY AND DO WONDER IF YOU COULD NOT FIND SOME SUITABLE ART CLASSES IN LONDON OR MELBOURNE STOP THE FRENCH HAVE NEVER BEEN TERRIBLY TRUSTWORTHY NOT THAT WE MEAN TO BE UNKIND STOP SELLING PAINTINGS TO TOURISTS IS NOT DESIRABLE STOP YOUR FATHER WILL CONTINUE PAYING ONE POUND A WEEK WHILE YOU

ATTEND THE ACADÉMIE JULIAN STOP I HAVE BEEN TRYING
TO MAKE ENQUIRIES ABOUT THE ACADÉMIE JULIAN BUT
NO ONE SEEMS TO HAVE HEARD OF IT STOP ARE YOU SURE
IT IS REPUTABLE STOP PLEASE LET US KNOW WHEN YOU
ARE SETTLED AT MRS RIX'S APARTMENT STOP
    WITH LOVE
    MOTHER AND FATHER XX

Jack read the telegram aloud to Aunt Elizabeth and, seeing her worried
frown recede, he knew she was every bit as relieved by his parents'
words as he was. Jack had never been one to defy his parents, but he
had made up his mind on this. He was going to go to Paris, even if they
had insisted he was to return home immediately. However, to have
them accept, even reluctantly, made him feel so much better. Elated, in
fact. With his parent's approval, the impromptu side trip felt legitimate.
Jack was going to Paris!

PART II
PARIS

CHAPTER 15

*A*lthough Jack had set the alarm for six am, he woke long before its shrill call. Rushing across the room to silence it, he hoped its shrieking trill had not violated the apartment's noise rules. The small collapsible traveller's clock had been a parting gift from Aunt Elizabeth and Uncle Robert.

'A little something for you to remember us by,' they'd said, handing over the small package at London's Victoria Station, his aunt dabbing her folded handkerchief to her eyes as Jack boarded the train. Though it had only been two days since they'd waved him off, now, standing at the window of Mrs Rix's apartment looking down on the Passage Dantzig, it seemed a lifetime ago.

Sounds of predawn street life gradually displaced the morning silence. Wrapping a woollen blanket around him, Jack stood peering out the dormer window through the misty grey light. Directly below, an enormous wagon, groaning under the weight of dozens of milk urns, was being drawn along the narrow street by a pair of black horses, their hooves clattering against the bluestone cobbles. He watched as two men dressed in overalls and matching caps battled to steer a wooden cart forward, filled to its low sides with a mountain of onions. Every sway and bump in the pavement caused a few loose spheres to escape with a bounce, then roll along the ground, resting in the indents between the cobbles. Even at this early hour, he could make out the steady movement of pedestrians tramping the footpaths, mostly men: caps low, newspapers tucked under their armpits, metal lunchboxes in hand, heading, no doubt, off to work for the day.

Jack walked to the table and collected the well-worn note to review today's route for the hundredth time. Roger had provided minutely detailed information to assist Jack on his journey, from his departure in London by steam train to Dover, the ferry ride across the channel to Calais and then instructions for his ticket purchase for *La Flèche d'or*, the luxurious train that delivered him to the Gare du Nord yesterday. Jack had felt embarrassed, thinking that after all his dithering concerns about his parents, Roger must have concluded that he was dealing with an incapable schoolboy who needed to be led by the hand. Nonetheless, he was enormously thankful for the instructions Roger had provided, which had paved the way for a smooth journey from London to Paris and were already proving to be useful today.

It was hard to believe that only yesterday morning he had arrived at the Gare du Nord and, following initial confusion as to which way to turn in the bustling station before consulting Roger's instructions, managed to purchase a ticket and make his way to Line 12 to board the train that took him to Convention Station. For all the new experiences Jack had undertaken, he reflected that train travel had a universal rhythm. Stations, tickets, platforms and the rickety motion of the carriages themselves bore a comforting familiarity, confirming to Jack that he would be fine. Of course he could navigate this strange country.

The sense of familiarity had continued as he'd followed the exit signs leading him out of the station. Turning left, Jack had walked with purpose, guided by the arrows on the scrawling map that Roger had sketched, striding two blocks along the Rue de la Convention, crossing the wide road and turning right at the Rue de Dantzig. After another three blocks, a signpost marked an odd, narrow street sharply angled to the right. The Passage Dantzig. Jack had been pleased with himself for accurately navigating the roads to his journey's end, but his confidence departed in an instant, replaced by a sense of being utterly alone in a foreign world–a dangerous foreign world–as he found the Passage Dantzig abuzz with all manner of people. A rough-looking crowd, its members lounging at various points along the way, had chatted rapidly in languages incomprehensible to Jack. Amid the voices, he'd heard bottles clinking and the strumming of a mandolin which had provided a soft accompaniment to the soulful crooning of an ancient gentleman, his closed eyes suggesting a yearning for times past and love lost. As Jack had ventured forth, there was nothing for it but to pass a group of people huddling around an iron brazier that had been set up in the middle of the footpath. From it, a stream of thick black smoke billowed, near horizontal, and providing meagre warmth against the cooling afternoon air.

Warily, Jack had woven through the crowd, unsure whether to raise his eyes and say hello, therefore announcing his presence, or to look down at the pavement and hopefully remain unnoticed. No one paid any attention to him, thankfully. As he'd edged further along the street, an unusual three-storey building had captured his attention. Circular, and with a strange turret rising from the centre of the roof, it looked more like an enormous beehive than a habitat for humans. Piles of debris cluttered its entry: abandoned chairs and loose drawers, wooden crates and a mountain of derelict-looking bicycles that lay twisted upon each other, absent of wheels, seats and even handlebars. As Jack reached the wide entrance, he noticed a cluster of people gathered near the gate. Artists, with their easels set up for work, were gathered around a young woman leaning against a stool, her arms holding a basket of colourful flowers, as if for sale. The girl had winked at him, even as she held her pose, and he'd smiled back. Her low-cut blouse, exposed shoulder and bare feet conveyed a timeless story of urban poverty and Jack had wondered if she was posing for artistic effect or whether she did, in fact, sell flowers like the raggedy girls with their heavily laden baskets of blooms he had noticed around the Gare du Nord when he had arrived in Paris.

Transfixed, he'd stood watching until he was approached by a tall, lanky man bearing the sharpest cheekbones Jack had ever seen. Stringy black curls fell well past the man's collar and a heavily paint-stained shirt hung loosely over his equally paint-splattered baggy trousers. Jack was relieved when the man's face had opened into a broad, friendly smile that was utterly oblivious to the set of crooked, tobacco-stained teeth now on display to the world. Jack had felt embarrassed, realising he had been caught out gaping at the artists at work, and immediately attempted an apology, hoping the English words would be understood.

Brushing his apology aside, the man had replied in a strong European accent of unknown origin.

'You want a room?–I'm leaving today. You can have mine if you want. Only three centimes a day. It's pretty rough, just a bed and an easel–but what more does an artist need?' The man had laughed. 'Cheap models.' He waved his hand towards the group painting in the courtyard. 'You see the concierge. Alf. He'll get you sorted.'

He pointed towards a faded sign by the gateway. *La Ruche, Studio Accommodation, Artistes Welcome.* Jack shook his head and found himself gesticulating and pointing further up the road, explaining that he already had an apartment waiting for him. 'No worries,' smiled the man. 'Good luck. Paint well, my friend!'

Continuing his walk along the Passage Dantzig, Jack arrived outside a narrow apartment building with the number seventeen etched in cast iron and attached to the front door. Looking upwards, he'd counted six floors. It was an attractive building, each level bearing two matching front windows overlooking the road, each adorned with ornately curved wrought iron grids. He'd been relieved to see that it was in considerably better condition than the strange-looking building down the road. Not only in better condition, but cleaner too, he'd noticed as he ascended the yellow stone stairs and entered the small foyer. To the right was an office-like window opening and a bell. Given the absence of human activity, Jack had rung it. Within seconds the round, cheerful face of a lady appeared, her cheeks bright with a rosy glow, providing a bold accompaniment to her even brighter red hair, the whole effect shrouded in an almost overwhelming scent of sweet perfume.

'*Bonjour*, monsieur. Can I help?' she had asked, smiling. Jack explained that he was here to collect the key to Hilda Rix's apartment and continue the lease on her behalf for the next few months.

'Pleased to meet you,' she replied, turning to the wall behind her and selecting a square-ended key attached to a round brass plate engraved with a swirling number three. 'Mrs Rix, she tells me all about you, Jack. And me, I am Mimi.'

Jack had listened as Mimi relayed a series of instructions in quite good English, relieved to find that language was not going to be a barrier here. 'Ash cans need to be down by eight am; fresh milk is available immediately outside the building every morning after six am; mail can be collected from the counter anytime between eight and eight. No tipping water outside the windows. No painting on the walls. Visitors,' a wink, followed by a stern instruction, 'quietness is essential. No drunkenness. No fighting.' Her frown for emphasis reverted to her smile. 'Rent: five francs, to be paid weekly in advance, Friday at the latest. You will be glad to be a little more... wealthy... Rooms up the top may be cheaper, but they wear out the knees very quickly. Welcome to Paris,' she concluded. 'I love our Australian artistes. Very friendly. Very nice. And they are not mean with their tips like the Italians.'

Jack assumed this was a hint and, despite suspecting the same flattering phrase was repeated to all new residents, amended according to nationality, he discreetly slid another centime onto the counter, glad of Roger's advice that a store of coins in his pocket would be useful.

As he'd climbed the narrow stairs to the third level, dragging his suitcase behind him, Jack was indeed thankful that he'd travelled light and that his apartment was not on the sixth floor. Opening the door at the top of the second flight of stairs, he entered the apartment. High ceilings, large windows and white walls immediately created a feeling of airiness and space. Paintings lined the walls, some framed, most not. A small wooden table sat under the window, a chair on each side. The musty odour of an old couch, its broad arms showing signs of wear, filled the air. Jack guessed this living room also doubled as a studio, judging by the large easel standing against the wall, drawing books and loose sheets of paper haphazardly piled beside it. Walking through, he'd quickly realised the only other rooms were a bedroom off to one side of the living area and a kitchenette with a storeroom opening off the far end. Jack returned to study the paintings on display, deciding he liked some of them but thought others were mere splashes of paint. Experiments, perhaps? Standing before a group of photographs pasted to the wall, he guessed that he was finally facing Mrs Rix, an attractive fair-haired woman with a broad smile who featured both alone and with assorted men and woman in the various photographs. Jack thought she looked friendly.

A note with his name scrawled across the top, on the centre of the table, caught Jack's attention. He carefully read through what proved to be a list of instructions, mostly reiterating those outlined by Mimi only minutes earlier.

Make yourself at home in the bedroom. I have cleaned out the top two drawers and the whole wardrobe. The bed springs have long gone, but the mattress is cleaner than most you will find in Paris, and the bedding is fresh. You will find a laundrette down the road for washing, though no doubt Mimi will offer to sort this out for you. There is a tub for washing on the first floor and water can be delivered daily – just let Mimi know if you want any, she'll look after you. Street life can get a little rowdy on the Passage; however, the neighbours are friendly. Mostly artists. Doing it pretty tough. They love a chat and will appreciate if you occasionally join in for a beer and song. Even more if you take a guitar and a bottle of scotch! 'Bonjour' will get you a long way on the streets of Paris – use it frequently. People are much more helpful when you do!

The note concluded by offering best wishes to Jack, followed by the name *Hilda Rix* written with a sweeping flourish, and then a PS that included the addresses of a couple of friends who would assist if Jack needed anything, and then a PPS explaining that Hilda did not expect to be back in France inside three months, quite likely not for six and, in any case, was happy for him to stay even if she came back early. *We will cross that bridge when we get to it.* Jack liked her, thinking how her way with words engendered an easy friendliness and that, somehow, she reminded him of Margaret.

Jack had spent the remainder of the afternoon settling into the apartment and revisiting Roger's notes in preparation for the art classes that were starting the next morning. He wanted to buy a small collapsible easel, a few larger brushes and some canvas; however, Roger had advised that, while there were many art stores in Paris, some carried better quality goods than others, and he'd encouraged Jack to be wary of using cheap paint.

'*Sennelier* on the *Quai Voltaire* is the best place in Paris for supplies,' he'd told Jack. 'Opened by my old friend Gustave over forty years ago. Mention my name. He will look after you. However, I suggest you wait and see what Monsieur Simon suggests you buy. All the masters have their own preferences when it comes to pigments. Better to wait.'

Darkness had settled on the street early and, just as Jack had been kicking himself for not thinking ahead to buy some food for his dinner, a light knock sounded on the door. Mimi stood on the threshold, smiling as she offered a steaming mug of soup, a long, thin stick of bread and a slab of cake wrapped in brown paper. 'I thought you might be getting hungry, yes?' she said with a laugh.

Jack had thanked her profusely, relieved to avoid a night of hunger and relieved that he did not have to venture onto the darkening Passage Dantzig searching for food, for the noise level from the street was escalating with every passing hour. As the evening had worn on he'd repeatedly found himself drawn to the window, fascinated by the shadowy scenes below that were visible in the eerie glow of the gas street lights, and he was sure that even more people were gathering each time he looked out.

Eventually, fatigue had set in and Jack had fallen onto the creaky bed. However, sleep had been evasive, and he'd lain awake, listening to the lively conversations of men and woman whose voices were so loud they sounded like they were in his room, singing and laughing, the languages unrecognisable. At one point, a drunken argument between a man and woman had pierced the night air and Jack had been alarmed by the slurring alcohol-fuelled abuse bandied between the two. He'd returned to the window and was relieved to witness the intervention of an older woman who, speaking in a sharp voice, separated the pair with a not-so-gentle shove.

Eventually sleep had arrived and this morning, as Jack looked down onto the street, the only evidence of the previous night's activities were bottles strewn across the cobblestones and an assortment of chairs that had been left scattered on the sidewalk. Fascinated, he continued to watch until golden sunlight began to filter between the buildings, casting glowing fingers of light across the Passage Dantzig. Spurred into action, he wasted no time getting dressed, packing his satchel with pencils, charcoal and the drawing pad that never left his side these days, and headed out of the apartment and onto the narrow road.

CHAPTER 16

The smell of warm bread and coffee wafted through the air, luring Jack towards a small stand set up at the end of the street. A sign advertised milk, bread and *café au lait* for sale. Sipping the hot coffee, Jack was glad its bitter taste was compensated for by the sweet, crusty roll. Standing while he ate, he watched a lone figure in the distance, possibly female, immense and reasonably strong judging by the way she was slopping water from a metal bucket along the gutter and following through with determined sweeps of a broad broom. Her rhythmic sloshing echoed through the street as she attacked the pavement with fury. Each stroke seemed determined to scrub away the very souls of the revellers who had made merry into the early hours, their bottles, cigarette stubs and stench of urine lingering.

Passing *La Ruche*, Jack peered into the courtyard. All was quiet this morning, and he imagined the late-night revellers with sore heads and seeking relief that only slumber could provide. Guided by Roger's map, he reversed yesterday's steps to work his way back to the station. Roger had warned that he would have quite a trek across town to the academy; however, on the upside, the new Métro now made getting around Paris much easier.

Turning out from the Passage, into the Rue de Dantzig, a young woman struggled to steer her cluster of straggly haired goats along the footpath. Jack wondered where on earth she was going? He watched, fascinated, when she paused to accept an enamel bowl from a lady standing on the path, then squatted beside the lead goat, her nimble fingers wringing a white stream from its swollen teats. As he passed, Jack could hear the shushing sound as the tiny jets of milk landed in the bowl. Amazing. This was a scene he would love to paint.

Deviating from yesterday's route, he turned left at the Rue des Morillons, lured by the shafts of sunlight spilling onto the cobblestones, confident that a right turn at the next block would lead him to *Convention Station*. From there the ride to Gare Montparnasse, where he disembarked and crossed to Line 10 and continued to Mabillon, had been straightforward, and it was only a matter of a short walk along the *Rue de Seine* to the academy.

Standing before the closed door of *Académie Julian,* Jack realised that, in his quest to avoid being late, he had arrived almost an hour early. Rather than stand waiting, he decided to explore the streets nearby and, lured by the glimpses of the river, he walked towards it. Closer to the city centre, the cobbled streets were streaming with people and Jack looked all about him with fascination. As a gaunt woman approached him, he realised the bundle she held close to her was a young child. Her gait was peculiar and he heard her muttering softly, her head bobbing and turning to the left and right, a picture of agitation, as though fearing some ghost from her past was pursuing her. On reaching Jack, she paused and held out her hand, still muttering as she gazed into his eyes. Her heavily lined face was brown and haggard, her age difficult to determine. Was she the child's mother or grandmother? Jack dug into his pockets and placed a couple of centimes into the gnarled claw extended towards him, and her brown eyes softened.

'*Gracias...*' The word fell onto his ears with a softness and unexpected dignity, and Jack felt moved to pat her shoulder, smiling down into the wary eyes of the child beside her. Nodding, the woman patted his arm and resumed her head-bobbing shuffle. He wondered at the dismal circumstances that had reduced her to wandering the streets of Paris, begging for centimes.

Continuing along the riverfront, Jack spotted a man standing within a domed metal space, one of a few he'd noticed along his walk, and was shocked to see that the man was relieving himself into the vessel. He realised that the ornate domes were in fact public urinals and made up his mind that, if this was the extent of privacy the public latrines offered, he needed to make alternative arrangements.

The pungent odour of dog faeces followed him and Jack, seeing the heel of his boot was soiled, scraped it against the side of the gutter. Dogs were everywhere, some held in check by decorative leads while others were carried in their owners' arms. Others ran freely alongside their owners, while still more seemed to run wild amongst the pedestrians, creating a nuisance. A man who was placing a cart of fruit outside his shop kicked away a small tricolour puppy who had paused and sniffed at the wheels. The dog yelped as it skirted away to avoid a second attack and Jack imagined gangs of dogs roaming the streets, seeking scraps and dodging kicks, with the cunning of street urchins.

Eventually, he returned to the Rue du Dragon to find the academy's blue door now open, not into the foyer of a building, as he'd assumed, but rather into a charming courtyard, now abuzz with people. Walking through, Jack had an overwhelming sense of disconnection, as though he had stepped onto a theatre stage depicting a scene from centuries past. Amid the most diverse group he could ever have imagined, he stared in wonder. Older artists, identifiable by their outdated flowing smocks gathered at the wrist, their layers of paint splatters a testimony of eons of experience, clustered together oozing the aura of accomplished practitioners. Groups of excited young people, chatted excitedly, the mix of languages revealing they'd arrived from across Europe to study art in Paris. Others stood alone, and, while some like himself gazed curiously around the unfamiliar environment, others leaned against the walls of the courtyard with detached, impatient expressions; returning students, perhaps?

A small café operated out of the back of a cart, surrounded by people eager to purchase sweet-smelling breakfast rolls and steaming cups of coffee for a few centimes. Two stray dogs sniffed for scraps between their legs.

Unsure what he should do, Jack decided to follow the lead of the others and simply stand, waiting for something to happen. Not for the first time in the last few weeks, he questioned his sanity. Nothing about his paintings and so-called talent made him feel connected to this time, this place or the people he stood amongst, and he wondered what possessed him to allow a bunch of crazy Bloomsbury artists that he barely knew to direct his destiny to this moment, to this place – a cobbled courtyard in Montparnasse, standing amid general mayhem and barely able to understand a single word that emitted from the chaos surrounding him.

Out of the corner of his eye, Jack noticed a bustle of movement from an arched doorway where a thickset lady with tight black curls and equally black eyes had emerged. Her words rang across the court-yard - French, Jack assumed. Not understanding her instructions, he remained still, looking for cues from those around him. A group of young women stepped forward and ventured up the stairs. Determining that this was a call for female students, Jack waited, his eyes firmly fixed on the arched entry, from where he expected his instructions would be delivered sometime soon.

He did not have to wait long, for within minutes a second person, a young man this time, requested that students of Monsieur Simon follow him. Although, again, the phrase was announced in French, Jack gleaned the word *Simon* and guessed it referred to the teacher Roger had organised for him. He joined the dozen or so men of assorted ages that trailed behind the youth along a dark hallway, up a flight of stairs and into a room with spectacularly high ceilings. Feeble sunlight attempted to infiltrate the dusty skylights, supplemented by beams forcing their way through the windows and, glancing through them, Jack realised that the room offered a stunning view across the rooftops of Paris towards the spire of the Eiffel Tower. The Eiffel Tower! It was the clearest Jack had seen the famous landmark since he'd arrived, and it thrilled Jack to know that he would enjoy this view for the next three months.

The room reverberated with the hollow sound of footsteps as the last of the students shuffled in. It was minimally furnished: large tables

speckled with paint of every conceivable colour, surrounded by a scat-
tering of stools. Heavy wooden shelves lined the rear wall, and along
the sides, glass-fronted cupboards displayed an array of jars and
bottles, many looking like they had been sitting undisturbed for
decades. A muddle of ancient easels lay against each other in a back
corner. At the front of the room, a tiny man with scruffy white hair and
a drooping moustache was deep in concentration, carefully arranging a
set of wooden blocks to appear as though they'd been scattered
haphazardly. Cubes, rectangles and balls in red, yellow and blue made
up a painstakingly crafted illusion.

Apparently satisfied with the effect, he finally looked at the new
arrivals with a welcoming smile.

'*Bonjour, amis*. Come in, come in,' he called, beckoning them
forward with a two-handed motion. 'You have bought paper, *oui*?' He
signalled to a pile of papers and charcoal sticks for those who may not
have. 'There are easels down the back, some so old, I think Methuselah
must have used them! Find a space, and draw, draw, draw...' His hands
made a squiggling motion universal in its meaning, and Jack surmised
that minimal words accompanied by sweeping gestures had proved to
be the quickest way for the master to communicate with the students of
various nationalities in his classes.

'Charcoal or pencil?'

'What paper?'

'How large?'

Monsieur Simon shushed the questions with a sweep of his hands,
indicating that anything was acceptable - just draw. Jack glanced
uncertainly at the other students and then followed a couple to the back
of the room, where they wrestled easels from the tangle. In the afternoon, he planned to buy his own – something lightweight and portable,
yet big enough to take a good-sized canvas, and that could easily be
slung over his shoulder. He returned to the table, first moving forward,
close to the arrangement of blocks, and then, reconsidering, moving
back. He finally settled on a vantage point a few feet from the table,
light streaming across his shoulder and illuminating the blocks in a
pleasing manner. After setting up the rickety easel, Jack pulled his

drawing book from his satchel, opened it to a fresh page and set it up. When he selected a thin piece of charcoal from his paintbox, it felt awkward in his hand, as though he'd never held a pencil before. Then, with sweeping movements, Jack began loosely sketching on his pad, glancing up every few seconds at the blocks. As he concentrated on the paper before him, he relaxed with every stroke.

Within minutes, the assembly of disparate individuals morphed into a cohesive collection of artistes, quietly focused on their drawing, the scratch of their tools over pads the only sound in the room.

Moving amongst them, Monsieur Simon looked over shoulders, nodding with approval here, making a quiet suggestion there, but largely leaving the students to their work. Jack, after creating a light outline of the table and the geometric shapes thereon, sketched in the shape of the man standing directly opposite him, whose frown reflected deep concentration as he also worked on the drawing task from his vantage. Jack then decided to add a second figure further beyond, to the right. Absorbed in the drawing, he deftly added the outline of Monsieur Simon and then worked across the page, using cross-hatching to develop a strong three-dimensional effect. Monsieur peered at Jack's work, smiled and chuckled as he moved on.

Time passed quickly and, after forty-five minutes, the master called the class together, requesting that they display their sketches along the front of the room. Stepping forward, one-by-one, the men set their easels in a row, the drawings generating appreciative murmuring from the class.

Jack's earlier reserve had diminished, warmed by the kindly manner of the teacher, the familiar act of drawing and the connection he could feel with the other students, created by the intensity of the shared drawing task. He smiled at the young men nearest to him whom he'd noticed entering the room earlier, speaking English with the flattened accents of Americans. Brothers, he guessed, for they looked very similar. They nodded towards him and he extended his hand – 'Jack Tomlinson.'

'Reg Hoover, and my brother, Keith.'

'Is that your drawing on the end? Well done,' Keith added.

'Very good, very good.' Monsieur Simon commanded the attention of the class and it seemed that every phrase that he spoke required an echo to reinforce it. 'Good interpretations of a common subject, each with their own style. *Oui?*'

The students agreed, marvelling at their diverse representations of the blocks from their various vantage points, some having created painstakingly detailed images of the shapes, others light, loose outlines. They'd also used a range of techniques to depict the reflections of light on the flat planes of the objects, and some, like Jack, had added dark cross-hatching or blending to portray the shadows created by the strong sunlight pouring through the dormer windows. One or two students had added features of the room, such as the table or the high windows. Only Jack had added human figures to the scene which drew appreciative murmuring from the group.

Monsieur Simon briefly commented on the range of techniques used, admiring one drawing for its clean lines and another for its clever shading of the negative spaces surrounding the blocks. Finally, he pointed to Jack's inclusion of the artists in the room, laughingly commenting on the handsome Monsieur who hovered in the background.

Suggesting the class would be ready for a break, he led the students to a room at the end of the landing. They were pleased to see the wood stove had been lit early and the cast-iron kettle was bubbling, steam pouring from its spout. A teapot, milk jug, sugar and spoons were set out on a table beside the stove, and an assortment of cups, albeit chipped from years of use, rested on the shelf above the table. Monsieur suggested that they may prefer to bring their own mugs in future rather than risk contracting some disease from the cracked crockery on offer.

For the next twenty minutes or so, the students politely conversed, enquiring where each was from and discussing their painting experiences as they sought common ground. Most had demonstrated competent drawing skills, and they'd enrolled in the art school for a range of reasons. One gentleman, Marcello, whom Jack assumed was Italian, had quite good English. Jack listened as he explained to the American brothers that he had been painting in watercolour for years and wished to develop oil painting skills. With a chuckle, Marcello said he now had to learn to paint backwards: where watercolour always began with the lightest colours on the paper first, oils started with the darkest. Another student, Rondel, was an experienced art teacher who'd been trained in classic techniques of realism. Like Jack, he had enrolled in Monsieur's class, hoping to gain skills in the modern painting styles for which Paris was renowned. Jack glanced at a thin young man standing towards the back of the room and, as their eyes met, he smiled with a nod. A foreigner, judging by the long, oily black curls and swarthy skin; he wondered if the young man spoke English. He chuckled to himself. Foreigner? He himself was the foreigner, probably from even more distant horizons than anybody else in the room, he realised.

Following the break, they returned for a second drawing exercise. This time, Monsieur arranged a pewter mug, a wine carafe and a loaf of bread with knotted crust. He sliced through the latter and placed it on a wooden board, then completed the setting by carefully positioning a slab of yellow cheese in the foreground.

'Your Parisian platter,' he said, explaining that no Frenchman could survive without their daily dose of wine, bread and cheese.

In this session, Monsieur Simon took the lead, describing the deliberate manner he'd used to create a triangular arrangement of the objects by balancing the vertical lines of the wine carafe with the horizontal lines of the breadboard. How he'd taken advantage of the sunlight – the contrast of shadows and light effectively infusing liveliness and energy into the scene. With a few strokes of charcoal, he then sketched the main shapes. Stepping back to view his progress, he explained the value of getting the proportions of the setting accurate before attending to details. Next, he demonstrated where flashes of brilliant sunlight would be highlighted, glinting off glass and metal to create strong contrast, and how to squint their eyes to check their composition and ensure a balance of dark against light, ideally a two-thirds, one-third ratio. Finally, and with great speed, Monsieur Simon began shading, varying the intensity. Before the students' eyes, the image popped forward as if three-dimensional. The wine bottle was so lifelike, Marcello joked that Monsieur was lucky: he merely had to draw his daily ration of wine, then reach out to grasp the bottle's smooth neck.

Once the demonstration was completed, it was the students' turn to reproduce the still-life, and the class was once again enveloped in silence, focusing on their work as they tried to remember the steps and reproduce the techniques of the master. Jack was pleased with his effort and yet, although well-practised and skilled at drawing, he felt surprisingly tired by the depth of concentration and silently acknowledged that his finished effort was a poor second to Monsieur's.

It was midday before they knew it and the end of the lesson, although Monsieur Simon explained that they were all welcome to remain painting into the afternoon if they wished. In fact, students were free to work in the room as often as they liked between the hours of seven am to five pm. They just needed to let the academy's janitor know that they were there, lest they be locked in overnight with only the ghosts for company. And a few good-sized rats. He chuckled. He then thanked the students for their hard work before requesting that they meet in the courtyard at nine o'clock the next morning, from which they would take a short walk to the *Musée du Luxembourg* and indulge in a banquet of art across the ages. Jack was a little disappointed at this announcement. Although he had enjoyed his time wandering through art galleries in London with Margaret, he had really liked this first day with charcoal and paper, and could not wait to be painting. The notion of walking through the art gallery like a bunch of schoolboys did not particularly excite him, but he consoled himself with the knowledge that there would be many weeks of painting in this very room ahead of him.

Thinking that this afternoon would be a good opportunity to purchase paints, Jack approached Monsieur Simon.

'So, Jack, is it? Roger's young friend? You liked your lesson today, *oui?*'

'I did, Monsieur. It is wonderful to be here.'

'Yes... Paris... it has a magic. I hope that you enjoy your time here, very much...'

'Roger suggested I check with you before buying some paints. He said that you might have preferences. I thought that I may get them this afternoon.'

'Yes, certainly. Of course, you may have your own favourites, but some are essential–prussian and cobalt blue, cadmium yellow, red ochre and emerald green. Plus, some cobalt violet and zinc white. And of course, you may like to try *Sennelier's* own creation–Chinese orange.'

Watching as the master reached for a sheet of rough paper and used a stick of charcoal to record a list of colours, Jack nodded. 'Roger also said to go to *Sennelier*. Over near the river somewhere.'

'The river! *The Seine*, Jack. *The Seine*. Named after the goddess Sequana. She runs through the heart of Paris, both dividing and uniting us, carrying our largest ships and our tiniest rowing boats, perfect for an afternoon of romance in the sunshine.' He winked at Jack and then, with a flourish, he turned the page over and sketched out the route to the *Quai Voltaire*, signing the drawing with the swirling letters *LS*.

After Monsieur left, Marcello encouraged anyone interested to meet at the *Café La Rotonde* at two pm. Close by, in Montparnasse, it was a popular place for artists, he told them. Renowned for its cheap coffee and warm soup, and of even greater significance, worth visiting to see the walls which were lined with hundreds of paintings, many by famous artists – a legacy of Parisian painters who had exchanged their work in payment for coffee and baguettes to avoid starvation. While the invitation was extended to all, Jack decided to stay with his plan to purchase his art supplies. He was happy to be alone and absorb the morning's lesson and, besides, if he planned to eat that night, he also needed to buy some food.

<hr>

Sennelier was only a short walk from the academy and, when Jack arrived, he found the store was already crowded with other students, like himself, replenishing their art supplies.

He gazed around in wonder at the abundance of stock. Tall glass-fronted cabinets lined the walls, filled with every colour of paint imaginable in tubes, jars and tins. Pigeonholed displays were jam-packed with brushes, from tiny round ones barely a sixteenth of an inch through to large, flat brushes - two inches wide. Their bristles were made from sable, squirrel goat and horse-hair. Then there were small tacks and wooden frames for stretching canvas, and an assortment of easels from enormous contraptions for very large works to tiny light-weight ones that could be folded and carried.

'*Bonjour, monsieur.* Can I assist?'

'*Bonjour*, miss…' The French greeting felt awkward rolling off his tongue. 'Yes, thank you. You have so much stock. This is wonderful!'

'*Oui.* Yes, it is wonderful. We like to have something for everyone. And if we don't have it, we will make it specially for you.'

'Wow. I mean, thank you, but that will not be necessary. I have a list.'

The assistant smiled as soon as she saw his note. 'Ah yes, Monsieur Simon. He is a fine teacher. You will enjoy him. One moment and I will have your paints ready.'

While Jack waited for the paints, he selected a small easel. 'No, not that one,' the assistant said when she returned. 'Here, this one with the strap. A fine easel which you can carry like this… You will not upset the pedestrians.' She demonstrated how the easel folded down, compact and unobtrusive, and could be carried over his shoulder. 'And for you, today it will be two francs!'

After adding an assortment of brushes and rods of charcoal, Jack left, pleased with his purchases. Surprisingly tired, he retraced his steps back to the station, stopping to buy bread, milk, cheese, some slices of ham and a jar of jam at a general store along the way. These purchases relied on visual cues, as beyond her greeting, '*Bonjour, monsieur*' as he entered the store, he could not understand a single word uttered by the elderly woman seated at the counter and, conversely, she shook her head at each of his requests until they both resorted to a game of pointing, nodding and pantomiming. By the time he left, they were smiling warmly at each other, and she laughed as he again repeated '*Bonjour*,' shaking her head. 'No, no. *Au revoir–au revoir.*'

'*Au revoir.*' Jack enjoyed learning the new word.

'*Au revoir. Merci*!'

'*Au revoir, mercy…*' Now it was getting complicated. Jack laughed with a wave of his hand, determining that he must return to this shop with its friendly storekeeper–that is, if he could ever find his way back again.

CHAPTER 17

The following morning, Jack again miscalculated the timing of the journey to the academy and was first in his class to be waiting in the courtyard, ready for the museum visit. He was considering taking a walk along the riverfront when a fellow student appeared. A man of similar age to Jack, his black shoulder-length hair topped with a cream cap and earnest manner seemed to set him apart from the rest of the class. Yesterday, Jack had observed him working at the back of the room, quietly completing the tasks set by Monsieur, but until this minute he had not found an opportunity to speak with him. Jack stepped forward with his hand extended.

'Jack Tomlinson, mate. Pleased to meet you. Great lesson yesterday.'

'Andrés,' the man replied in halting English as he shook Jack's hand. 'Yes. Monsieur is a very popular teacher. Helpful. A gentleman.'

Jack smiled by way of reply; recognising that Andrés struggled to speak English, he wanted to avoid plying him with questions. Nonetheless, the young man seemed keen to converse.

'You're English, no? American?' he asked, attempting to clarify Jack's unfamiliar accent.

'No, mate. Australian. I'm a long way from home.'

'Australia.' Andrés smiled broadly, his white teeth flashing. Jack wondered if he was the first Australian that Andrés had ever met.

'What about you?'

'Málaga,' replied Andrés. 'Málaga, Spain.'

Spain! Jack was pleasantly surprised, conscious that the boundaries of the world he had comfortably inhabited for eighteen years were again being expanded. It felt good to be conversing with a male close to his own age, and he was pleased that they would be classmates.

Over the next fifteen minutes, the remainder of the class arrived in rapid succession. Firstly, Reg and Keith, who greeted Jack like an old friend and then introduced themselves to Andrés. They explained how they were regular visitors to Paris, their father frequently visiting the city for business and, whenever they could, they seized the opportunity to attend the city's famous academies for lessons. Jack was amazed. He could not imagine his father indulging him with painting holidays.

Next to arrive was Raymond, the man who'd set up opposite Jack yesterday while they'd painted blocks, assisted by a silver-tipped walking stick to support his large bulk. He nodded at Jack and Andrés as he pulled a crumpled handkerchief from his jacket pocket and mopped his forehead. The exertion of his walk had left him somewhat breathless. For his sake, Jack hoped the walk to the *Musée du Luxembourg* would not be too long. Raymond was closely followed by a quiet little man of about fifty, dark-haired, with smooth olive skin. Jack wondered if he might also be Italian. His drawing of the blocks on the table had captured Jack's attention, it's multiple sharp, angular lines bouncing off the shapes, almost like echoes–repetitions boldly drawn before receding into the distance. It had reminded Jack of paintings he had seen in London's National Gallery, and he assumed the man was attempting modern techniques. Two more students appeared, chatting animatedly and calling '*Bonjour*!' to the others as they approached. Jack could see that the two men-strangers yesterday-had already formed a firm bond, no doubt drawn together by their similar ages–about forty–and cheerful personalities.

He jumped as the heavy carved door behind him opened with a loud creak and Monsieur Simon appeared.

'*Bonjour, Messieurs*,' he exclaimed, prompting a chorus of '*Bonjour, Monsieur*' in reply.

'Are we ready for our feast?' His eyes twinkling at the prospect of the morning's excursion; the master's enthusiasm was inspiring. His right hand held a wad of cardboard slips, which he immediately began distributing.

'To each of you I give the key to joy, wonder and beauty,' he said. 'These are yours to use as you wish over the next three months. They will give you entry into most museums and galleries in Paris. Make sure you wear them out!' Monsieur reverently pressed a small folded card into each student's hand as though bestowing a priceless gift. Swiftly, he then turned and headed down the stairs, a wave of his hand beckoning the group to follow. At the base of the stairs he steered them to the left, and left again, and they followed him down a street so narrow that Jack could stretch his arms out and almost touch the buildings on each side, prompting laughter from Andrés.

Looking skyward, where a strip of blue was visible between rooftops, Jack marvelled at the age of this ancient street, lined with houses five storeys high. Their side walls were attached to each other, like his aunt and uncle's in London, but these buildings were much older. Yellowing, the stone walls showed signs of buckling and bulging. Possibly even ready to collapse at any second, he thought, then assured himself that they had probably stood for hundreds of years and so unlikely to fall at this very minute. To Jack, this narrow street was extraordinarily picturesque, its buildings endowed with charming entrances, their carved doors bearing ornate iron hinges; flower pots, perching precariously on narrow window ledges, a reminder of spring. Many of the ornate wrought-iron balcony railings were adorned with the flapping evidence of the morning's washing. Jack inhaled deeply, recognising a familiar perfume–geraniums–from his own mother's garden, their sweet perfume blending with the earthy odour of dog and goat droppings lying in wait for less observant pedestrians than himself. He listened to the voices ringing through open windows as families prepared for their day, words indiscernible to Jack, combining with the tinkling of pianos and rasping of violins. He hoped the small children practising their instruments enjoyed their music lessons more than he ever did. Together, the sights, odours and sounds of this tiny street converged in Jack's mind to form an image of the daily lives of Parisians that he knew that he would never forget. Charming, energetic and colourful. If only he could see into the closed doorways.

Andrés caught his eye. 'Paris! It is truly wonderful, Jack,' he said.

'Yes. To think I have only been here for three days now. I love it. I think I might stay here forever!' Jack replied, causing Andrés to laugh again with him.

On reaching the end of the narrow lane, the group turned onto a broad street, teeming with rushing pedestrians whose footsteps spilled around leisurely women who chattered, arms linked, and barrow boys balancing heavy stock for delivery. Again, as everywhere it seemed, there were dogs, some attached to their owners by way of short leads, others running loose. Shops displayed their wares on the pathway and the enticing odours of croissants, sweet buns, fresh bread and coffee emitted from a small corner café. The cobblestone road was chaotic with motor vehicles, buses and horse-drawn carts banking up behind boxlike two-storey trams that lumbered along fixed metal rails. The air was constantly pierced by shrill squeals of metal against metal as they braked for passengers to dismount–a familiar sight to Jack, reminiscent of the green trams of Melbourne's city streets.

However, Monsieur Simon's eyes were fixed on a distant destination and he seemed oblivious to the cacophony of the morning bustle. Maintaining his brisk pace, he led them around stalled vehicles and stepped over horse manure as they crossed the road.

'Come along! Not so far now,' he called over his shoulder, causing Jack and Andrés to step up their pace.

Passing through large iron gates, they entered an exquisitely manicured parkland with tall trees, expanses of green lawn and colourful garden beds lining a long central driveway, its atmosphere one of serenity in contrast to the busy streets they had just left. Jack wondered if there was anything to be found in Paris that was not interesting or charming or beautiful.

Continuing to the end of the driveway and turning sharply to the left, the group finally found themselves before their destination, the *Musée du Luxembourg*. Numerous tourists were gathered, waiting for the doors to open. A group of young men with short-cropped hair jostled on the broad stairs. Their laughter and loud voices drew amused looks from some visitors, frowns from others.

'Students from the *Academy des Beaux-Arts*,' Andrés whispered to Jack. 'Not always so well behaved!'

On the stroke of the half hour, the doors opened and tourists and students entered. Monsieur waved to the attendant seated at the entry desk, who smiled and waved back, calling *'Bonjour, Monsieur Simon'* before returning to the task of admitting a large group of chattering Americans. Jack suspected the master was a familiar figure at the gallery.

Ushering the group through the turnstile, Monsieur declared with a dramatic sweep of his arm, 'Now we will take a journey through the ages. We will walk in the steps of the masters. We will feast on their works. We will learn their styles, analyse their techniques and imagine their influences. From them, we will see where art has been, where we are now and, where you, my *étudiants*, may take painting into the future.'

With that, Monsieur swept forward, beckoning the students to follow him into a room–its enormously high ceilings a work of art in themselves with decorative plasterwork–where dozens of very old paintings hung in rows. Once the group had clustered around him, Monsieur began his exposition on art history.

Jack had enjoyed his visits to London's National Gallery, with Margaret chatting nonstop and making him laugh with her serious acceptance of the most ridiculous artworks, drawing the frowns of the attendants. In honesty, however, he had not been terribly excited at the prospect of being dragged around a dusty old gallery behind Monsieur like a class of schoolchildren. He would have preferred to remain at the atelier, themselves painting, rather than gazing at old paintings. Monsieur, however, proved to be a marvellous guide, bearing an extensive and detailed knowledge of both artists and individual artworks. His gift for storytelling enraptured the students, unlike the guides who had led Jack and his schoolmates through the Melbourne Museum in years gone by and seemed more intent on vaunting their knowledge, oblivious to disinterest of their audiences. In contrast, Monsieur's passion and energy proved contagious.

Moving rapidly through the early works, the master described the focus on religious experience – saints with contemplative expressions, biblical visions, dreams, Madonnas. Continuing down the broad corridors, Monsieur explained how portraiture had developed, first with stiff images of significant leaders, soldiers, royalty and wealthy patrons, then shifting to more relaxed settings: men standing beside their seated wives while children gathered at their knees.

Huddled around their teacher as ducklings to their mother, the group moved along the corridor as a single unit, straining to follow Monsieur Simon's words as they gazed upon one painting after another. Together, they observed the finest details of ancient brush-work, including corrections and repairs that had been made over time, revealed by scrutinising the texture of the oil for changes. Standing back, they viewed each painting in its entirety, listening as the master described interesting compositional techniques that had been deliberately employed to move viewers' eyes around, across and into paintings.

'Even the greats make mistakes,' Monsieur Simon claimed, pointing out flaws in a number of works, such as Édouard Manet's barmaid in *Bar at the Folies-Bergère,* whose reflection in the mirror behind her was clearly at odds with her posture, and then there was the unnaturally long neck and grotesquely large feet of the beautiful woman featured in Botticelli's *Birth of Venus*.

Jack listened intently to every word, fascinated by the world-famous paintings and the stories behind their creations. Artists that he had heard about in his classrooms–men of ancient times who held no interest for sixteen-year-old schoolboys–suddenly were being viewed in a new light. Jack began to identify connections. The transmission of styles across times and nations. The influence of religion and politics. The symbols cleverly embedded in works that provided codes for those who knew how to read them. A compass to show wisdom. An hourglass to show we must use time wisely. The personal tags that artists left on their paintings, barely visible unless one knew where to look.

'It is like a hidden message,' Monsieur explained. 'A tiny word here, an unobtrusive object there. The meaning revealed only to those clever enough to interpret them. You must all go to the *Musée du Louvre* and see Jan van Eyck's *The Arnolfini Portrait*. Full of symbols, it is, but also tagged with the artist himself. So clever! A hint—look at the reflection. That is your homework!' Monsieur's eyes teared with laughter at this reference. 'Ah, we artistes, we can be so very sneaky sometimes!'

Standing before the paintings of the Impressionists inspired awe, and Jack could not wait to attempt their style as soon as possible. Even though the portraits and river scenes were overly colourful and the brushstrokes loose and untidy, he could see the beauty and romance of these paintings.

From Monet's beautiful garden scenes to Renoir's portraits of patrons relaxing in cafés or rowing on rivers, Jack marvelled at the ways that these artists had captured everyday life in energetic strokes. Monsieur Simon pointed out Renoir's clever use of complementary colours—the way he'd position a red umbrella against a green dress; an orange cup against a blue tablecloth—was no accident, he assured the students.

It was humbling to admit that, yes, Jack may have a skill—a talent to reproduce—but there was so much more to creating a great painting than making something look real. In fact, many of the great works in the gallery had no bearing on reality at all! Now he suddenly felt as though he knew nothing at all about art and he felt hungry to learn, practise and improve.

It seemed that the more excited Monsieur Simon became, the faster he spoke, and hence the more difficult he was to understand. The group, spellbound by now, did not wish to miss anything, and so they clung tightly together, leaning in towards him.

'Now. To get really *intéressant*: the *modernes*,' he said, his eyes wide and his voice rising with dramatic effect, before waving his protégés onward. The first room, clearly popular, was already full of pamphlet-waving, loudly chatting tourists.

'Not to rush.' Monsieur steered the group away from the largest crowd into one of the smaller side rooms.

'Here, a van Gogh. You may have heard of him!' he said with a chuckle, pausing before *Sunflowers* as though personally responsible for introducing the artist to the group.

'Impasto – see how thick he lays on the paint. Uses the canvas as a pallet! And another van Gogh–see the many strokes.'

Jack was astonished by the effect of the scene before him: a bright yellow sunset, in the foreground a man in a field. Not worked with the brushstrokes that he was familiar with, but rather, the image was created by thousands of tiny dashes in as many colourful shades. Immediately beside it was a painting by Georges Seurat.

'*Bathers at Asniéres.* Point, point, point,' said Monsieur, his finger mimicking a jabbing brush to demonstrate the staccato motion used by the artist to build up his extraordinary works. 'Not a stroke to be seen, just thousands of jabs. And not just dots, but colours carefully selected to... what to say?... shimmer... on the canvas.' Monsieur's eyes shone, enlivened by his passion for technique and willing his students to feel the power and excitement of colours vibrating and dancing on the canvas.

~

'Must have taken forever,' Jack whispered to Andrés. Seurat's scene reminded him of his painting set on the Yarra, yet it was vastly different from the realistic style he had aspired to achieve, for his parent's anniversary painting.

Not all paintings were to Jack's liking. The group moved into a room exhibiting the works of a well-known Spaniard, Salvador Dali. Monsieur described the contemporary artist's reputation for arrogance and controversy which had rippled from Spain to Paris to London and even to America.

'Not all artistes are... polite, sadly,' he informed the students. 'Sometimes a great gift comes with great arrogance.'

'Tell us about him,' Ted drawled, his brother nodding expectantly beside him, sensing an interesting story.

'Oh, Dali... he respects no one. Not even the parents who bore him. His poor father could barely tolerate him in the end and, when Dali even disrespected the memory of his own dead mother, well, that was the last straw. His father threw him out.' Monsieur's hands swept the air as if it was infused with a nasty odour. 'Of course, Dali knew everything. Far more, even, than the ignorant Masters of the Royal Academy!'

Jack listened curiously, not at all surprised to hear that the awful works before him were created by an equally awful person.

'Honestly, the professors must have wondered what they'd struck when Dali, only seventeen years old, told them he was more intelligent than they were, so how could they possibly assess his work!' Tears formed in Monsieur Simon's eyes and he rummaged to retrieve a hand-kerchief to mop his face, the story amused him so much. 'It makes me laugh so to imagine the astounded faces of the old professors when the young upstart put them in their place.'

Again, looking at the works, Jack found little to be impressed with. He could not conceal his distaste for the odd images – distorted bodies, their genitals obscenely enlarged, the animal-like fusions contorted in incomprehensible ways on barren landscapes–and his doubt that they could be viewed seriously.

Jack turned to Andrés and asked, 'Who in their right mind could even consider these paintings "art"?'

'Aha,' exclaimed Monsieur, overhearing his incredulous reaction. 'There lies the eternal question: "What is art?"'

This did, indeed seem to be an eternal question, and Jack listened eagerly, interested in the master's views on the topic he'd heard debated from the decks of the *Ormonde* to the dining table of Charleston, to the museums, cafés and taverns of London and now here, in the *Musée du Luxembourg,* in Paris.

In rapid, excited phrases, Monsieur extolled Dali's case for representing that which was not real, searching the exhibition to show Jack examples of the Spanish artist's earlier works, portraits and landscapes that were far less controversial.

Jack remained unconvinced, however, and, while happy to accept the Fauves' wild use of colour or the Cubists' geometric representations that they had just viewed amongst the contemporary works, he believed the sexualised images of Dali to be disturbingly obscene.

'*Amigo*, you are upset, no?' Andrés looked apologetic, as though personally responsible for the works of his fellow countryman. Guilty by association. Jack felt a little foolish and unsophisticated at the way he'd reacted so strongly to Dali's works. He certainly did not want the gentle young Spaniard to feel the need to placate him.

'No, no,' he said. 'It's just that I don't understand this sort of thing. I don't know anyone who would hang a painting like this on their walls. If anyone I knew back in Melbourne did, they would create a stir, I'm sure.' Jack tried not to sound as upset as he felt as he imagined Streeton's painting of the Victorian mountain range, the Grampians, in his parents' lounge room, replaced by one of Salvador Dali's works. He envisioned the shocked expressions of visitors to the house. His mother's church group. His father's business associates. It was beyond thinking about.

'Yes, as in Spain. Dali is quite eccentric, you would say. Not your typical Spanish artist. Many reject him.' It seemed that poor Andrés was trying to convince Jack that the Spanish were not a bunch of heathens. 'We have many great artistes. You will see Pablo in a minute. Another contemporary, but not so... what would you say?... controversial. Perhaps you will like him better...?'

The works of Pablo Picasso, who Monsieur described as one of the most popular artists in France, credited for changing the way that people viewed art, were exhibited in the busy room which they had bypassed earlier that morning, and which was still crowded with tourists and student groups alike. As Andrés had predicted, Picasso's paintings were less confrontational than those of Dali. However, Jack had mixed feelings about these, as well. He'd loved Picasso's earlier works, the portraits of his mother and sister which revealed the popular artist's extraordinary talent when he was as young as thirteen. His later paintings seemed to be child like and primitive in comparison. Jack could not understand why Picasso had discarded his extraordinary gift for realism to produce the strange contorted images before them.

To appease Andrés, Jack kept his opinions of Picasso's work to himself, and even questioned his own judgement. What did he know? Tourists by the hundreds were making a beeline to the exhibition. They all seemed to believe that Picasso was one of the greatest artists of the twentieth century. Who was Jack to question the judgements of the public and, apparently, the critics?

All too quickly, it was midday, and the group clustered together as Monsieur finished up the morning session. 'Tomorrow, do not be late, *mes étudiants*. We will study the works of Derain and Matisse. We will work on our colours, and you will be *sauvage* and *passionne* like the Fauves. I am already excited just thinking about it!'

After two mornings together, the men in Monsieur Simon's class were developing close ties and, overall, the class shared a pleasant camaraderie. Jack was pleased that, by arriving early this morning, he had met with Andrés and, after sharing the walk to the *Musée du Luxembourg* together, they had remained by each other's side throughout the morning.

'Jack, would you like to join me and come to my aunt's café for lunch? She has fine olives and cheese. You will not be disappointed, *amigo*. Perhaps we could go sightseeing this afternoon?'

'Yes... I would like that. That sounds great, mate.'

'Ha, mate! What a world. I do love Paris!'

~

Exiting the museum, Jack and Andrés descended the stairs together and followed the pavement towards an enormous pool. It was picture perfect, an octagon complete with cascading fountains rising high above them, their spray falling to create sparkling ripples over the water's surface. The glorious sunshine had enticed picnickers to the gardens and today it was surrounded by people, some feeding bread to the snow-white swans drifting majestically across the water, others sitting along the edges enjoying the warmth of the day and watching small children under the watchful eye of their nannies, running along the pools edges, guiding colourful yachts with long poles.

Beside Jack and Andrés, two small boys, charmingly dressed in identical shorts, white caps and navy-blue jackets, each complete with a row of neat red buttons, set up a loud wailing as the buxom lady accompanying them removed their yacht from the water and demanded that they follow her, *aussitôt*. Winking at Jack, Andrés leapt forward, landing on his hands and walking for a dozen or more steps before righting himself directly in front of the suddenly attentive boys.

'Could you help me, *messieurs*?' he asked them. 'I have lost my way and I don't know where is up and where is down.' Andrés' forlorn expression and comical hand gestures immediately had the boys laughing hysterically.

'Why, up is there,' replied one, pointing to the sky.

Andrés gazed up and with sadness in his voice, asked, 'But how will I ever get there?'

Jack joined in the laughter of the boys, whose tears were now forgotten. Following Andrés through the gardens, he was so glad that he had met this new friend with the contemplative air and thoughtful conversation that seemed at such odds with his haphazard appearance and spontaneous humour.

CHAPTER 18

*J*ack followed Andrés out of the park, onto the streets and, after weaving through narrow lanes, they eventually arrived at the Seine.

'Not much further,' Andrés said and Jack noticed that his friend had a hint of breathlessness, surprising as they had not been walking that fast. He deliberately slowed his steps. This section of the town was busy, a combination of industry and warehouses, although scattered amongst the bustle of commercial activity were multi-storeyed residential dwellings and cafés.

It was to a café with dark green-checked cloths covering tables on the pavement that Andrés led him. Inside, a counter displayed an assortment of foods that looked tasty, although somewhat foreign to Jack's experience. Dried hams hung from the ceiling, and enormous jars of olives lined shelves. Loaves of bread as well as the familiar crusty baguettes Jack had noticed all over Paris – were heaped in a large wicker basket. A range of cheeses were arranged under the glass case, including an enormous wheel of *comté*, as well as a smooth cylinder of goats' cheese and smooth yellow balls the size of quail eggs. Gazing around the walls, Jack could see a Spanish influence. Large posters showed matadors fluttering embroidered red capes before vast bulls, whose forelegs pounded the dusty arena, their heads low, preparing to charge their bejewelled adversaries. Other posters displayed flamenco dancers, decorative fans held aloft in dramatic poses, males and females both exquisitely dressed in ornate, traditional Spanish clothing.

Standing behind the counter, slicing olives into a yellow ceramic bowl, was a young woman with gleaming black hair pulled into an intricate bun, an ornate clip providing adornment above her perfectly shaped right ear. Her thick black eyelashes framed dark eyes, and her lips held a sweet curve which, on Andrés' appearance, broke into the most dazzling smile that Jack had ever seen. When she caught sight of Jack and realised he was with Andrés, the smile softened a little as shyness set in.

Jack was mesmerised. In truth, he had not had many close meetings with beautiful young women in his life. There were the Fitzgibbons' girls – he'd known them for years – and Margaret, of course. He had felt very comfortable with her, as indeed, she did not allow anyone to feel otherwise. However, this lovely girl with a spectacularly beautiful smile disarmed him and he felt stuck for words.

Andrés, oblivious to the pounding of Jack's heart, was polite in his introduction, speaking slowly, carefully choosing his words in English.

'Jack, I would like you to meet my baby sister, Sofia. Sofia, this is Jack from Australia.' Sofia giggled and swatted at Andrés' left shoulder. Stepping back, out of her reach, he laughed in reply. The two clearly shared a personal joke.

'Don't you "baby sister" me,' Sofia scolded, her English, like Andrés, understandable despite her strong Spanish accent. Turning to Jack, she explained, 'I should have been first, only that he yanked me back by my hair and made me bald!' It emerged that Sofia may well have been Andrés' baby sister, but only by a matter of chance – in fact, they were twins, arriving minutes apart. The warmth of their relationship shone like a beacon and Jack tried to imagine what it must be like to have, not just a sibling, but a twin sister with whom to share your whole life.

Sofia, stepping out from behind the counter, hooked her arm through Andrés'. Looking over her shoulder at Jack, she spoke directly to him and he felt his heart skip a beat as her eyes locked on his briefly.

'Come. Outside. It's a beautiful day. Let the sun kiss your cheeks and warm your bones. Maybe it will even warm your memory,' she said with a firm glare directed at Andrés, her eyes crinkling with humour that Jack found enchanting. She led the boys out the front door, settled them at a table and, announcing that she would be back in a minute, turned back inside. Andrés spent the next few minutes explaining how their Aunt Christina had left Málaga with her French husband many years ago, coming here to the sixth arrondissement, where together they'd opened the *Café Española*, its Spanish theme proving popular, setting it apart from the hundreds of other cafés in Paris.

Andrés described how Sofia visited the markets in the early morning, returning to serve in the café from ten am to two pm. Their aunt's elderly husband had recently taken ill, and she was grateful for Sofia's help. Andrés and Sofia had come to Paris specifically for him to attend the *Académie Julian*, hoping also to make some contacts with Parisian galleries that would be willing to take his work on consignment before they returned to Málaga, their hometown in southern Spain. Jack listened with interest. Sofia placed a carafe of water on the table and set out wine glasses, which she filled from a tall green bottle. Andrés continued his conversation with Jack as she returned with a tray. After placing an empty plate before each young man, she proceeded to fill the space between them with bread, a variety of cheeses, a plate of sliced ham, a small bowl of olive oil and a mushy mix which drew an enquiring look.

'*Tapenade,*' Sofia stated and Andrés showed Jack how to tear a slice of bread and dip it in.

Jack tried to concentrate on Andrés' words, but was distracted by the graceful movement of Sofia's hands as she playfully laid cloth serviettes with a flamboyant flourish, in front of first himself and then Andrés. With a cheeky giggle, she curtsied as she backed away from the table. Minutes later she returned, this time bearing a second plate holding two large slabs of a rich-looking fruitcake and a bottle of wine to refresh their glasses. And then, with a start, he noticed it. A ring with a small green stone, a diamond on each side sparkling in the sun's rays. Engaged?

Hardly surprising, really. After all, she was extremely lovely. In her early twenties, he guessed, a little older than himself. Beautiful, and bound to have many admirers. Too bad. For a tiny moment, he had wondered....

Jack enjoyed Andrés' company more than he could have imagined. Pulling out their drawing books, they discovered that they shared a common fascination for human subjects.

'Your work is wonderful, Jack,' Andrés said, looking at his drawing of Margaret. 'The hair, it gleams in the sunshine, and her face, it glows with joy!'

Sofia appeared at that moment and nodded in agreement with Andrés. 'Very beautiful, Jack. You are a good artiste, si... Your girlfriend?'

'No, no.' Jack shook his head, suddenly feeling embarrassed, and closed his book to focus on Andrés' sketches.

They showed traits of the more modern techniques that Jack was quickly becoming familiar with. Impressions of facial features rather than realistic details. Sharp, exaggerated lines and angles combining to create intense, vibrant images. Jack commented on a series of sketches depicting an ancient medieval building perched high on a cliff face.

'The *Castillo de Gibralfaro*. Tourists love these paintings.'

Jack was intrigued. 'Tourists? Do you sell paintings?'

'*Si*... yes... Sofia and I, we have a small *galleria* on the mountain. It was our father's, but now we manage it. Tourists come up the mountain to see the castle, and very often they call in to the gallery. Especially now that Sofia has opened the café.'

'A café?' Anything about Sofia was interesting to Jack.

'Yes, Sofia is never so happy as when she is cooking. It is her... passion... that and art, although she is not a painter. A curator, *si*. Very good with the gallery.'

Turning the pages as they spoke, Jack could hear the passion in Andrés' voice and realised that, for him, painting was so much more than a hobby or a source of income. Beyond aspirations of wealth or fame, it was his life. Andrés lived to paint. To experiment with colour and line. To test theories. To learn from the masters and develop his own style so that his work would be deemed important and sit proudly beside that of Spain's many great artists. Andrés explained to Jack how he hoped the months at the academy would be an opportunity to be noticed, to gain a reputation.

'We Spanish have our masters, for sure,' Andrés said. 'However, it is the French who are viewed as the experts of modern art.' He described how the Spanish artists were considered poor second cousins to the French and how, for a Spanish artist to truly be successful, he must gain recognition in Paris. Picasso, born in the twins' hometown of Málaga, became internationally renowned, as were Miro and Dali, following exhibitions in Paris. Andrés hoped that by studying with French masters he too could develop his techniques and get a chance to exhibit to a French audience. Perhaps even at the prestigious Salon d'Automne that would take place in October, known to launch the careers of many great artists. Additionally, many private salons in Paris provided further opportunities for recognition.

Jack, rather, viewed his time at the *Académie Julian* as an indulgent extension of his European holiday. Certainly, he hoped to develop his skills, but he knew he was just taking a side path from his real life and the responsibilities of adulthood that awaited him, seizing an opportunity that had been set in motion by the Bloomsbury artists. In three months he would return to Australia and take up his position at Goldsbrough Mort & Co.

He looked at the young Spaniard's straggly, unruly hair topped with a dark blue beret, his ill-fitting clothes and paint-splattered shoes. To Jack, in some ways, it seemed that Andrés had come from another world. Not just his appearance, but his intensity. Given that painting was the essence of Andrés' life, Jack imagined he was oblivious to what he ate, how he dressed, or even his grooming.

Andrés asked about Australia. Sharing the uniqueness of his country, Jack sketched on his pad – the language that overcame all barriers – and Andrés laughed at the image of a mother kangaroo, complete with the tiny pointed ears of a joey peeping out of the apron-like pouch on her belly. He called Sofia over to see the drawing, and Jack was inordinately pleased to hear her chuckle with delight. Engaged or not, he saw no reason why he could not make Sofia smile and he immediately drew the rounded face, fluffy ears and bright little eyes of the beloved Australian koala to prompt more of her laughter. He followed with a quick sketch of the unlikely construct of the platypus, with its duck bill, beaver tail and otter-like feet, swimming underwater.

At two twenty-five, Aunt Christina arrived, a vivacious dark-haired lady straining under the weight of a basket of clean linen for the café. Andrés immediately leapt up to relieve her of the heavy load.

'*Muchas gracias*,' she said, and turning to Jack, smiled. '*Hola, joven amigo...*' For the next few minutes, she spoke to Andrés and Sofia in rapid Spanish, of which Jack could not understand a single word. He grasped that she was apologising for being late back to the café, words Sofia dismissed with a 'No, no,' shaking her head firmly. The wave of her aunt's arm in a shushing motion indicated that Sofia was being told to finish up for the afternoon, confirmed as she reached behind her waist to undo the ties of her apron and stepped behind the counter to hang it up on an iron hook.

'So, big brother, I thought that today we would walk along the Seine and then follow the *Rue de l'Université* to the *Tour Eiffel*.'

Andrés looked at Jack. 'She has my life mapped out for me, amigo. I work all morning and then she demands every minute of my afternoons! When am I supposed to paint?'

'Well, if I didn't get you away from your paintings occasionally, you would never get any exercise at all, and we would see none of Paris. Consider it research for your subjects.'

'Okay, okay... Jack, would you like to join us? There is no better tour guide than Sofia – she knows more about this city than the Parisians themselves. And she knows every crêpe stand from here to the Spanish border!'

'I certainly do!'

'I would love to join you, if that's okay.'

'Of course. The more the merrier,' Sofia replied, her smile again making his heart flutter in a most surprising way.

It was a lovely afternoon and Jack enjoyed the company of the twins. As they set off down the street, Andrés and Sofia maintained a constant flow of chatter, teasing each other and sharing news about their morning. They had already been in Paris for over a month and had familiarised themselves with the local environment. Jack noticed how quick they were to nod at the Parisians they encountered with a *'Bonjour'* and cheerful smile.

Jack found the walk along the Seine fascinating, its banks lively with boat builders and pedestrians enjoying a stroll beside the languidly flowing river on the fine summer afternoon. Fishermen at regular intervals cast their circular nets into the broad waters. Watching as a man jerked his rod and quickly wound his reel, Jack was not impressed by the small wiggling fish that was lifted onto the bank, flapping and gasping for air. Looking at the murky sludge of the Seine, he compared it to the crystal-clear water of Melbourne's Yarra. No doubt the Parisians had washed, discharged effluent and spewed industrial waste into this river for centuries, turning fresh water brown, its banks clogged with debris and responsible for the unpleasant odour wafting through the streets. In contrast, the Yarra River was relatively untouched and Jack hoped that it would not suffer the same putrid fate in the course of time.

The Eiffel Tower soared above them, its needle-like spire piercing the clear blue sky. Standing beside it, the tower was enormous and, for Jack, it was thrilling to be here, in the presence of the famous edifice. Even though it was Monday, hundreds of tourists gathered at its base, preparing to climb the stairwells that promised a wonderful view of the city. In unspoken agreement, he and the twins joined the lines which moved quickly and, in no time, were ascending the stairs.

'¿Estás bien, Andrés?' Sofia asked sharply, turning back towards Andrés, who was lagging behind them as they neared the final deck.

'I'm fine, Sofia. Don't worry about me,' Andrés replied, rolling his eyes at Jack.

'He gets breathless, sometimes,' Sofia explained to Jack, without taking her eyes off her brother.

'We can stop here if you like,' she suggested, indicating a widening of the stairwell and, for a few minutes, they paused while a few dozen people overtook them, resuming their climb once the stairs were clear of fellow tourists.

When they arrived at the final observation deck, the view across the city was stunning. It was a clear day and the Seine, meandering through the city, looked like a large snake. Numerous bridges enabled people and vehicles to cross from one side to the other, and they laughed at how the people looked like ants. In the distance, a number of famous landmarks dominated the skyline, and Sofia listed them to Jack.

'*The Arc de Triomphe, Sacré-Coeur, Notre Dame.*' He tried to concentrate on her words as she leaned into him, encouraging him to follow the direction she was pointing as she named each building.

～

It was four-thirty when they finally descended the tower, and if anything, the crowds at the base had increased as tourists arrived to view the city by night.

'We, too, will have to come back at night time,' Sofia said. 'The lights of Paris would be wonderful to see.'

Jack watched as she retrieved a large city map, which was starting to show signs of wear, and a notebook from her bag. First, she made an entry in the notebook and then she traced a neat line along the road they'd walked and drew a circle around the tower.

'See, Jack? Our lives are being mapped every minute of the day,' Andrés complained theatrically.

'Well, if we are going to see everything about Paris, we need to be methodical,' said Sofia. 'Otherwise we'd just walk around in circles and never know where we've been or where we want to go back to.'

'See those numbers?' Andrés said to Jack. 'What do you think that they are?'

Jack shrugged. He had no idea.

'Crêpes!'

'Crêpes *and* croissants,' Sofia retorted.

'The numbers?'

'That is how many crêpes Sofia eats at each place!'

'Six! Eight!' Jack eyed the map while Sofia pushed Andrés.

'I joke. It's the rankings, Jack, the rankings. Sofia gives them all a mark out of ten. We discuss them in detail. Are they fresh? Are they soft? Is the flavour perfect? It's quite a science!'

'Laugh you may, but I have my reasons. Now, I want to have a walk along that row of stores.' She pointed across the road to where colourful striped awnings blew in the summer breeze.

Andrés glanced at Jack. 'A good opportunity for some sketching, amigo?'

'Yes, wonderful… If Sofia doesn't mind, that is.'

'She will be happy sniffing out crêpes, never you mind.'

'Well, we will save crêpes for later, but I do want to look at the cafés here.'

'She is stealing secrets from the cafés of Paris to take home,' Andrés explained. 'We will take Paris to Spain – no one will want to come here anymore. Not when they've tasted Sofia's famous crêpes high on the hill above Málaga!'

'Yes, and the Málagians will love it. You wait and see,' said Sofia. 'They will be coming to buy my coffee and cake instead of your paintings!'

For almost an hour, Jack and Andrés sketched scenes from around the base of the tower until Sofia returned. Moving between them, she admired their work.

'Oh, Jack, you are very good. Andrés said you were. Was it you who added the figure of Monsieur to the blocks yesterday?'

Andrés raised his eyebrows at Jack. 'See, she has to know everything. I have no secrets – Sofia extracts them under torture.'

Just at that moment, a lively group emerged from a small booth, and Sofia insisted that she, Andrés and Jack cram inside it and have their photograph taken.

'Today, we must remember. A celebration of new friendships and Paris.'

Jack was happy to oblige, although as he followed Andrés and Sofia into the confined space, his arms and legs suddenly felt cumbersome and he was not sure what to do with his hands.

'Come in closer,' Sofia said, hooking her arms around both Andrés and himself, pulling him in so close that he felt distracted by the sweet scent of her hair. 'Don't move....'

They waited for the bright flash of light, which never seemed to happen at the right moment and, when Sofia discovered that Andrés had pulled comical rubbery faces in the first photograph, she chided him, insisting they take a second set. Jack happily accepted the copies that Sofia handed to him, thrilled to have a photograph of her, of them all, on this wonderful day of sightseeing.

∾

Later, walking towards Montparnasse, it felt quite natural when Sofia took hold of both his and Andrés' arms and, keeping them close to her, steered them to the left.

'Here, this is where we need to go,' she said, leading them into a café with bright red seating and mirrors along its walls. '*The Café de Flore*! Famous for its coffee and bound to serve crêpes, I would think!'

'Sofia, you will be as wide as you are tall if you are going to eat crêpes every time you see them. Don't you know that it is almost dinnertime?'

Grinning at Andrés in reply, Sofia produced her coins. 'What about you, Jack? Are you going to try one?' she asked.

Of course, he said yes, and so did Andrés. Jack loved the milky coffee and the tissue-thin pancakes rolled into logs that oozed sweet, orange-flavoured syrup over his hands.

CHAPTER 19

*F*or Jack, waking up in Montparnasse each day seemed like a dream. Was this really his life? He could scarcely believe it! Beyond the excitement of living in Paris, it was the sense of freedom he felt, taking responsibility for his own needs, for the first time in his life. Carrying a key to an apartment, coming and going, as he pleased, without explanation; organising his washing; purchasing supplies of milk, coffee, sugar, bread and jam. Notwithstanding, when Mimi suggested that she could provide him with a bowl of soup or stew for a couple of centimes each day, he'd gladly accepted. It was a relief not to have to cook evening meals for himself. Furthermore, he loved the enticing aromas that seeped down the stairwell when he returned to his apartment each afternoon and looked forward to seeing what surprise awaited him beneath the cloth-covered saucepan on the bench.

In no time at all, the streets of Montparnasse became familiar to him, and Jack enjoyed his pleasant routine. Rising before the sun each day, he made a cup of Sanka, spooning the bitter powder from the tin and – endeavouring to make the instant coffee palatable – adding three, and sometimes four, heaped spoons of sugar; a drop of milk from the small enamel jug he kept in his refrigerator and, finally, hot water

147

that he boiled in a saucepan on the brass paraffin burner. Sipping his coffee, while chewing on a bread roll lavished with a generous spread of butter and jam, Jack liked to sit at the window, watching as the sun's rays filtered onto the *Passage Dantzig* while the street came to life. By six-thirty, he was ready to move and enjoyed stepping out into the narrow street, invigorated by the crisp morning air; intoxicated by the sense of independence. Most days, he'd greet the milk lady with a wave of his hand, and, if she would meet his eyes, the angry street sweeper who'd stop her hectic movements and watch expressionlessly, her wet mop beside her, as Jack passed by. He'd nod to everyone who crossed his path on the way to the station with a cheery '*Bonjour*,' the phrase increasingly familiar on his lips, even if often preceded with 'g'day, mate' – the easy Australian greeting he found so difficult to abandon.

Train travel became a thing of the past when, in his second week, returning home one afternoon, Jack noticed a bicycle propped at the entrance to La Ruche, an ancient-looking contraption with a large basket on the back and a crudely drawn sign slung over its handlebar. Nearby, a man was busily stacking bags, an easel, enamel pots and a large wooden paintbox into an overloaded wagon. Obviously departing for somewhere – warmer, more comfortable lodgings if his finances had improved, his paintings noticed by a wealthy patron, or perhaps he was returning home, his dreams of achieving success as an artist shattered, having exhausted his financial reserves. Assuming the bike was for sale, Jack did not hesitate as he felt for the coins in his pocket. He handed two francs over, then straddling the rickety machine and, taking care to avoid the deep ruts between the cobblestones, he wobbled down the street towards his own apartment. Each morning thereafter, Jack retrieved the bicycle from the storeroom beside the office and felt as if he owned the world as he wove through the awakening streets of Montparnasse. Inspired by Sofia's adventurous approach to life, he frequently turned left or right at the street corners, losing himself and finding himself again as he made his way to the academy.

Jack and Andrés were usually first to the academy, arriving a full two hours before lessons officially started, taking advantage of the quietness of the building to work on their paintings. Andrés always arrived with a brown bag bursting with crusty rolls, small jars of olives, well-wrapped slices of ham and cheese, and some biscuits or fruitcake for their morning break.

'Sofia is convinced you're going to fade away.' Andrés laughed the first time he'd shared the feast, washed down with *café au lait* from the café next door to the Academy. Jack had felt embarrassed when Andrés arrived the second day with another large bag of food packed that morning by Sofia. Arriving at the café after lessons, he thanked her for her thoughtfulness, pulling out his wallet to pay.

'No, no, you are my guest. It is easy to add a little extra for Andrés to share with you.'

'Yes, but you would not accept money for my lunch yesterday.'

'No. Jack, it is nothing. A few olives and cheese!'

Jack decided that that there was only one way to break the deadlock. 'No worries,' he had said. 'I will just have to go to some other café for my meals, which would be a shame, because the food here isn't too bad, although the waitress is a bit bossy.' For this he had received a slap with Sofia's dishcloth and her reluctant agreement to accept two francs each Monday in advance for the weeks' morning tea and lunches she provided.

When he arrived at the academy, Jack liked to set his paintings along the front board and scrutinise each in turn, weighing up what he needed to add in order to finish them. And then would come the point when he just knew the painting was done. The image would reflect a sense of wholeness and completion. It asked nothing more of him. That was when he knew it was time to put his brushes down and walk away. To continue to paint was to ruin the picture. Not everybody identified that moment, not even Jack sometimes, and it would take Monsieur Simon to prompt him.

Currently, he had four paintings under development in addition to the exercises Monsieur Simon set each morning. The first lessons had focused on the styles of the modern artists, emphasising the way each had used colour in recent decades. Following their visit to the *Musée du Luxembourg*, as promised, the master had given the class demonstrations on the techniques of Henri Matisse and Paul Gauguin. Next, they'd analysed the ways that line had been used, focussing on Wassily Kandinsky and Pablo Picasso's semi-abstract portraits. Finally, the master had introduced brushwork exercises, and the class had completed whole paintings using metal knives, lavishly adding dabs of oily pigments onto their boards – small boards, as who could afford to waste so much paint on large ones? This, they'd pushed around, adding more colours, blending and scraping, achieving all manner of effects, many of which were destined to end up in the trash bin.

After their morning break, the students worked on their own designs, implementing the styles and techniques they'd learned on still lifes, streetscapes, landscapes and portraits. Jack was pleased with his achievements. He found Monsieur Simon to be marvellously patient and valued his gentle suggestions and words of encouragement, which guided him to take risks and acquire the skills to move away from the traditional, realistic style he had perfected over the years towards a modern expressionist style.

'Your work - it is very good, Jack. You have a gift to draw, that is beyond doubt. But here we are learning to add energy and movement, to make our works pull... tug... on hearts and minds, evoke the passions, *oui*?' Jack was reminded of Roger Fry's and Clive Bell's comments in the dining room of Charleston.

Frequently, Monsieur encouraged them outdoors to paint *plein air*.

'Onto the streets, *mes étudiants*, for we must paint Paris! None of you came to this wonderful city to sit in a dusty old room, did you? Come along, quickly, while the beautiful sun shines sweetly upon us!'

Gathering art satchels and slinging easels over their shoulders, the men followed Monsieur Simon down the stairs and onto the streets to explore all manner of interesting paint-worthy subjects – the cafés tucked along the alleyways; the ancient bridge crossings, fishermen and boats along the Seine; the beautiful gardens of the *Jardin des Tuileries* and, of course, the magnificent towers and soaring steeple of the wonderful *Notre Dame*.

Jack had always enjoyed drawing outdoors, and he loved these opportunities to set up his easel on the streets of Paris with his classmates. He didn't even mind when tourists, excited at seeing real artistes at work, interrupted his painting to ask questions. Happily, he smiled while they took his photograph; an artist on the streets of Paris. It was funny really, he thought, how in the eyes of the tourists he was part of the iconic Parisian world. One of the thousands of artists who, along with the poets and novelists, had travelled from London, New York and Rome to absorb the energy and be part of the exciting bohemia of Paris in its 'golden age'.

The locals were not always tolerant of the influx of foreigners, though, and when Monsieur lined the class along the *Champs-Élysées* to paint the *Arc de Triomphe*, many an impatient tutting could be heard as the pedestrians had to step around them. One angry woman had lashed out at the master.

'You should know better, clogging up the pavement!'

'Relax... There is beauty here for everyone to share,' he had replied.

'Do you think we should move?' Jack had asked. However, the master did not seem concerned at all.

'Not to worry,' he reassured the students, 'she will get over it.'

∾

Most afternoons, Jack left the academy with Andrés, pushing his bike along the pavement with one hand. They analysed their morning's lesson as they walked to the Café Española. There, they continued chatting over bread, ham, olives and wine while waiting for Sofia to finish her day's work.

'How did my artistes go today?' she'd ask, always interested in their progress.

'Oh, so-so. Monsieur Simon thinks that we should be exhibiting at the Louvre, but we had to decline...' Andrés would say.

'Where are these masterpieces? I need to see evidence, not just talk about how wonderful you are!'

Every few days, Jack or Andrés carried a painting back to the cafe and Sofia would frown in concentration as she analysed it, surprising

Jack with her perceptive analysis of their work. Frequently, she'd reflect the same opinions of Monsieur Simon. Jack recognised how seriously Andrés valued her comments as, together, they discussed his methods and considered how else he might approach the composition.

He found himself eagerly and yet apprehensively awaiting her opinion on his own work, glowing when she praised his brilliant choice of colours, his spirits dampened when she was less confident of his execution.

'Jack, this is a little...conservative... don't you think? Perhaps... see... if you pulled this line here... or maybe darkened this area here... you would have drawn the eye into the centre... teased the mind,' she would say as she tilted her head, eyes squinting into his work, searching for signs that were only visible to experienced appraisers.

Jack always listened carefully, invariably agreeing with her recommendations, and, as he worked on his paintings he often caught himself wondering, 'What would Sofia think of this...?'

~

By two pm most afternoons, they were usually out on the streets, exploring the sights of Paris. An easy friendship developed quickly between himself, Andrés and Sofia and they laughed, talked and teased each other constantly. Sofia's warm affection for her 'big brother' now extended to Jack, and he loved it when she'd call, 'Come on, Jack, don't lag, stay with us,' and he'd feel her arm reaching out and hooking through his as they set out along the streets.

Sofia was relentless as she teased Jack, repeating 'G'day, mate,' every time he greeted the fishermen, street vendors and even the pedestrians they encountered on their adventures before quickly adding '*Bonjour*,' remembering Mrs Rix's advice in her note to him.

'G'day Mate... sorry... Bonjour,' she'd parrot after him, then, squealing, she'd weave and duck, trying to escape from his grasping arms, begging him to release her from his firm headlock, promising she would stop repeating his words. And then, of course, she'd do it again.

Sofia had appointed herself their tour guide, determining that each afternoon must include a new adventure. She methodically recorded these journeys on a large fold-up map of Paris, as well as inserting notes and tiny sketches into the pages of the green notebook that she carried everywhere.

First, they focused on the main attractions of Paris. *The Louvre*, of course, as well as every other gallery that they passed, making use of the free entry tokens that Monsieur had issued to the students.

Together they weaved back and forth, crossing from the Left to the Right Bank, exploring the various arrondissements of Paris, quickly making sense of their organisation by numbers, spiralling in a clock-wise direction from the city centre like an enormous snail.

They walked back alleys and river banks and returned to the Eiffel Tower to see the night lights.

And they spent hour upon hour in the cafés of Paris, where Sofia would spread out her map and update her journal, making plans for their next walk. The food was amazing – ham and cheese baguettes, bowls of soup and slices of salmon quiche. Jack was sure that he'd never eaten anything so tasty. Additionally, they sampled every variety of crêpe or croissant Paris had to offer. Research, Sofia called it as she recorded descriptions in her notebook, and Jack was always happy to participate, sharing discussions about which were the nicest flavours, the best toppings, the lightest pastries and the finest, softest crêpes.

Beyond the practical benefits cafés offered for escaping the weather, making plans or tasting the delicious food, they loved the atmosphere of the crowded rooms. *Le Dôme, La Closerie des Lilas* and *Café de La Rotonde* were all popular amongst the artists of Montpar-nasse, and Jack, Andrés and Sofia squeezed their way between the wooden chairs in search of empty tables at every opportunity, deter-mined to embrace the Parisian artiste experience.

~

Paris was full of beauty. Statues and monuments of years gone by could be found in all manner of obscure places. And then of course there were the gardens and courtyards, many locked behind ornate gates, offering only glimpses of beautiful interiors. Jack and Andrés would trail after Sofia as she sought destinations of interest, Andrés grumbling when his sister led them into inconsequential alleyways, particularly when their meandering suddenly ended in brick walls.

'What on earth are we doing here?' Andrés would exclaim, staring in exaggerated amazement at a blank wall before them while Jack collapsed in laughter as he listened to Sofia defend herself with some story about the historical significance of the ancient construction.

'Andrés, this is a very special remnant of the old city walls – *The Wall of Philip Augustus*,' Sofia read from her notes, then pointed high above. 'See the walkway up there... This wall is seven hundred years old, at least – built to keep Paris safe while the king joined the Crusaders!'

'If I wanted to look at a pile of old rocks, I would have stayed home and gazed at the *Castillo Gibralfaro*! What are you, some sort of crazy woman? All the wondrous sites of Paris and you bring Jack and me to stare at an old stone wall!'

Andrés surprised Jack with his gift for mimicry and magic tricks. He loved to entertain children, his face twisting into humorous expressions, eyes crossing, lips rubberlike in their contortions, hands masterfully flapping like bird wings or producing coins from strange places.

'He just can't help himself,' Sofia told Jack as, for the third time that morning, he had two little girls howling with glee at his gorilla impersonations, quickly reverting to a serious expression every time adults looked over. The parents smiled knowingly, guessing the source of their daughters' amusement.

'Ten years ago, he spent months in hospital with the Spanish flu. The days were long and boring, so he amused himself by entertaining the younger children and making them laugh.'

They bought fishing lines and attempted to catch bream from the murky waters of the Seine. Jack proved to be the most skilled, hooking three glistening 'monsters', while Sofia caught and lost one, much to her irritation. It was a fun-filled afternoon and Jack marvelled that he found such wonderful friendships ten thousand miles from his home.

~

Increasingly, Jack's thoughts drifted to Sofia. Sofia the woman. He could not deny how much she affected him with her warmth and laughter. His mornings were filled with excited anticipation, the thrilling knowledge that he would be seeing her in a few short hours.

As he and Andrés walked towards the café after their lessons, Jack could feel his pulse quicken, and he struggled to focus on their conversations while his mind digressed, sifting through fanciful imaginings of what the afternoon might bring. He was conscious of a warmth flooding over him, a slow burning that started at his neck and moved towards his hairline when Sofia met them with her usual greeting, '*Hola*, Andrés. *Hola*, Jack,' and hugged him on their arrival. At first, Jack had been awkward in his response, but Sofia had teased him, exclaiming, 'Jack, you are stiff as a board! Relax, I promise I won't hurt you.'

The nights were agony when, tossing and turning, Jack's mind refused to settle. He would review the minutest details of the afternoons they'd spent together, warmed by the nuances of the smile that Sofia directed towards him, the light touch of her hand on his arm as she offered him tapas at the café or when she leaned into him in the street as she pointed out an object of interest. Her behaviour confused him. She never mentioned her fiancé and Jack certainly never asked, but he knew that they constantly exchanged letters and postcards; she was forever seeking out post offices to purchase stamps and send letters. He tried to content himself with the knowledge that, to her, he was like a brother, and yes, she may have a sisterly affection for him, but that was it.

Weekly, Jack sent postcards home to his parents, his brief messages crossing the ocean and passing the long letters his mother sent to him. Thankfully, the six-week delay in mail delivery provided Jack with a satisfactory buffer that enabled him to ignore his mother's probing questions about his life in Paris. She clearly missed him, but had revised her original misgivings about her only son heading off to unknown and uncivilised foreign shores, now expressing the view that 'seeing a bit of the world was good for a young man' – no doubt repeating the consoling refrains of her friends at her morning teas.

Jack ensured his messages described a structured lifestyle, including his lessons in the morning and the tourist-like activities that he knew they would not necessarily enjoy but accept that he would take advantage of. Deliberately omitted were descriptions of the many hours he spent in cafés with Andrés and Sofia, the lively discussions and debates they participated in over glasses of wine and mugs of beer with painters bearing all manner of accents, and the way that his own knowledge and opinions were developing as he absorbed the surrounding conversations.

CHAPTER 20

*J*ack had been in Paris for almost a month when, clambering down the stairs, two at a time, to collect his bicycle, Mimi called out, waving an envelope with unfamiliar writing. It was a letter from Margaret and Jack opened it immediately.

Dear Jack,

Finally, I'm free to get away for a few days and my first thought was that I must come see you, drag you out of the taverns and extract you from the arms of the Parisian beauties. I feel so excited just thinking about you there in Paris, stomping the cobblestones, bumping into Picasso and Hemingway and painting up a storm. How are the classes? Are they able to teach you anything or is the brilliant Just Jack showing them a thing or two? I am so envious of you being there. I asked Roger why he hadn't waved his magic wand to get me a place at the Julian, but he just said there are many good painters, and then there are brilliant ones. So, I guess there is a message in that for me! Mind you, one day I, too, will be a student in Paris, mark my words. Anyway, enough of that for now because I will see you on Saturday! I am thinking the Musée du Louvre, ten-thirty on the front steps or what-ever entrance they have. We'd better say 'the main entrance', in case there is more than one. Oh, the Louvre, the Louvre – makes me tingle just thinking about it!

See you there!

Affectionately yours,

Margaret

Jack smiled as he read the scrawling handwriting. Margaret's bossy manner and cheeky comments leapt off the page as though she were right beside him. He realised how much he'd missed her and could not wait to see her again. Furthermore, he looked forward to introducing her to Sofia and Andrés. He had mentioned Margaret to them numerous times and knew that they were curious about her.

Mid-morning Saturday, he rode his bike to Aunt Christina's apartment. There, he and the twins planned their route and, after considering taking the Métro, they agreed that they preferred to walk. It was, after all, a beautiful day.

Sofia was full of cheek as they walked, plying him with questions about his 'Australian girlfriend'.

'She's not my girlfriend, Sofia!'

'Ah, Jack. Sometimes a man doesn't know these things…'

'What things, Sofia? Are you saying that I don't know my own mind?'

'Well, a picture paints a thousand words, *si*?'

'What picture?'

'Ah, the picture of the beautiful woman in your book.'

'Woman! What woman?'

'Sofia, leave Jack alone. He can have as many beautiful women as he likes in his book.'

'Not many – just one. With sparkling eyes that look at you with love!'

'She is mad, Andrés. Your sister is quite crazy!'

The banter continued as they crossed the Seine at Pont Neuf and with a sudden movement, Jack grasped Sofia's waist and lifted her high, pretending that he was going to throw her over the side of the bridge.

'No... no...!' Sofia was laughing so hard as she squirmed in his arms that Jack could barely hold her.

'Andrés, mate, give me a hand, will you? She is like a wild yellow-belly thrashing about on the end of a line. A bit skinny, though – we'll have to throw her back.'

'Yellow-belly! I'll give you yellow-belly, Jack... and skinny...!'

They were still laughing when they approached the Musée du Louvre a few minutes later, and Jack immediately noticed the quizzical look in Margaret's eyes as she advanced towards them.

'Jack, so good to see you,' she said, hugging him tight and then, adopting the manner of the French, kissing him on each cheek. Her spontaneous affection made him blush, as he was conscious of Andrés and Sofia watching with barely concealed curiosity. Never one for understatement, Margaret continued, 'Look at you. I would swear you have grown two inches'–she laughed–'and is that a beard? No, couldn't be!'

She did not let go of him, and Jack found himself also laughing with pleasure. Margaret was exactly the same and, yet, somehow different. Her hairstyle had changed in the few weeks since he'd seen her, now fashioned stylishly short, cut square along her chin line. The madness of her unruly curls extended horizontally, accentuating the smooth lines of her fair skin, and her clear blue eyes were sparkling with delight at seeing him again. Margaret's dress had a touch of eccentricity; she looked like one of the dapper young males that strolled the pavement of the *Champs-Élysées* in her loose-fitting jacket and baggy trousers. Even her voice, with its broad Australian accent, sounded foreign to his ears after the last five weeks of being surrounded by Parisians, European fellow students and, of course, Sofia and Andrés' lyrical Spanish accents. What hadn't changed, though, was her warmth and humour.

'Margaret, leave me alone,' he said, still laughing. He realised that in her eyes, he also had changed in the few weeks since they had last seen each other. His hair was longer, for one, and while he had not intentionally grown a beard, his routine of shaving every two or three days had been abandoned in the absence of a decent razor. Additionally, he must appear a little scruffy. While he had kept up with laundering his trousers, vests and shirts by delivering a basket of dirty clothes to Mimi on Fridays to find them neatly washed and ironed by Saturday afternoon, they were still inclined to be rumpled as they got tumbled over in the basket on the dining table throughout the week, and paint stains had become a permanent fixture on almost everything he owned.

Turning to the twins, he introduced them. 'I would like you to meet my friends, Margaret. Andrés and Sofia.' He continued, 'And this is Margaret, bossiest woman in the world. Watch out or she'll have your lives turned upside down before you know it!'

'Well, some people need their boring lives turned upside down, Jack, so you can be very thankful that I rescued you,' she retorted, before turning towards the tall, young Spaniard and the petite, dark-haired girl by his side. They'd smiled shyly as Jack made the introductions, and he could see their surprised expressions when Margaret stepped forward, welcoming them each with a hug.

'What have you two been up to?' Margaret asked them, waving her finger in their faces. 'I sent a nice, quiet boy to France and now I find him a man of the world–an artiste–navigating the streets of Paris like a local. Congratulations to you both! Well done.'

'*Si. Gracias*,' they replied, smiling broadly.

Suggesting that they walk down the Avenue des Champs-Élysées for lunch, Jack led the way through the Jardin des Tuileries, the beautiful gardens at the entry of the Louvre. They looked along the roadway to where the Arc de Triomphe stood proudly in the distance.

'I had forgotten how much I love Paris,' Margaret said to Jack, as the foursome were swept along with the crowds thronging the busy pavement. Today being Saturday, it felt as though everyone had stepped out to enjoy the sunshine, and Jack felt a surge of elation, relishing this moment spent with these special friends on this street, which at this minute, he was sure was his favourite place in the whole world.

As they walked, Margaret plied Jack with questions, wanting to know about every detail of his life since she had waved goodbye to him five weeks earlier. How did he manage the Paris Métro? What was his apartment like? Did he like *Académie Julian*? How many students were there? Had he learned anything? What had he painted so far? As they walked and talked, they passed numerous cafés, their tables full, and they finally arrived at the large, chaotic roundabout marking the end of the shopping stretch, its centrepiece the wonderful *Arc de Triomphe de l'Etoile* towering above them. With unspoken agreement, Jack, Margaret, Sofia and Andrés stepped between the vehicles, crossing to the centre island, where they began climbing the steep circular staircase housed within the right side of the arch. Within minutes, they emerged at the top and gazed out in silence. Today the view of Paris, with its clear summery sky, was spectacular. Sounds from the street far below drifted up to them – car horns blasting, voices shouting and even good-natured laughter–and they moved from side to side, looking down below to where cars, lorries and horse-drawn carriages eased into the roundabout, almost coming to a standstill as they weaved through the chaos created by the twelve converging roads, attempting to avoid the collisions that threatened to occur every few minutes.

Eventually, Jack suggested it was time for lunch and they descended the stairway, crossed the road and returned along the avenue. Arriving at the *Café Royal*, he spotted an empty outdoor table and quickly claimed it. For the next hour, he, Margaret, Sofia and Andrés chatted and Jack was pleased to see how well his friends got along together. Their conversation was relaxed, and they shared similar humour as they watched the endless parade of glamorous people streaming along the *Champs-Élysées*: young ladies in colourful dresses, jaunty hats elegantly accessorised with matching parasols, the dapper men escorting them wearing pin-striped suits and carrying fashionable silver-tipped walking canes.

Margaret, as usual, led the conversation. She inquired how Andrés and Sofia had come to meet Jack and made a cheeky comment about how he had developed an eye for beautiful women. The words created an awkward silence. Margaret, recognising her gaffe immediately, bridged it with a line of questioning about Málaga. She was fascinated to hear that Andrés had painted for years and immediately insisted that he show her his paintings.

'Don't show her,' warned Jack. 'She will take over your life, pack you off to a foreign country and send you on a crazy adventure. Just look at what she has done to me!'

Laughing, Margaret punched his arm while Andrés and Sofia looked on, their smiles shrouded with a hint of confusion indicating that they had not fully understood the exchange.

Margaret also brought news from London. 'Now, Jack, I don't mean to organise your life, but Roger is coming over this coming Friday and he has arranged for you to meet Miss Stein on Saturday.'

'Who, Margaret, is Miss Stein, and why on earth does Roger want me to meet her?' Jack was constantly surprised by Margaret's manner of planning his life.

'She is quite an experience, believe me. Roger brought her to Charleston years ago, and I'm sure the place has not been the same since. They spoke of her visit for ages. Her name is like royalty to Ness and Duncan. She lives on the Left Bank and has enormous influence on the American art scene. It would be good for you if she likes your paintings.'

Jack smiled at Andrés and Sofia, rolling his eyes as if to say, *here she goes again!*

'No, Jack. You must listen to me. Miss Stein is an institution. She came to Paris years ago and never went home. Writes a bit and encourages all the new artists. You know, she introduced Picasso to the Americans. And Matisse. Has an eye on out for all the up-and-coming talent and recommends her discoveries to her wealthy American friends. It a wonderful thing that Roger had organised for you to visit her. Miss Stein's opinion has the power to turn starving artists into millionaires. A nod from her and you are set!'

Jack shook his head in amused disbelief, accepting that his destiny, at least for the following Saturday night, had been decided.

Over the next few days, Margaret joined Jack, Andrés and Sofia in their afternoon jaunts around Paris as both tourists and artists, absorbing the sights, wandering into every gallery they passed, from the quaint and eclectic to the expensive and sophisticated, chatting to the street artists, sampling the delicacies from market stalls and cafés and, of course, pulling pads and paints out at every opportunity. At night, they roamed amongst the cafés and bars of Montparnasse and Jack was pleased that for once he was able to show Margaret something new. He enjoyed seeing her excitement as they sat amongst the artists who gathered in search of warmth, companionship and cheap food. Not only painters, but writers and poets also, all simmering with creative energy, where raucous laughter and bellowing conversations were fuelled by bowls of steaming *garbure*, thick crusty bread, cheese and endless carafes of cheap wine.

Repeatedly throughout the week, Margaret reminded Jack of Saturday's meeting with Roger before they went over to Miss Stein's house, encouraging him to review the works he had completed over the last six weeks. Monsieur Simon had nodded in approval when Jack told him of Roger's plan for him to meet Miss Stein, offering support when Jack discussed his colour choices and ideas. During his classes, Jack sensed the critical eye of the master frequently being cast over the two large canvases he was completing that week. The extra time and attention involved nods of support coupled with gentle suggestions.

~

Jack was amazed at Margaret's capacity to draw people out, learning more about the twins' background in one hour than he had in the last month. He had been so occupied with their busy schedule, it had never occurred to him to inquire about the intricacies of their lives in Spain.

'Our mother died giving birth to us,' Sofia explained sadly in response to Margaret's questions about their childhood one afternoon as they sat on the side of the *La Fontaine des Quatre-Parties-du-Monde* running their hands through the streaming water as it cascaded across the pool. They'd just arrived and were enjoying the sunshine and beauty of the park after having spent the morning exploring the catacombs of Paris and their mood was subdued by the hours they'd spent underground, walking the damp, dark network of tunnels located far below the city, housing the bones of thousands of Parisians. Sofia described her mother's taxing pregnancy, lengthy labour and the unexpected arrival of twins – good-sized twins, each over five pounds, with lusty lungs, keen appetites and a determination to survive. Their father, while broken-hearted at the loss of his young wife, raised the twins in a loving home, high on the hill above Málaga, with the help of his sister. He was a talented artist in his own right, who supplemented his income teaching art at the local school while developing a small gallery on their finca. As a young man, he had known Picasso, who was the same age. He had even sat beside him while taking drawing lessons at Málaga's Escuela Provincial de Bellas Artes, taught by José Ruiz y Blasco, Picasso's father. Like most Malagians, he'd been proud of Picasso's achievements and the Cubist style he was famous for. Sadly, the twins' father had died suddenly only two years earlier, leaving his small gallery, cottage and attached studio to his children along with a bank account that provided a moderate income to assist in maintaining the property.

Andrés had been producing paintings to sell in the gallery since he was fourteen, brightly coloured modern works that sold for a few pesos each and appealed to the American tourists who increasingly ventured into southern Spain, enchanted by the sparkling beauty of the Mediterranean Sea and attracted to the historical features of the towns. Sofia also played an active role, managing the gallery. With a good head for business and a keen eye for quality artworks, developed under her father's guidance, she selected local pottery and fine leatherwork to carry on commission. Andrés, clearly proud of his sister, enjoyed the opportunity to describe Sofia's accomplishments. He explained how two summers ago, she had rearranged the gallery and courtyard to create space for a tea room, now popular with visitors who ventured up the hill to take photographs where panoramic views of Málaga were framed against the glistening backdrop of the Mediterranean, as well as to roam the ancient *Castillo de Gibralfaro*. Financially, the twins had sufficient means to survive, if they managed their pesos carefully. Furthermore, numerous paintings in the gallery that their papa had acquired over the years were increasing in value, and hopefully, would provide a buffer should they be forced to raise funds in a crisis. Works of Picasso, of course. Plus a series of beautiful beach scenes by Sorolla and works of Joan Miro and Juan Gris, modern Cubist artists that had fascinated their father.

And, while Jack knew that Andrés presence at the academy was due to a prize for his painting, it was Margaret who recognised the prestige of the annual prize granted by Madrid's Prado Museum. That Andrés had won the modern portraiture section, complete with one hundred thousand pesetas, was no small feat. After deep consideration, the twins had agreed this money should be used to further Andrés' painting by studying in Paris, the centre of the art world.

Sofia had researched the various teachers and convinced Andrés that Monsieur Simon was a good choice – highly sought after, with many students who achieved respect as professional artists. It was Andrés who had insisted that if he was going, Sofia must join him. She, of course, was concerned about their gallery and worried about the additional costs her joining him would create. However, the first obstacle had been quashed when their father's sister, Aunt Jovita, and their cousin, Stefan, had agreed to care for the finca and run the tea room while they were away.

The twins had known collusion between their aunts had occurred when, unexpectedly, a letter had arrived from their mother's sister, Aunt Christina, insisting that the twins stay with her during their time in Paris and so, eliminating the second obstacle of their proposed visit to Paris. They'd been thrilled by Aunt Christina's offer and, as it turned out, their visit had mutual benefits for her elderly husband had succumbed to a bout of pneumonia, and she was having difficulty managing the early morning starts at the *Café Española*. Sofia had been thrilled to help out, insisting that she worked all weekdays through to one-thirty, so her aunt could take advantage of the twin's visit, to have a good rest.

The next day, Margaret arrived at the café with a request that the afternoon be spent climbing the Eiffel Tower. However, before they set off on the long walk to the seventh *arrondissement*, she insisted that Andrés show her his drawing book, which she'd spied protruding from the bag behind his chair. She shook her head in wonder at his loosely drawn sketches and colour samples and, encouraged by her interest, Andrés retrieved two small canvases from the back of the café – completed paintings that he had brought back from the Academy a week earlier. Like Jack, he favoured portraits; however, in these Andrés had used sweeping broad brush strokes in high-intensity colour and heavily layered paint, a technique known as impasto. His talent was indisputable, his paintings showing a completeness and mastery that many accomplished artists never fully achieved. Margaret loved his work and was unrestrained in her praise, and Andrés smiled with pleasure at her words.

Saturday finally arrived and Margaret primed Jack for his visit to Miss Stein's house. As he packaged the paintings that he'd selected for Roger to peruse, he was overcome by doubts. He hoped that Roger would not be disappointed in the fruits of his labour under Monsieur Simon's guidance.

'Do you think they are alright?' he asked Margaret.

'Jack, they are wonderful. Roger will love them, I am sure. So will Miss Stein!'

To Jack, Miss Stein sounded like a fussy old lady, similar to the many who'd sit on his mother's sofa with her 'best china' teacup poised on their laps; only this one, apparently, had a fondness for art and money to pander to artists. However, Margaret firmly set him straight.

'Jack, you must understand how important this meeting is for you,' she implored.

'Why don't you show Miss Stein your paintings?' Jack teased in reply. 'I'm sure she could shoot you to international fame and make you a millionaire.' He laughed, remaining ever reluctant to take any of this too seriously.

'No, Jack, I am serious. If I had half of your talent, I would jump at the opportunity. Gertrude Stein is an institution. Paris has always had its salons, with wealthy patrons supporting starving artists. The difference is that she is American. She writes columns for American newspapers that people read. They take notice of her. Paris may be setting the pace for modern art now, but New York is watching. And, not to mention, it's where the serious money is. Not everyone was born with a silver spoon in their mouth, nor talent oozing from their fingertips,' she finished, looking at Jack accusingly, again chastising him for his habit of failing to recognise his gift or the opportunity it held for him.

Andrés and Sofia nodded their agreement. While not familiar with Miss Stein, they well understood the value of patrons who could assist artists to become recognised. And, as Jack had earlier concluded, for the twins, art was not about being rich. Artistic renown, however, led to sales and sales meant being able to paint without starving - a freedom elusive to most artists.

'Lucky for you,' Margaret went on, 'Miss Stein owes Roger a favour.' When Jack looked enquiringly at her, she explained that, while she was a columnist, Miss Stein's true desire was to be a published author. It had been Roger's recommendation that led to the publication of her first book. It emerged that Roger Fry was not only an artist and renowned critic but also edited one of the United Kingdom's most prestigious monthly magazine dedicated to the arts, *The Burlington Magazine*. Jack was taken aback as he realised the extent of Roger Fry's sphere of influence and elevated status.

'So again, my friend, Just Jack: you must not blow this opportunity.'

Jack sobered, realisation dawning upon him that Margaret's endless prattle, generous spirit and boundless enthusiasm for life and art were not only grounded in a clear understanding of the political, social and economic forces behind the art world, but supported by a network of very important people. He felt somewhat ashamed that he had not taken the pending meeting with the esteemed Miss Stein more graciously. He must seem spoiled and unappreciative of Margaret's efforts, which he now saw had secured him an opportunity that few artists ever received.

CHAPTER 21

*A*s arranged, Margaret brought Roger to Jack's apartment at four pm on Saturday afternoon to sort out his portfolio and prepare for the meeting.

'Well done, Jack. I knew Monsieur Simon would do the trick,' Roger exclaimed as he set Jack's paintings out along the wall, reminding him of a world ago when he had done the same in the dining room of Vanessa Bell's home in Sussex. Roger did not say much more, but he had a look of excitement about him as he held up paintings and drawings, keeping some, discarding others and sorting the final selection into the order he wished for them to be revealed to Miss Stein.

Rather than lugging the bulky folder of artworks on the train, Roger flagged a taxi to take them to Miss Stein's apartment on *Rue de Fleurus*. The door was answered at once and they were ushered in by a small, dark-haired lady with the distinguishing feature of a very hooked nose, who introduced herself as Miss Toklas.

Chatting continuously, she led them to a lounge room so over-crowded with furnishings, artefacts and paintings that Jack hardly knew where to rest his eyes. A rotund woman with an attractive, heavily featured face and thick, dark hair pulled loosely into a bun sat in an armchair by the fireplace. Lying at her feet, his head resting on his front paws, was a small, wiry-haired dog, whose bored expression did not change with the influx of strangers into the room. A dog who had witnessed many visitors, Jack guessed.

The woman stood to greet Roger with a hug, indicating they were old friends. Jack was surprised to see that despite her large size, she barely reached his shoulder.

'Gertie, how are you?' enquired Roger with a broad smile, and the two immediately embarked on a conversation about mutual friends in New York, London and Paris. Miss Toklas bustled amongst the guests, offering refreshments from a sideboard where a range of cut glass carafes held brightly coloured liqueurs. Accepting a small glass of framboise, Jack took a sip and its fruity flavour flooded his tongue with warmth. He wondered what his parents would say if they could see their son at this moment.

Standing against the fireplace, he looked around the room silently. The walls were covered in paintings, some mounted in heavy gilt frames, others set in plain wood and still more leaning up on small tables and whatnots. The room was also filled with interesting objects: colourful glass ornaments, wooden carvings and brass sculptures. Perhaps they were gifts in grateful token of Miss Stein's patronage from around the world.

Beckoning Margaret and Jack to follow her, Miss Toklas retreated to the far corner. After settling them there, she picked up her needle-point and briskly jabbed the needle into the cloth as she directed a series of questions towards Margaret. Listening with interest as she enquired after Ness and Virginia, Jack realised they had met before. When Margaret explained that Jack was staying in Mrs Rix's home in her absence, Miss Toklas looked at him with interest. Jack sensed his status was elevated by his association with the woman whose apartment he lived in, even though he had never met her.

He studied the paintings around the room, pleased that recent experience now enabled him to recognise some styles. Matisses, identifiable by their outlandish colours that had little bearing on reality. He also recognised a Derain, possibly the original of the copy Jack himself had reproduced as an exercise in class. Immediately above Miss Stein's chair hung a painting of a nude - a girl with flowers - and, looking closer, Jack noticed the distinctive signature – Pablo Picasso.

Suddenly he was conscious of a conversation including his name. Returning his focus to Miss Stein, he found her gaze upon him, somewhat intimidating.

'So. Jack. You are an Australian with some talent, Roger tells me,' she said in a loud drawl, her American accent magnifying her presence. Jack, interpreting her words as somewhere between a question and a statement, was reminded of standing in the principal's office, unsure what his answer should be.

'Don't be shy, son. I don't know what it is with the young people of today. They either never stop talking, telling you how fabulous they are, or they don't have a thing to say. Tell me about yourself. So few Australians come here, I'd hate to think you were mute! Mind you, it would be a good thing if more Australians got out and realised that art is not all gumtrees and rivers. Who have you studied with?' she asked.

Jack determined that he needed to speak up or risk being assessed as dim-witted, so he formulated what he hoped was a sensible reply that would elevate her impression of Australians.

'Well, in fact, I never had formal lessons beyond school,' he answered, 'but, in saying that, I have always drawn and painted. For as long as I can remember. Here in Paris, I have been studying with Monsieur Simon. Mr Fry recommended him.' Jack was surprised at his formality in suddenly calling Roger 'Mr Fry'; the gravity of standing in front of what seemed like a one-woman judge and jury, and perhaps even executioner, had inflamed a nervousness within him.

'Well, well, well. An original. Not only Australian, but also undiscovered. Let's see what we have here.' She indicated for Jack to open his drawing portfolio. Roger had selected eight of Jack's works: two from his original portfolio, delegated to be revealed first, five from works completed over recent weeks in Paris, and finally, the charcoal drawing of Margaret that Jack had completed on the *Ormonde*. Jack set out his pictures, one by one, in the agreed sequence on a sideboard that seemed positioned there for the purpose of allowing Miss Stein to view works and deliver edicts.

He watched as Miss Stein studied each canvas carefully, as though inspecting for flaws. She then stood back, taking in the overall impression of the group and called over to Miss Toklas, 'Alice, come and have a look at these.' Together they moved along the wall, studying each painting, occasionally directing a comment to Roger, while jabbing a finger at his works. Jack wondered how anyone could spend so long looking at any single picture.

Roger gave a reassuring nod towards Jack as he tried to make sense of their comments. *Touching realism, compositional gestures, linear connection and vitality.* It was as if they were talking about someone else's paintings.

The wait was unnerving and Jack sensed that Margaret, standing beside him, yet to be acknowledged by the great Miss Stein, held her breath in anticipation. She jumped at the sound of her name.

'Margaret,' Miss Stein said as she examined the large charcoal portrait that had captured Roger many weeks earlier. 'So. You are the clever girl who discovered Jack. Well done, girl. Well done.'

Jack exhaled as relief washed over him. Again, he marvelled that the opinion of strangers, not least this intimidating woman, suddenly seemed significant in his appraisal of himself as an artist.

To Jack, she said, 'Young man. See this and this and this'–selecting three paintings–'and this.' She added his drawing of Margaret. 'I want you to put together a dozen or so paintings over the next... say... four weeks? Has Paris got you for that long? Roger and I will exhibit them and show you off. How does that sound?' She turned away and Jack sensed that Miss Stein did not give a hoot about what he thought, assuming his agreement was a given.

'Splendid,' said Roger, saving Jack from answering – a good thing, because he was not altogether sure what to say, his number one thought being that he was going to be on a sailing boat to Australia at that time.

'I knew you would like Jack's work,' Roger continued.

'Well,' replied Miss Stein abruptly, 'it is all very well for me to like him. Blind Freddy can see he has talent. We just need to make sure that the Americans like him.'

She turned back to him. 'Now, Jack, don't disappoint me. It is in the colour. That is what Americans are looking for. Get your marvellous portraits right, get the colour right and you are in.'

In, thought Jack, nodding frantically, overcome by the thrill of being on the threshold of something exciting, but somehow, shadowy and indeterminate. Although a surge of trembling ran through him, Jack could not conceal his smile. Without doubt, he had been presented with an opportunity more far-reaching than any art show he had ever entered as a schoolboy.

Breathing deeply, he calmed himself. Of course, he could do this. Painting was what he loved. Margaret, Roger, and now Miss Stein, all liked his paintings. He just needed to get on with the job. And, he mused, in six weeks he would be on a boat back to Australia, so if Miss Stein was disappointed in him and the Americans did not like his work, who cared? Such was life.

Even as Jack pragmatically assessed the opportunity, he knew that he was kidding himself. More than anything he wanted to paint wonderful paintings, applying skills he had acquired with Monsieur Simon. Works that not only 'people' liked, which had always come easily, but works that people like Miss Stein and Roger liked. Important paintings. Paintings that inspired conversations beyond how lovely or how lifelike they were, which he had been told all his life. He itched to get back into the studio to start planning.

'So, that is sorted,' said Roger. 'Now, Gertie, can I bother you to have a look at another couple of paintings? I don't think you will be disappointed.'

Jack, surprised to hear this, wondered if Margaret was in fact going to test herself before the great Miss Gertrude Stein after all. He was even more surprised when he saw that the three canvases Roger was setting out on the sideboard were, in fact, Andrés'. The works were in the bold hues that Andrés executed so well. The first showed a busy streetscape which Jack recognised as the beautiful Rue Saint-Antoine.

Deep blue, green and violet contrasted with orange and red, creating a rich, lively scene. Pavements abounded with diverse characters and close examination revealed quirky features. A child scrambled upon an ivy trellis, attempting to retrieve an orange balloon floating just beyond his reach. A tall, thin man walked on his hands, making Jack laugh. For that was exactly what Andrés had done in the *Jardin du Luxembourg*, after their museum visit with Monsieur Simon.

The next, Jack recognised, was a painting Andrés had completed in class under the guidance of Monsieur Simon: the portrait of a young fisher-lad filling his metal bucket with glistening bream on the banks of the Seine. The poverty of the boy was evidenced by his thin frame, bare feet and oversized trousers torn at the knees, but beautifully counterbalanced by the abundance of his catch and the glow of excitement on his face. The third canvas was a painting Jack had not seen, yet immediately identified. Andrés had captured Sofia bearing a tray, prominent in the foreground, laden with small bowls and dishes – an offering of delicacies to delight the palate. The background depicted a room with the suggestion of paintings of assorted sizes displayed on its walls. No doubt the setting was the *Galleria Toulouse*, set high in the hills behind Málaga. Sofia was smiling broadly, her beautiful face expressing hope and optimism, her eyes sparkling in the way he knew so well, animated by the joy of living. Titled *Opening Day*, it was a stunning work, reflecting Sofia's spirit and energy while playing on the viewer's emotions in a way that made Clive Bell's theory of art make sense. This was truly art.

Jack listened as Roger explained to Miss Stein how the pair to this painting had won the esteemed Prado Museum Portraiture Prize last winter. Roger added that he had never met the young artist before, in fact only seeing these paintings himself this morning when Margaret had brought them to him. However, he had been so impressed that he believed that she must see them too.

Gertrude looked at Margaret with renewed interest. 'My, you are quite the spotter, girl. Well done, yet again.'

Margaret's eyes shone at the praise. Jack was also glad to find that he was not the only one who was at a loss for words in the formidable presence of Miss Stein. There were not many people who could shut the indomitable Margaret up!

Turning to Roger, Miss Stein spoke with concise purpose, like an army general with a battle plan ready for execution. 'Okay. Here is what we'll do. A combined exhibition – two emerging artists. Their styles are different enough to hold their own, and I am sure I can find enough Americans to spend their dollars. How does that sound?' It was a statement rather than a question.

'Just as I hoped, Gertrude. I could not agree more. We will invite every Londoner and American in Paris and reveal our young men, the Australian and Spaniard, together.'

Their conversation was interrupted by a loud knock on the door indicating another visitor. Gertrude quickly gathered the paintings and handed them back to Jack to return to his satchel. 'And so, the evening begins,' she said, amusement in her voice as she winked at him.

~

Over the next few hours, dozens of guests moved through Miss Stein's living room. Some were American visitors in Paris paying homage to the well known expatriate. Others, artists and writers, hoping that Miss Stein might favour their work and prove a valuable connection – perhaps a reference or introduction that would further their career. And then there were those who just wanted to say they had been to the renowned address, *27 Rue de Fleurus*, and that they'd rubbed shoulders with the Who's Who of the Parisian art world. Jack's understanding that Miss Stein was no ordinary person was now complete, and he was amazed to think that here he was, receiving a private audience in her home. And more than that, his work had impressed her!

The evening progressed with friendly chatter, revealing an intense interest in the developing trend for modern art in America. An elderly New Yorker associated with Columbia University cornered Roger for over an hour, amused by his cunning invention of the term 'Post-Impressionism'. This deft manoeuvre, testimony to Roger Fry's capacity to influence the art world, had been an insightful attempt to appease British conservatives by aligning the works of modern artists - who they'd disdained - to those whom they respected - the French Impressionists - when he had brought Manet and Cezanne to a London audience two decades earlier. Again, Jack's esteem for Roger increased, and he realised how much he had underestimated the crazy Bloomsbury group to which Margaret had introduced him. He only wished that Sofia and Andrés were here, now, and he could not wait to see Andrés' face when Roger revealed the plan to exhibit both their work together. He hoped that Andrés agreed!

The steady flow of wine and beer made for a pleasant evening, the ever-present Alice looking after the few women present and ensuring that a seemingly endless supply of sandwiches and small pastries were available.

'Ness warned me to expect this - for the women to be ignored by Miss Stein.' Margaret whispered to Jack as they watched the older lady, now surrounded by no less than ten males.

'Apparently she doesn't like females very much. Only has time for artists-and writers-she takes them under her wing, too. She believes that their work must come first and, if they are silly enough to fall in love, it is at the peril of their career. And the married ones-Hemingway and Joyce–their wives are totally ignored! Makes the women furious. Especially when Miss Stein gives their husbands marriage advice - tells them that their wives shouldn't waste their money on clothes and food. Insist that they should buy paintings rather than eat!'

Margaret snorted. 'I think Miss Stein just wants to be the Queen Bee, fawned upon by the males around her. Or maybe she's just another one, who only sees men as serious artists.'

'Surely not,' replied Jack, knowing how sensitive Margaret was on this issue.

'Well, artists can be pretty nutty. Ness says Miss Stein's even more fanatical about art than they are at Charleston and, as you know, that's saying something!

'Why do the women put up with it?' Jack asked, looking across at the ladies clustered to one side of the room.

'It infuriates them, but it's a double-edged sword. Miss Stein's approval helps sell their husbands' books and paintings. Probably feathering her own nest, really, as the more famous her protégés become, the more valuable her collection becomes.'

'But let's not complain, Jack. The single-mindedness of Miss Stein is going to make you and Andrés famous!'

Jack was slowly getting used to the idea that works of art could actually be extremely valuable and that some people were earning large sums of money for single paintings. He was astonished to hear that Picasso's paintings were fetching two hundred American dollars. It would take most people months to earn that much money!

Suddenly, Jack noticed eyes on him and realised that Miss Stein had just indicated to those gathered around her that he was an emerging artist.

'Save your dollars for his inaugural exhibition in June.' She laughed. 'This boy is worth collecting!'

Jack felt himself reddening as he tried to look like a confident artist of soon-to-be-revealed merit.

'How about a preview?' asked the tallest of the men, his belly hanging over his belt, cigar wavering precariously as he spoke in a loud American accent, eyeing the portfolio leaning against Jack's chair.

'No, no, you'll have to wait,' she replied, winking at Jack.

Later, she expanded. 'It's all in the marketing, my boy. The greater the mystery, the more they will pay, so we will reveal nothing and keep them sniffing.'

～

Jack and Margaret could not wait to catch up with Andrés and Sofia and share the news. They met on the doorstep of Aunt Christina's apartment at ten-thirty on Sunday morning.

As they'd anticipated, Andrés was overjoyed, sure it was the opportunity he had been waiting for. He kept pacing and speaking to Sofia in rapid Spanish, his excitement visible in his frenetic movements.

'Andrés, we need to meet with Roger, today. He goes back to London tomorrow and wants to speak to both you and Jack, together.' Margaret said.

'Yes, certainly, yes. That will be very good. Very good!'

They made their way to Roger's hotel, hearts beating in anticipation as the concierge phoned the room, advising Roger that his visitors had arrived.

Half an hour later, over mugs of coffee and sharing a platter of pastries, Roger outlined the plan.

He and Gertrude would locate a place. In fact, he already had somewhere in mind.

Gertrude was marvellous at this sort of thing. She and Roger would organise everything; all Jack and Andrés had to do was paint.

Sofia's experience in promoting her brother's work through the gallery and seeking opportunities for him to gain recognition through prestigious art competitions and exhibitions quickly became evident. It was equally obvious that the business-minded twin had no intention of being excluded from ongoing decisions about Andrés' art. Without hesitation, she quizzed Roger about the nature of the exhibition, how paintings would be presented and priced, as well as the percentage of the takings that Andrés would receive.

Margaret and Jack were astonished by Sofia's cool head and assertive manner in the face of such excitement. However, Andrés just shook his head and smiled. 'She doesn't trust anyone to manage my work,' he said, 'least of all me.'

Sofia, glaring at her twin, sharply retorted, 'Well, my big brother, the issue is that you would not know one end of an account from another, as long as you have a brush in your hand and a piece of canvas in front of you. I guess one of us has to make sure money comes in and the bills are paid!'–to which Andrés sheepishly nodded in agreement.

Roger, impressed by the depth of Sofia's knowledge of curating, agreed that she would be included when they next met with Gertrude. He was equally generous in his praise for Andrés.

'Paris is full of artists that are passionate about their work, Andrés.'

177

he said. 'However, it is a rare gift to discover passion that is accompanied by the extraordinary talent that you display.'

'And, Roger, who did the discovering?' Margaret asked cheekily.

'Yes, Margaret. Well done to you... I will have to employ you as my new spotter now, won't I, lest somebody steal you away from me!'

Embarking on an earnest discussion with the young artists, Roger encouraged them to stay true to their art, but bear in mind Miss Stein's American audience. He outlined the importance of a cohesive and yet diverse portfolio and suggested appropriate subjects that he knew would please a range of tastes.

Andrés and Sofia well understood Roger's advice, having enough experience to recognise that, for an artist to be truly successful, he required finely balanced commercial success as well as critical acclaim, unless, of course, he was enormously wealthy! Should an artist produce too much 'commercial art' he would not be deemed 'serious', while to become engrossed in a personal style, regardless of audience taste, was to starve. The ideal was to be able to produce paintings that were unique, masterfully crafted, pleasing to the eye and the appropriate size for ease of transportation and display in the homes of buyers.

Jack, less conscious of the vagaries of the art world, still selected subjects according to personal instincts. He was, however, pleased with his progress in implementing the techniques Monsieur Simon was teaching and happy to do anything both Roger and Miss Stein suggested, without question.

CHAPTER 22

At five pm that afternoon, on leaving Roger's hotel room, Margaret hugged both Andrés and Sofia farewell. Andrés had developed a mild cough, and Sofia insisted that they should return to their aunt's apartment and have an early night. For once, Andrés did not argue. Margaret had two hours before her train would leave the *Gare du Nord*, so Jack decided that he would stay with her.

They settled at the station tea room, sipping on hot chocolate and reminiscing about the last four months: the voyage from Australia to London, their painting expeditions and his Uncle Robert and Aunt Elizabeth. Margaret had been meaning to visit them and thought that she would, that very week.

Time passed quickly and, fifteen minutes before the train was due to depart, they made their way to platform eleven. Margaret gave Jack one of the tight hugs he had become used to, reminding him to get his paintings sorted for the exhibition and promising that she would be back in three weeks. An uncharacteristically awkward silence followed, and Jack guessed that she had something on her mind.

'What is it, Margaret? Is everything okay?'

Her response was not what he expected.

'She is beautiful, Jack. Just right for you. Don't mess this up.' Margaret's words expressed urgency.

Jack stepped back in astonishment.

'Don't you look at me like that,' Margaret said. 'You know exactly what I mean. I see you. I see Sofia. The way you look at each other. Life is short, Jack, and you are not in Paris for much longer.'

'Yes, but she's engaged,' Jack replied.

'Engaged! What! No... are you sure? I am sure she's not. Why on earth would you think that Sofia is engaged?'

'The ring. Haven't you noticed it?'

'The ring... heaven forbid! What is that supposed to mean? As far as I know, the Spanish wear wedding rings on their right hands. Are you sure you are not jumping to conclusions?'

'No... She never said that she wasn't... She sends postcards and things...' Jack trailed off. Had he jumped to conclusions?

'For crying out loud, Jack. Girls announce when they are engaged, but they certainly don't advise everyone that they are *not* engaged.'

'So, you don't think that the ring is an engagement ring?' Jack asked.

'Ask her. There is no better way to find out.'

Jack felt confused. He'd been sure the ring with the green stone surrounded by diamonds had signified that Sofia was engaged. It was the sign that all men looked for. A ring on the left hand told them that a woman was taken. To stay away. And to follow Margaret's advice and ask? He could not begin to imagine how he would pose such a question.

'But what on earth would she think if I asked her?'

'She might think that you were interested in her, Jack. That wouldn't be a bad start, would it?'

'Yes, and she might think how ridiculous of me, to even hope that she could like me in return.'

'Of course she likes you!'

Jack's heart skipped a beat. Margaret thought that Sofia liked him! Still, he sought clarity. 'Yes, but as a friend. In a brotherly sort of way?' His words came out more like a question than a statement.

'Jack. You cannot be so blind. She adores you. And why wouldn't she? You are actually an okay sort of bloke, you know. Now... you've got–what?–barely two months left before you go home. I'm serious, Jack. Do NOT go home wondering if you might have had a chance with Sofia. You will regret it for the rest of your life. And you will be ruined for having a decent relationship with anyone. Forever, you will be dreaming about Sofia, the beautiful Spanish girl you let get away in Paris, and no poor bloody Australian girl will ever be able to live up to your fantasies. Do you hear me?'

'And who did you leave behind?' Jack asked, half joking, half hoping to divert Margaret from the tirade she was launching at him.

He was sorry he asked, for tears sprang to her eyes. Tears that she brushed aside angrily, her hand movement restoring her face to its usual control.

'You don't need to say anything, Margaret. I was joking.'

'It's all right, Jack. I try not to think about this too much, for it still seems to hurt, so I will say it fast,'

'We were both seventeen and, to be honest, he was very much like you. James, to be precise. Jim, we called him. I adored him. Met him at Max Meldrum's school. We set up beside each other and started talking, and the conversation never stopped. He had already left school – had a good job with the electrical company and he certainly loved to paint. He was good, too! Each Thursday evening he'd come to Max's, and I just lived to see him. And then we started meeting up on the weekends, after he finished work. For over six months, we painted from one end of Melbourne to the other and talked and fell in love. He adored me, and I him. He was big and strong and fair, and he was always smiling,' Margaret glanced at Jack and he could see that the image of Jim was as real to her in that moment as if her lost love was standing with them. 'A bit like you, Jack, and with the same easy-going manner.'

Jack squirmed. It felt strange being likened to this man from Margaret's past, who'd obviously meant so much to her.

'Always laughing. Didn't take anything too seriously. Except the war. And the day he turned eighteen, he signed up. I begged him not to, but he wouldn't hear of it. His mind was made up. Had been for years, I suspect. Still, I can hear his voice. "How can I not go, Margaret?" he'd say. "You give me a good reason, and I will stay."

' "Because I love you?" I'd say to him, but he'd always have an answer. "Yes, but what about the boys over there? They have girl-friends and wives and fiancees and mothers who love them, too. They need to get back home, don't you think? Some of them have been gone for years."

' "And some will never come back. Thousands have already died!" I'd argue, but that just made him all the more sure that he needed to go and support them.

' "I'm strong and able-bodied. I have no excuses. Heaven knows, we need to finish this thing off and the lads over there need all the help they can get. I couldn't live with myself knowing that others had responded to the call – gone to France and Turkey and Egypt – and I had just sat here on my hands." And so, of course, he went.'

Jack's heart sank, for he knew the end without it being said. He spared Margaret the words.

'So, he never returned…'

'No, Jack. He never returned. I waited and hoped and prayed. At first, there were letters. He'd completed his training and then they put him on a ship. Then there was silence. Weeks and weeks of silence. I used to visit his mother to see if she'd heard anything. And then, one day I went around there and, as soon as she saw me, the tears started. I knew straight away. She read me the letter. "Died a hero, blah, blah, blah!" What a lot of rubbish they dish out. He'd only been gone three months! He was no hero. He was a boy who felt he had to do his duty, and it killed him. God – the war was already as good as over. No one needed Jim to throw his life away on it. What a bloody waste!

'So now, I look at other men, and sometimes they look at me. But they are not Jim. The bastard ruined everything for me!'

Jack felt a lump in his throat. For Jim, who sounded so nice and brave and honourable. And for Margaret, trapped by a love that had bound her heart for over a decade, unable to move on. It seemed so sad and unfair. And such a waste.

'Promise me, Jack, you will at least have a talk to Sofia?'

Jack nodded without comment and Margaret continued, 'When I am back, I expect to see progress. I don't care if your romance is a blazing star that crashes and burns within a week, or if Sofia is the love of your life and you have ten screaming brats together. Just make something happen.'

With that, a loud whistle blew, prompting Margaret to give him another quick hug before she stepped through the open door of the carriage. The porter called for bystanders to step back and the train began its slow, ambling roll out of the station, leaving Jack gazing after her in bewilderment.

'At least she might have told me where to start,' he muttered to himself, not doubting for a second that Margaret would have expert opinions on that too.

CHAPTER 23

*J*n hindsight, Jack realised the following Friday afternoon's
events had borne the characteristics of a well-rehearsed
play. One whose scenes had been set long before the moment when he
and Andrés walked back from their morning's lessons and Andrés had
explained that he would not be able to go to Montmartre with Jack and
Sofia, following lunch, as they'd planned.

'Are you unwell?' Jack asked, surprised.

'No… I just need to go back to Pont Neuf and review my sketches
of the afternoon crowds crossing the bridge on their way home from
work.'

'We'll come with you,' Jack offered. However, Andrés shook his
head.

'No, you and Sofia must go,' he replied. 'Sofia has been waiting all
week to go to Montmartre. She'll be disappointed if we cancel and you
know how cranky she gets if she doesn't get her own way!'

Jack laughingly agreed, although he could not really recall any time
when Sofia had been particularly cranky.

When they arrived at the *Café Española*, Sofia's reactions seemed
odd. Her usual warm greeting and excited, 'So, what has my *artistes
extraordinarios* achieved today?' had seemed muted and, after a quick

hug, she'd turned away. Today, it was Sofia who'd blushed and Jack noticed her dress, one he had not seen before, in a light, flowing fabric with orange and yellow polka dots scattered across a pale green background. Its matching green belt cinched at the waist, the full skirt emphasising her slender figure, and the bright colours were perfect for a summer day in Paris.

Jack had not dared to believe that Sofia looked forward to spending time with him as he did her. However, neither was he silly, and it suddenly occurred to him that both Andrés' and Sofia's behaviour had Margaret's fingerprints all over it.

I don't believe it, he thought, then chuckled. Of course he believed it! Margaret had been directing his life from the minute they met. Why would she stop now? Clearly, she had played Cupid, speaking to Andrés, no doubt convincing him to give Jack and Sofia time alone together. Jack knew that Andrés would be no match for the persuasive Margaret, who always had definite ideas about everything and was nothing but generous with her advice. She had quite possibly cornered Sofia and given her the same little talking-to that she had given Jack, this time girl-to-girl.

Sofia placed the usual carafes of water and wine before Andrés and Jack, accompanied by two sets of glasses, a routine Jack had adjusted to over the weeks. However, instead of hovering for a few minutes to chat as she usually did, she quickly placed bowls of *cazuela marinera*–a beautiful Malagian seafood broth–and a plate of soft white bread before them. As she moved around the table, Jack studied her hands, looking at the sparkling ring that had held so much significance. Perhaps Margaret was right, and it was not an engagement ring at all.

Over their lunch, Jack tried to stay focused as he and Andrés discussed Miss Stein's upcoming exhibition, a conversation that seemed to surface hourly over the last week, be it to comment on the progress of their works and decisions about their selections or just to ponder the excitement of it all. Who would come? Would anybody? Frequently, they fell into nervous teasing about all the things that could go wrong.

'Sofia, did you hear Miss Stein had an accident this morning? Not expected to live!'

'Oh, no, Sofia, the academy was vandalised this morning. All of our paintings have been destroyed!'

'Jack, I hope you will still be my friend when all my paintings have "sold" stickers on them and yours are left hanging...'

Just as they finished their meal, Sofia arrived at the table, ready for their afternoon excursion, her bag in hand. She looked startled when, with a sudden motion, Andrés pulled out his chair and excused himself, mumbling awkwardly that it was time to head off, explaining to his surprised sister that he needed to complete his sketches along the Seine and insisting she and Jack have a lovely afternoon together. He left them staring at each other. While Andrés had already prepared Jack for this change of plans, he clearly hadn't done the same for Sofia, and her blush returned. So! Sofia had not been forewarned of this little ploy, Jack realised.

They watched Andrés' retreating back in silence, and then looked at each other, as if to say, 'What next?'

'Okay, Sofia, looks like it's you and me today.' Jack laughed, extending his arm, hoping his aura of confidence concealed his rapidly beating heart.

With a shy giggle, Sofia stepped forward and hooked her arm through his in her usual manner. She began chatting and Jack discovered he need do no more than accompany her in a gentlemanly fashion, steering her across the busy street, holding her arm as she stepped onto the bus before him and guiding her to the single empty seat halfway down the aisle. Sofia, clearly cut from the same cloth as Margaret, did not draw breath as she launched into an account of her early morning shopping trip to the local market, offering detailed descriptions of her purchase of a leg of ham and how the delicatessen's shopkeeper had 'accidentally' overlooked adjusting his scales and tried to charge her almost double the price for the café's order of goat cheese, a favourite with their regular customers.

Jack could not help but smile to himself, sure that Sofia's continuous chatter, operating on double-time today, was a cover for nervous excitement. For him, it was a godsend because, in her nervousness, he was able to gather composure. Her breathless speech gave him time to think about his reactions, and his instinct was to provide a calm and reassuring presence to the sweet girl beside him.

~

They arrived at Montmartre in no time at all and wandered along the rue des Abbesses, admiring the wonderful buildings, the tidy streets, the colourful doorways and the rows of black iron grills upon the windows of the apartment blocks. There was nothing they could fault. Jack bought them ice-cream cones and they continued their walk, looking at the beautiful houses – mansions really, and eventually they found themselves peering through the large entry gates of the *Parc Monceau*. Nannies in black dresses with white aprons wheeled huge, ornate prams along the pathways and they could see a gleaming red and gold open carriage drawn by pairs of horses. The view was beyond charming, and by unspoken agreement, he and Sofia entered. At every turn, the park offered one surprise after another. Tiny replicas of ancient buildings – a pyramid, windmill and even the recreation of ancient roman ruins. Garden beds had been planted with the flair of an artist - flowers colourfully arranged to please the eye. A beautiful pond formed the centre-piece, now invaded by hundreds of birds that were being fed handfuls of grain by a man in overalls. From time to time, they came upon statues and they tried to guess who they were. The only name that Jack recognised was that of Frédéric Chopin.

~

The afternoon was everything Jack could have hoped. Beautiful spring sunshine, the park lively with tourists, entertainment and companionable ease between himself and Sofia. While each had recognised the subtle shift in their relationship, two significant events flagged the change from friendly affection to something more. First,

Jack, in a moment of spontaneity, bought Sofia a pretty coral necklace from a street vendor who was standing outside the park as they left.

'Something for the beautiful lady.' The elderly gentleman stepped before them, his hands splayed, colourful strands of beads spilling over his fingers in display.

'Why yes, certainly we would like something,' Jack replied without hesitation.

'No, Jack, that is not necessary,' Sofia said.

'Sofia, I want to buy you a necklace. Which one would you like?'

'Thank you… perhaps this one?'

'This one it is, then. Thank you, sir.'

For all of Jack's man-of-the-world negotiating to purchase the necklace, his hands trembled when, at Sofia's insistence, he placed the triple strands of orange coral around her neck, finding the fingers which commanded squirrel-hair brushes to make the finest of lines on canvas suddenly clumsy in their struggle to navigate Sofia's wavy tresses. The faint scent of her sweet perfume was intoxicating at this close range. She laughed as she helped him, holding her hair high, exposing a smooth, slender neck and, after he had attached the clasp, she turned to him, her mouth so near he could feel her soft breath on his face while he distractedly repositioned the necklace.

A second event that marked the change occurred in the late afternoon, when the sun was beginning to cast long shadows over the streets. They had walked the lengthy blocks from Montmartre, weaving southward, knowing that eventually they would arrive at the Seine.

'Jack, we are lost, surely,' Sofia exclaimed once or twice, her smile suggesting that she did not really mind.

'Sofia, trust me. If the setting sun is on our right, we are heading south. Can't go wrong. I've got the instincts of an Aboriginal tracker. Stick with me and you will never get lost!'

Even Jack was surprised when they emerged halfway along the Champs-Élysées. Without thought, he turned to the right towards the Arc before crossing the busy road and returning in an easterly direction.

'How about we find a bite to eat, Sofia? Will your aunt miss you for dinner?'

'No, she will not mind, Jack. That would be lovely.'

They passed about three cafés, all with empty seats, and Sofia looked at Jack enquiringly, but he just shook his head. They continued walking until Jack stopped outside the plate-glass doors of a very fancy restaurant, complete with a doorman resplendent in a white blazer decorated with gleaming gold buttons and a breast pocket embroidered with a flowing 'C'. The restaurant's name, *Le Grand Colbert*, was visible in bold letters, gold on black, above the broad windows.

'Here,' said Jack. 'Let's try this one.'

'Jack! It will cost a fortune!' Sofia responded. 'Andrés will think I've gone mad if I spend our savings here. Besides, I am not dressed for such a fancy place. What are you thinking?'

'Nonsense,' said Jack firmly. 'My treat, and you... you look beautiful...' Without waiting for the protest that he knew was coming, Jack steered Sofia towards the open door. The doorman, whose facial expression had not faltered at their exchange, smiled with a half bow as they entered the restaurant.

Glancing around, Jack was pleased. It was as impressive as he had hoped it would be, with stunning chandeliers cascading from the ceiling and the floor laid in glistening swirls of tiny mosaic tiles.

'This way, sir, madame.' A serious-looking maître d'hôtel guided them to a small table for two by a window opening directly onto the street.

Allowing themselves to be seated, they accepted tall glasses of cool water and then were finally alone.

Gazing across the table, Jack had one of those moments when he could barely believe what was happening. Here he was, alone with Sofia in a beautiful restaurant. She returned his gaze with a gentle smile, but he recognised the telltale sign of her nerves as her chatter launched into overdrive while her hands fidgeted, first with the serviette, unconsciously dismantling the complex arrangement of folds which formed an exquisite swan from the heavily starched white linen, and then repositioning the salt and pepper shakers. She realigned the cutlery, forming neat, straight rows of the knives and forks arrayed to the left and right of her setting. In a sudden attempt for composure, she joined her hands together to still their frenetic activity, only to recommence their fiddling seconds later.

Surprised by his composure, Jack reached across the table, his hands taking Sofia's firmly and holding them still as she was about to adjust the salt and pepper shakers for the third time. No words were said, but at that moment, the transformation was complete. Jack and Sofia simultaneously knew their friendship had finally turned the corner it had been tentatively approaching over recent months.

Jack insisted that they have all four courses on offer, commencing with an *apéritif* – Kir Royal, the champagne and *crème de cassis* cocktail served in sparkling crystal flutes and accompanied by a small platter of *pissaladières* – small onion and anchovy tarts. They laughed at the entrée options, giving up on their efforts to interpret the menu written in beautifully scrolled lettering – in French. Assisted by the waiter, they ordered the *escargots de Bourgogne*, Sofia insisting that snails were an essential culinary experience for Jack.

For the main meal, Jack selected *coq au vin* and Sofia the *boeuf en croûte* and, by the time their dishes were served, the wave of shyness that had washed over them, triggered by the imposing atmosphere of the formal dining room, had thankfully receded. Relaxed and enjoying each other's company, they discussed the grandeur of the room, the fastidious attention of the waiter and how odd they must appear in their casual street clothes compared to the other diners – women dressed in sparkling headwear and tasselled dresses accompanied by men in black three-piece suits.

Following their main course, they agreed they were full. However, Jack maintained that the dining experience would not be complete unless they tried *Bombe Alaska*, having witnessed the spectacular flaming dessert ceremoniously delivered to diners at tables around them.

As they relaxed, their conversation turned towards life experiences. While, over the weeks, Jack had gleaned aspects of Sofia's and Andrés' childhood in Málaga and had, in turn, spoken of his life in Australia, the intimacy and quietness of the dinner table prompted more personal revelations.

Jack described his childhood. The loving parents who, he unashamedly confessed, doted on him and were anxiously awaiting his return. He laughed even as he sympathised with them, describing to Sofia the shock they must have experienced when the London holiday they'd planned for him had taken its southern diversion across the English Channel, admitting that his parents would find his life in Paris as an art student incomprehensible. Jack described growing up as an only child and the craving to draw which had been in him for as long as he could remember. He admitted to moments of acute loneliness, fantasising about life with a brother, confessing his envy of the closeness that Sofia shared with Andrés, and hoped he didn't sound silly for expressing such feelings. When Sofia enquired about his friendship with Margaret, Jack realised she had harboured some uncertainty about the role that the outspoken, bossy woman held in his life. Having seen the sketch he'd made of Margaret in the last week of their journey on the *Ormonde*, Sofia had drawn her own conclusions.

'You thought that Margaret was my girlfriend?' Jack was stunned.

'Well, yes, Jack. I did, actually.'

'But... she's old!'

'Not really. And anyway, I am old also... two years older than you, *si*?'

'Yes, but that's nothing...' Taking her hands between his, Jack looked down at the ring Sofia wore on her left hand. 'And I take it you're not engaged?'

'Engaged!' Sofia seemed to think that was extraordinarily funny. 'Why on earth would you think that, Jack?'

'I don't know. Just a thought.'

Holding Sofia's hand firmly, as if the very action would bind them closer, Jack laughingly described his meeting with Margaret on the *Ormonde* and how she had immediately designated herself as 'director' of his life. He told about how she had introduced him to her relatives, the Bloomsbury artists, and the day he had stood nervously while Roger Fry scrutinised his paintings, subsequently arranging for him to attend *Académie Julian.* To Jack, the events he spoke of seemed surreal, as if they'd happened in someone else's life – as did this moment, sitting here with Sofia. And yet, somehow, it all sounded so right.

In turn, Sofia described her childhood in Málaga on the Costa del Sol. Jack watched her face light up as she spoke of her home, the finca high above the town, bought by her parents as newlyweds over thirty years ago. Her love of cooking began when she was fourteen and started experimenting with various recipes to cure their home-grown olives. She described the process to Jack; crushing the hard fruit, inedible when picked, submerging them for weeks first in fresh water – changed each day – then in salty water, changed every two days. Taste testing, to make sure the bitterness of the natural fruit had gone. Only then were the olives ready for marinating! Sofia's passion for her olives was evident as she explained the pleasure of trying out different herbs – fennel, rosemary, garlic – and seasonings such as paprika, mint, peppers and then citrus fruit for added flavour. Her favourite: their very own oranges.

She described the many fiestas in Málaga and the surrounding villages, nestled high in the hills and along the coastline, lively events with street stalls, parades, dancing for both young and old, where men and women relished opportunities to dress in traditional Spanish costume and celebrate all manner of national and local traditions. The annual olive harvest and religious festivals were a regular source of community gatherings, as were a constant stream of baptisms, weddings and holy communions.

Jack enquired about the two things he associated with Spain. First, bullfighting, to which Sofia screwed up her nose. 'Too cruel,' she replied, shaking her head. She laughed when he next asked about flamenco dancing and acknowledged that, yes, she like all young Spanish girls, had attended dance lessons and loved the opportunity to put on a ruffled dress, mantilla and high heels at the many festivals throughout the year.

Without them realising it, hours slipped away, and the restaurant emptied. Jack considered taking a taxi back to Montparnasse, an uncommon luxury; buses, trains, trams and walking were the usual modes of transport for the trio. However, reluctant to end the night, he suggested they wander along the *Champs-Élysées* and across the *Pont Neuf*, and then – when their legs wore out, or perhaps his ears got sore from her endless chatter, he teased – they would flag a taxi. Sofia replied by punching him in the arm, in 'a most unladylike way for someone who has just been dining in a fancy Parisian restaurant!'

Jack paid the bill and tipped the waiter as he had seen his father do many times following formal dinners with business contacts, and he felt a strange sense of truly becoming a man as he touched Sofia's elbow and escorted her through the open door of the restaurant onto the sidewalk.

The street they entered, visible although strangely remote from the quiet intimacy of their window seat in the restaurant where they'd sat a few minutes earlier, was abuzz with life. Well-dressed men and elegant women, bearing extraordinary headwear and extravagant clothing, paraded along the *Champs-Élysées*, the sound of their heels clipping the pavement mingling with soft words and low giggles, as if the twinkling lights and late hour of the evening inspired a delightful nocturnal charm. Horse-drawn taxis mingled with motorised vehicles, competing for curb-side space, and muttered growling and cursing between drivers was audible as they cut each other off in their attempts to pick up and drop off laughing couples and foursomes. Adding to the confusion, long chauffeur-driven saloons idled beside the pavement, personal drivers on hand to relocate their employers to any of the theatres, restaurants, galleries and clubs that remained open until the small hours of the morning. Hazy light emitting from hundreds of electric bulbs gave the avenue a soft glow.

Lively music filled the air, drifting through the open doorways of nightclubs, whose patrons were spilling onto the pavement. Jack and Sofia stopped and watched a group of musicians performing. The music was jazz, performed by black entertainers whose presence throughout Paris had been a constant source of surprise to Jack. His only experience with dark-skinned people were the Aboriginals in Australia, most often relegated to the role of servants. Certainly,

Australian Aboriginals were not celebrated entertainers like the people of colour here in Paris. Indeed, the adults Jack knew frequently debated the position of Australia's Aboriginals, who had few rights and were granted little respect. Many adults, including his parents, believed they were destined to die out. It was only a matter of time, and that those living needed to be 'looked after' on missions and reserves. A couple of the boys at Jack's school were endlessly vocal on the subject, insisting that the only thing causing Aboriginal people's awful living conditions and their terrible death rate was the government policies and the way employers treated them, claiming it was the Aborigines who did all the work to build up the big rural sheep and cattle stations that made Australia rich, and yet they received miserable rates of pay. Jack and his mates had called these students The Ministers, sure that they were set for a future in politics. Despite the teasing, Jack often felt they had a point when they started their rants about the rights of Aborigines to have fair wages, should be free to leave the missions, travel and even to marry without having to ask permission. They also insisted that the common practice of removing children from their parents, and placing them in institutions, was cruel and unnecessary.

Looking at the black musicians on the stage, aglow with the enjoyment of their performance, applauded and cheered by the crowd, Jack knew in an instant that the boys at school, The Ministers, were probably right.

～

Sofia paused, peering into a room that was erupting with the powerful sounds of a female's voice accompanied by saxophone, trumpet, double bass and piano. Dancing couples could be seen through the hazy smoke, their feet moving in complicated steps to the latest incarnation of the Charleston.

'Come on, Jack, let's go in.' She tugged him towards the doorway.

'No way,' Jack said, shaking his head.

'Yes – come on! It will be fun,' Sofia implored.

'Sofia, I've never danced in my life. You will be so embarrassed, you'll walk out and leave me lying in a heap on the dance floor.' Jack's words were drowned out by the music as Sofia determinedly pulled him through the door and he allowed himself to be towed through swaying bodies, trying to avoid creating carnage as he dodged between waving long-stemmed glasses and smouldering cigarettes as she made her way onto the dance floor.

Firmly holding Jack's hands, Sofia demonstrated simple moves: sway to the left, sway to the right. They shuffled together, Jack laughing so hard it took all of Sofia's strength to hold him upright. At that minute, his happiness trumped self-consciousness as he reasoned that nobody in this room knew him, so why care what anyone thought? Besides, he was with the most beautiful girl in the world and, for her, he would do anything.

Additionally, Jack was pleasantly lightheaded from the alcohol he had consumed and everything seemed fun, anything possible. At the restaurant, they had followed the *Kir Royal* with the latest Parisian fad recommended by the sommelier, a champagne and orange juice cocktail called a *Mimosa*; then a brandy and vodka cocktail, a *Pepa*, had followed the *Bombe Alaska*.

After swaying their way through three dances, Jack bought a *La Grande Parade de Paris* for Sofia and a beer for himself, which they consumed at the bar. This time, Jack led Sofia back onto the floor. At 11:30 pm, however, in a startling moment of clarity, he pulled Sofia aside.

∾

'Time to go,' he said with urgency. 'Andrés will have my head if I don't get you home safe and sound.'

Sofia laughed. 'Jack, I may be his little sister, but I am not a child,' she said. 'Besides, Andrés knows that you will look after me.' She seemed, however, happy to leave the noisy chaos of the club and have Jack to herself again.

They walked along the broad avenue and over the Pont de la Concorde to the Left Bank, where the street lighting suddenly diminished. When Jack sensed the presence of a shadowy shape scuttling past in the dark, he felt it wise to take a taxi to Rue des Saints-Pères to ensure Sofia's safe passage home.

Minutes later, walking hand in hand silently up the stairs of the apartment building, they were thankful to find its hallway lights still on. After collecting the key from her bag and opening the door, Sofia turned to Jack.

'Thank you for a wonderful day,' she said.

The softness of her expression and shiny warmth in her eyes left Jack in no doubt that the feelings he had for her were reciprocated, and he pulled her close, even as questions flooded his thoughts. What next? To start something, when he was leaving so very soon? And then, cupping his hand around the back of Sofia's head, he pulled her towards him and kissed her, first gently, softly touching her lips with his, and then firmly, surprised at how natural it felt.

'Thank you,' he said, pulling back, his nose touching hers as he looked into her eyes. 'I am sure that today has been the best day of my life. Let's see if we can do it again sometime very soon.' And with that, he let go of her, ushering her through the door of the quiet apartment.

CHAPTER 24

*T*hankful to see his bicycle leaning against the stairwell railing – brought home by Andrés, Jack guessed – he set out through the darkened streets toward the Passage Dantzig. He was surprised to see the streets of Montparnasse still bristling with life at this late hour. Numerous salons were conducting a lively trade and loud voices, drunken rantings, laughter and music spilled out onto the streets. While perhaps not so sophisticated as those on the *Champs-Élysées*, the Montparnasse establishments had an aura of earthiness borne of their patrons' diverse mix of nationalities. Artisans and writers, united in their fellowship of poverty, nonetheless found richness in their nightly gatherings of shared dreams, optimism and inspiration, not to mention a steady dose of alcohol-fuelled nostalgia, romance and debate. Riding at barely a walking pace, Jack breathed in the night air with a sense of intoxication. At this moment, he understood the magic of Paris: alive, in love, connected to a world where art was central, as necessary as the air he breathed, fulfilled by images of the shining eyes of a beautiful woman he could call his own.

Jack smiled knowingly at couples walking along with arms tightly entwined, feeling he now understood the joy of two hearts pulsating as one. It seemed as if every sound of the midnight hour was heightened.

Sole pedestrians scampered through the streets – a drunkard singing softly to himself, an old woman whose face was painted with the heavy makeup common to the street women, whose price and number of customers both diminished with age. Then there were the young *prostituées* actively plying their trade. Jack recognised some of them, regulars on these streets, and laughed at their friendly attempts at seduction. They, in turn, who were quick to observe every lone male who wandered past 'their corner', recognised him, for they regularly called out to him as he rode through the streets of Montparnasse in the evenings.

'Ooh, you are very late tonight, young man.' The call came from a tall girl, her white blouse hanging loose on her shoulders and plunging low over her expansive bosom.

'I think he is in love. 'Tis quite a smile he has on his face,' a second called. 'Or perhaps he just got his pleasure.'

'I'd be happy to put a smile on his face if the lad would like to spare a franc,' another said, to which Jack laughed back. He was certainly in love and did not mind sharing it. The streets of Montparnasse pulsated with energy in a rhythm that spoke to his heart, and he had never felt so blissfully alive in all his life.

~

The next day being Saturday, Jack met with Andrés and Sofia at eleven am. Over coffee, he and Andrés agreed they needed to add to their collection of sketches along the Seine in preparation for painting. Joking about the late hour of Jack and Sofia's return the evening before, Andrés suggested they would probably want to catch a taxi everywhere today, too tired to walk.

Jack and Sofia did their best to behave as usual. However, the shift in their relationship was impossible to ignore. Every time they caught each other's eyes, they smiled as if sharing a secret joke. Aloud, they recalled the liveliness of Montmartre the previous day or how lovely their dinner was, reliving the magic moments that they'd shared.

They stopped by a wharf along the riverside where wine barrels were being rolled off a barge and loaded onto horse-drawn wagons for delivery to the various bars of Paris. The boys settled along the banks, opening up their sketchbooks, leaving Sofia to meander amongst the tiny alleyways to gather inspiration for her own *Galleria Toulouse* café.

~

For Jack and Andrés, preparing paintings for the exhibition was now their priority. While still following their pattern of early starts, morning classes, and lunch at the café, their approach to the works they created took on a more serious nature. Monsieur Simon, thrilled with his young students' opportunity, continued to offer careful guidance where requested, but he mostly left Andrés and Jack to develop their styles. An old friend of Roger Fry's, he had known of Roger's plan to show Jack's works to Gertrude Stein, should he prove worthy, from the beginning. Unbeknownst to Jack, Roger had made regular enquiries on his progress and was pleased when Monsieur Simon had agreed with him that Jack had extraordinary talent and, furthermore, was very receptive to his teachings.

Most afternoons were still spent walking through the streets of Paris, sitting in a warm café or wandering along the river. Andrés frequently decried the shift in relationships among the trio as Jack and Sofia walked, arms entwined. Where she used to hook her hands through each of the boys' arms, more often than not, now she and Jack walked hand in hand, leaving Andrés to wander alone in front or behind.

'You've stolen my best friend,' he'd whimper theatrically to Sofia, tugging at Jack's arms in a bid to reclaim him.

At this, they would laughingly take Andrés by the arms between them.

'*Amigos*, must I do handstands to get your attention?' he grumbled one Saturday afternoon as they walked around the base of the Eiffel Tower. He promptly launched upside down, walking a few metres on his hands, to the amusement of hundreds of onlooking tourists.

However, with increasing frequency, he left Sofia and Jack to explore Paris together while he returned to the Academy to work on his paintings, determined to make the most of the opportunity that had come his way.

~

As crucial as the rapidly approaching exhibition was, Jack could not summon the same degree of single-minded commitment to it as Andrés did. For one, he had never shared Andrés' lifetime of yearning and effort to achieve artistic fame and its associated freedoms, a world that was still foreign to him. Secondly, he was in love and that, in itself, was an enormous distraction. Thoughts of Sofia constantly infused his mind, of the joy she brought into his life as well as the looming date when they would each return to their own lives. Sofia constantly apologised to him, feeling guilty for taking him away from his painting, and together they would make bargains – if they went out today, Jack would paint tomorrow – plans they rarely adhered to, and Jack found it difficult to care. He had no desire to spend his days hovering over oil and canvas when confronted with the ever-present knowledge that his time with Sofia was ending very soon. In a few short weeks, the exhibition would be over, followed by Jack's last two weeks at the academy, and then he would be making his way back to London and onto the *Ormonde* for the six-week journey home. He could not bear to think about leaving Sofia. The return sea voyage, this time without the distraction of Margaret's company, followed by a life in Australia, seemed meaningless without Sofia by his side, and interminably depressing. His mind tossed and turned relentlessly, grappling to find a solution.

~

As if sensing Jack's apprehension at the thought of return, his mother's letters became overwhelmingly enthusiastic about his pending homecoming. Mimi delivered them as regular as clockwork each Thursday.

Jack would take the familiar thick cream envelope from her, collect his bicycle from the foyer's side storeroom and, after carrying it down the steps, leaned against it and quickly scanned his mother's words. It always amazed him that, as soon as he began reading, it was as though his mother stood before him. With every word, he sensed her undercurrent of anxiety. Jack suspected that, with his side trip to Paris and delayed return home, his mother was fearing she may never see him again. Notwithstanding, she bravely compensated for her worry with overstated enthusiasm. Firstly, she spoke of how fortunate he was to have a position with Goldsbrough Mort & Co; how generous they had been to hold it open for Jack, especially with so much unemployment; how keen Mr Johnson, head of the finance department, was to see him start. Then – how splendid it would be for him to arrive home in time for the football finals. Everybody was predicting a Collingwood versus Carlton Grand Final. Next, she wrote of bumping into Mrs Fitzgibbons – of how her girls were looking forward to hearing of his adventures. Especially Katherine. Had he remembered to send them postcards? She hadn't liked to ask. Jack had a suspicious feeling that his mother and Mrs Fitzgibbon may have embarked on a matchmaking plan, his mother no doubt hoping the lure of the attractive Katherine Fitzgibbon, ripe for an engagement, might secure his speedy return.

Not losing sight of Jack's newfound commitment to painting, his mother also proved surprisingly resourceful in exploiting this angle to sweeten his homecoming. 'The Victorian Artists Society has an excellent reputation, and it offers a range of painting classes in East Melbourne,' she wrote. Another option was an art school in Caulfield. Marian offered to enrol Jack, securing a place for the following year's lessons if he wished. He was touched, appreciating the research his mother had undertaken on his behalf and her determination to demonstrate that Melbourne also offered opportunities for him to pursue painting as a hobby. If only she understood. Paris was more than art lessons once a week. It was living and breathing art – immersion in an environment that was steeped in history and yet rapidly changing, defining a new way of viewing art in the modern world and challenging the restraints of social boundaries. Concepts that Jack barely grasped, and yet he was captivated by the exciting promise that they offered. Totally beyond his parent's comprehension, he knew. And, Jack could not deny, it was about being in love with a girl with sparkling eyes so luminous that he felt he could drown in them. The sweetest girl in the world.

~

Sofia began to raise the topic of his return to Australia.

'So, Jack., will your parents kill the fatted calf and invite all your friends over for a feast when you get home?'

'What time will the ship leave London?'

'I suppose you will forget your Spanish girl when you arrive in Australia.'

Jack understood that she, like him, was trying to make sense of what the future held for them. Was this wonderful time together simply a magical holiday romance? A memory to be cherished, stored away with the coral necklace, along with the memories of their wonderful day in Montparnasse? Jack considered the option of asking Sofia if she would come to Australia with him. However, he knew that for her to leave Andrés would be unthinkable. He was her brother and only family. Her twin, connected in utero and life. They had compensated for each other's absence of a mother, supported each other during their father's dying days as they'd nursed him and ultimately stood side by side, sharing fathomless depths of grief as the wonderful man who had raised them was lowered into the ground. Jack knew he could not ask her to travel to the other side of the world and leave Andrés alone and, more than that, he knew what the answer would be if he did ask.

With the passing of each day, Jack's misery increased, and he found it difficult to answer Sofia's searching questions. Their plans, to write each week and for him to travel to Spain next summer, sounded fanciful and vastly inadequate - even as he spoke them.

Andrés, sensing the predicament that his sister and friend were in, half-jokingly encouraged Sofia to stow away on the ship to Australia. However, he also knew that she would never leave him, nor could he leave her, and so he left them to work it out. When Jack expressed his worries to his friend, Andrés replied with confidence, 'Jack, it will all work out. What is meant to be, will be.' And then in a cheeky attempt to lighten Jack's mood, he continued, 'I will listen to her cry for a while and offer consoling words... and then a handsome Spaniard will come along and she will forget you... No need to worry, my friend!' In response, Jack grabbed the laughing Andrés in a headlock and pretended to punch him.

~

Unlike Andrés, Margaret was far less philosophical and totally disinclined to leave Jack and Sofia to work out their dilemma. In fact, when she slipped across the English Channel to Paris the week before the exhibition, her comments to Jack were razor sharp.

'You are going home in three weeks! What about your painting? What about Sofia?'

When he simply shrugged in helplessness, she could not conceal her annoyance.

'Jack! What are you doing? Trying to live your life for other people? You owe it to yourself to stay in Paris and paint. And don't you think you owe it to yourself and Sofia to see if what you have is worth keeping? Just send a letter. "Sorry, I won't be coming home because I think I may be in love." Tell them you are fine and happy, and that you will stay in touch. Tell them you'll invite them to the wedding in due course. Tell them you have just been given an extraordinary opportunity that few artists ever receive. Tell them anything, but now is NOT the time to go home! Too much is at stake.'

Listening to her passionate plea for him to stay, Jack thought of Jim, the love lost to her when he had sailed out of her life across the sea and never returned, and wondered if she, too, made the connection.

~

May, Friday 14 arrived and Jack, Andrés, Sofia and Roger, who had arrived in Paris the previous evening, were to meet with Miss Stein. The exhibition was now only two weeks away, and it was time to make a final selection of their works to be catalogued, framed and hung. The morning was spent with Monsieur Simon who, assisting them to display their paintings, suggested a room at the academy for this important viewing. Although very old, it was a beautiful room, over fifty feet long and thirty feet wide, where the Academy's exhibitions were displayed, including the annual student exhibition to be held in three weeks, only one week after Miss Stein's.

Portable partitions were on hand, designed to increase wall space and allow the curator to control the presentation of artwork. Dragging one from a side storeroom, they placed it perpendicular to the long wall, opposite thin windows that overlooked the street. This created two alcoves, one for Jack's work, the other for Andrés'. Monsieur's enthusiasm was palpable as he paced the room waiting for Jacques-Noël, the academy's handyman, to assist them to move the clutter of furniture and shelves that had been stored in the room over the winter. Once an artist himself, many of Jacques Noël's extraordinary charcoal portraits hung in drawing rooms across Paris and beyond. Unfortunately, he'd been forced to forsake his craft over a decade earlier when a rare form of anaemia ravaged his body, year-by-year taking its toll, until the mere act of holding his charcoal stick became impossible. Nonetheless, art was his passion, and he'd happily accepted the job at the academy, thankful of the opportunity to remain amid the world of artists. For years, now, he'd set up the academy's annual exhibitions, and his expertise proved invaluable. He and Sofia took control of the presentation, consulting with each other as they arranged and rearranged the order for the paintings to be displayed, ignoring helpful suggestions from Jack and Andrés with a shake of the head.

'Go away. You are merely the painters – your job is done. Leave this to the experts,' Sofia laughed.

Monsieur Simon bustled around, straightening their paintings as they waited for Miss Stein and Roger to arrive, beaming and patting both Andrés and Jack on their backs. He repeatedly exclaimed how proud he was of them – how exciting it had been for him to watch the evolving skills of not just one, but two young men! How nice it was to see their friendship develop, devoid of the competitive ego that so often accompanied artistic relationships. Monsieur Simon joked that they must remember their old master and tell the newspapers how it was he who had led them to greatness. Repeatedly, he told them how pleased he was to witness their good fortune, explaining that, while many students had talent, few were truly exceptional, and rarely did one get such an opportunity as Miss Stein and Roger were offering.

A state of nervous energy pervaded the room when Roger and Miss Stein arrived on the dot of two pm and, after greetings were attended to, they quickly moved on to the business at hand. To everyone's relief, it became rapidly evident that they were pleased with the quality of work Jack and Andrés had presented.

'Jack, this is marvellous,' Roger exclaimed over his study of the gnarled hands of a fisherman, tanned and aged like old leather boots, contrasting with the salmon being scooped from his net, sunlight capturing their smooth golden scales as they tumbled into a wicker basket. 'So traditional in its subject, yet so modern in its expression.'

'Oh, Roger, what do you think of this? Definitely an important work.' Miss Stein scrutinised Jack's portrait of a young girl on a bustling city street. The spire of the Eiffel Tower rose in the background, a detail inspired by Jack's early morning rides to *Académie Julian*. The girl's face glowed with a dreamlike expression, her mind appearing to have transcended to thoughts of hope and consequence despite the bareness of her feet picking their way along uneven, cold cobblestones as she drove four stringy-haired goats before her.

'See how he has captured her life of drudgery and poverty juxtaposed against the modern buildings?' Miss Stein commented. Jack marvelled at the way her words made his painting sound so very important.

'Oh, this is good. This is good. Everyone will want this,' Miss Stein said, analysing Jack's Renoir-like street scene, a celebration of the flower stalls of Paris. The lively picture was further energised by a jazz quartet carefully positioned on the lower right according to the rule of thirds, recognised by all artists as a design strategy for balancing a composition in a most pleasing way.

As usual, Andrés' work was striking in his use of colour. Bold tangerines and deep blues created a dazzling impression, administered with broad and confident brushstrokes. Andrés' style evoked the aura of earthiness that always captivated city dwellers who, according to Miss Stein, were universally drawn to scenes depicting the rural life of the generations that had preceded them.

Miss Stein and Roger agreed upon eight paintings that would serve as feature pieces to be offered for ridiculously high prices, firmly positioning Jack and Andrés as emerging artists of significance. They then identified other works to form a more general display, affordable enough to be purchased and hung in the lounge rooms of the fashionable trendsetters of New York who followed Miss Stein's judgement. Her recommendations assisted patrons to accumulate quality private collections and, while many could not afford the works of Picasso and Matisse, whose prices had escalated with their increased renown, she regularly directed them to emergent artists, such as Andrés and Jack, who showed promise.

Sofia, who had stood quietly holding Jack's hand while Miss Stein and Roger viewed the works, stepped forward as their conversation turned to fine-tuning the details of the exhibition. They listened as she demonstrated her innate understanding of grouping and presenting art in a way that captivated potential buyers, enticing them to part with their money. Together she, Miss Stein and Roger spent the next hour taking notes and drawing sketches of the proposed display and Jack was amazed to see the depth of thought that went into displaying artwork firsthand.

'Don't people prefer to pick their own frames?' Jack naively asked to be told that paintings would sit in corners for years if not sold ready to hang, consequently diminishing the perceived value of the artist. It was important that paintings sold at the exhibition should be highly prized, immediately displayed in prominent positions in their new homes for their owners to show them off to their friends and create a ripple of interest that would generate further sales.

At the end of the monologue, after which Jack almost felt sorry he had asked the question, Andrés, who had managed to stand well back alongside Monsieur Simon, winked at him.

'Out of our league, mate,' he said, copying Jack's Australian manner of speaking. 'Best left to the experts. We are just the clods who push the paint around the canvas.'

Jack joined him as the discussion continued. Even Andrés shook his head, impressed as his diminutive sister asserted herself as agent for both him and Jack before the great Miss Stein. They listened with amazement as she inquired as to the pricing of the paintings as well as the division of funds. Jack proudly acknowledged that while Andrés may well be the talented artist, it was his sister who showed a solid head for business. Her years of experience curating and creating an income from the family studio and gallery were evident. Miss Stein, for all Margaret's claims that she rarely acknowledged female intelligence, was obviously impressed with the young Spanish woman whose youth belied her skills.

'Why are we exhibiting in Montmartre?' Sofia asked when she learned the location proposed for the exhibition would be across the river.

'We need to be where the prosperity is,' replied Miss Stein. 'Montparnasse may well be the heartbeat of Parisian art, but Montmartre has the glitter. We will lure the tourists and the Americans to our exhibition and they will spend, spend, spend.'

When Sofia expressed concern at the extraordinarily high price tags, way beyond both her imaginings and experience, certainly the equivalent of a month's wages for an average Frenchman, Miss Stein answered, 'No problem. There will be enough buyers to warrant high price tags. If we sell too low, we will be sold out too early. We need to be low enough that people can afford them, yet high enough for them to feel they have bought something valuable. If people want five-franc paintings, they can buy them from the street artists.'

Speaking with Jack and Andrés later that afternoon, Sofia calculated that if they sold all their paintings, they would receive eight hundred and fifty American dollars each, nearly a year's wages. Miss

Stein herself would collect the same, from which she would pay for the framing of the works, hire of the venue, printing of catalogues and most importantly, the wine and hors d'oeuvres that would be liberally distributed throughout the evening to encourage the opening of chequebooks.

CHAPTER 25

iss Stein's prediction of the interest that Jack and Andrés' exhibition would create proved accurate, for when they arrived at The Corvet Gallery at five-thirty pm in advance of the six o'clock start, keen attendees were waiting at the door. These were serious collectors who were determined to get the pick of the paintings on display. Friends of Miss Stein, they were confident that she wouldn't refuse them a preview, knowing their wallets, combined with their style, held sway.

Jack, Andrés and Sofia hardly knew what to do with themselves, so exciting and extraordinary did it all seem. Looking at the framed works, Jack could barely believe his eyes, amazed at how impressive their paintings looked hanging on the walls, each with a gold-edged cardboard tab on the side describing the work and its asking price.

To be here, seeing it all come together – the exhibition attended by Miss Stein's connections to wealthy Parisians and Americans – was astonishing. Jack mused at his parents' likely reaction. What would they think if they could see him now?

As the evening wore on, it seemed that every American in Paris walked through the doors at some time to view the works on offer and, of course, they all wanted to meet the artists. Also, there were a smattering of British, Italian and even Russian viewers. The majority of attendees had no intention of buying paintings, instead viewing the evening as a social event, there to be seen on their way to dinner or to the theatre. Additionally, many local artists dropped in to critique the works of the lucky young foreigners, harbouring jealousy and goodwill in a finely tuned balance. Roger had colluded with Miss Stein to ensure that the right art critics received invitations, those who were inspired by foreign artists and modern styles, and influential enough that their opinion pieces would be guaranteed publication in the newspapers.

The response to the paintings was enormously pleasing. Andrés' bold colours and Spanish influence were enthusiastically admired. Likewise, Jack's works were viewed with excited comments. His subject matter and portraiture skills were undeniably outstanding and interest was further enhanced by the intrigue of his Australian heritage.

Jack watched the crowd move in to study his brushwork and the fine detail of his paintings and then step back to take in overall impressions. Just as he had observed serious patrons do when they were analysing great art in galleries, he thought, astonished to think that it was his paintings they were viewing.

A few esteemed guests made appearances, including a scruffy, somewhat familiar young man introduced to Jack and Andrés as Ernie, later revealed as the young but hugely successful American author, Ernest Hemingway, accompanied by his wife, a stylish woman called Pauline. When Miss Stein introduced Jack to Ernest, she pointed out that he was a fellow Montparnasse resident. Although Jack did not acknowledge it, he had in fact seen the celebrated writer numerous times, sitting oblivious to his surroundings in the back corner of Café La Rotonde, furiously scraping his nib across the pages of the writing book on the table. Jack had observed Hemingway's manner of cursing quietly to himself whenever his pencil required sharpening, interrupting the flow of his writing, or silently staring into the distance, perhaps clutching for elusive words to immortalise on the sheets of his notebook. Ernest grudgingly expressed admiration for the paintings and Jack observed what appeared to be a negotiation with Miss Stein for his river scene, *Fishermen Working Their Nets on the Seine*.

A lively foursome spilled through the doorway and seemed to consume all the room's oxygen in an instant, so dominant was their presence. Loudly commenting on the 'marvellous paintings,' they sashayed amid a cloud of swirling smoke, emitted from the cigarettes inserted into fashionable long tortoiseshell holders which they cast about with exaggerated movements, carelessly dropping ash onto the polished floor. They accepted flutes of champagne from the passing waiter, who carefully balanced his newly stocked tray of refreshments, a difficult task within the crowded room. Roger quietly whispered to Jack that it was the Fitzgeralds - Scott and Zelda - with their friends, as though that should mean something to him. As Jack watched, Zelda demanded that Scott replace the champagne flute she had emptied within minutes while she darted from painting to painting, expressing loud gushing opinions on each. Scott, the quietest member of the group, seemed subdued, and Jack noticed him a little while later shaking his head when offered a second glass of champagne. Zelda chided him, 'Scott, what is wrong with you tonight? You're being so boring.'

Sofia, standing beside Jack, tutted, and he looked at her disapproving face. 'I don't like her,' she muttered to him. 'I hope she doesn't buy any of our paintings.'

Of course Zelda did, though, her eyes landing on Andrés' Cubist-styled cityscape that had drawn a continuous stream of appreciative comments throughout the evening.

'Oh, Scott, isn't it marvellous? We must have that for our living room!' she exclaimed in a tone that produced a satisfied look from Miss Stein. Jack suspected that Zelda was denied very little and could not help but feel sorry for Scott, who seemed to be exhausted by his very beautiful, very demanding wife. Having made their purchase, Zelda launched into a series of kisses that barely met their mark, farewelling half of the room as the foursome departed to go dancing at the Moulin Rouge, only half a block away.

They passed close by Jack and Sofia, and Scott paused. 'You painted this, right?' he asked, waving towards the painting they'd just purchased, now bearing a large red 'sold' sticker on the description tag.

'No, I am Jack. That was painted by my friend, Andrés.' Jack pointed across the room, where Andrés was speaking to a young woman about a painting that she was in the process of buying.

'He's very good. You both are. Enjoy your success!'

'Scott, you are holding us up.' His wife's voice was strident, and Scott grinned ruefully. 'I will have to catch up with your paintings another time, Jack. Pleased to meet you. And you, too, beautiful lady. I'm thinking that your Jack is a very lucky man.'

Sofia blushed.

'Wasn't he nice?' she said, watching Scott's departing back. 'A pity he is not so lucky with that awful wife!'

'Should I be worried?' Jack asked, looking at her with a quizzical smile.

'Very!' was her reply.

Just after nine, a sudden burst of excited murmuring rippled through the gallery, apparently generated by the arrival of an older man with a broad forehead and intense, piercing eyes. Ignoring the surrounding crowds, he immediately crossed to the walls where the paintings were displayed. Miss Stein appeared at his side, remaining silent as he studied the works.

'Good, good.' He nodded as he moved along, analysing each one, slowing on some, moving more quickly past others, suggesting he was able to assimilate the value of a painting with a glance. 'And where are the young artistes?' he asked, finally turning to Miss Stein.

Miss Stein called Andrés over.

'I believe you Spaniards may know each other,' she said, and the man smiled.

'I remember a little boy sitting with a big drawing pad at the back of his father's studio, *si*?'

Andrés smiled back. 'Yes. And I remember you also, Señor Pablo. My father followed your career closely, often speaking of your great talent. He was so pleased for your success in Paris.'

Picasso brushed the praise aside with a wave of his hand; however, the twinkle in his eye indicated pleasure. 'Perhaps I am not the only one doing well, Andrés. Your colours are phenomenal and - Impressionism - you make it your own!' Nudging Andrés' arm with his elbow, he chuckled. 'We Spaniards will show the world a thing or two about painting, *si*? But we will talk later. Now, *mi amigo*, please introduce me to this most talented young Australian *artiste* friend of yours.'

Andrés turned to Jack, who had been watching with interest as the enormously popular painter conversed with his friend. While Jack was not altogether sure that he liked Picasso's work, here was an artist who now had paintings exhibited in galleries in London, Paris and, no doubt, New York and, by all accounts, fetching astronomical sums. Andrés introduced them, still beaming with pleasure at being identified as Picasso's friend.

'Your work is very good, Jack. Very good. The Americans will love it. Nice. Very nice. You have a real eye for human experience. We will talk more, but not now. Please, you must both come to my studio. Tomorrow?'

Well, of course they could and would. Arrangements were made to visit Picasso at two pm the next day at the address he scribbled on the back of an exhibition catalogue and handed to Andrés.

Miss Stein certainly knew her business. As she had predicted, by the end of the evening, a red sticker was attached to every work that remained, indicating its sale. Triumphantly looking at Jack, she exclaimed, 'It is all a matter of numbers. If you ask enough people and create enough interest, they will come. Let the champagne flow and they will buy. They always do. And they get their money's worth because your paintings will be investments to them. Trust me, they will have increased in value by the time they arrive on the doorstep tomorrow.'

CHAPTER 26

*T*he next afternoon, Jack, Sofia and Andrés navigated their way across the Seine, catching the bus to Rue La Boétie in the eighth *arrondissement*. Sooner than expected, they found themselves standing on the doorstep of Number 23, looking at each other in anticipation. In the cold light of day, the thought of spending the afternoon with the great artist ignited a flicker of nervous excitement that was contagious. All three held their breath as Andrés pressed firmly on the brass doorbell and released a loud chime on the interior. They could hear the rhythm of light footsteps approaching from within. A lady opened the door, tall and graceful in her demeanour, her dark hair pulled into a low bun at the base of her neck, framing a perfect oval face and accentuating beautiful classic features which, however, were devoid of even a hint of welcome. Without smiling, she opened the doorway wide, ushered them in with a wave of her hand, directing them to follow her down the narrow passage.

'Pablo is waiting for you in his studio,' she said, her voice as absent of expression as her stony face, making Jack wonder if she was annoyed by them imposing on her husband's time. She led them to a room filled with tables, benches, easels and boxes. At first, they did not notice Pablo standing by a far window, gazing intently at a pile of clay that he was in the process of shaping into a female figure with impossibly voluminous breasts, matched by equally distended buttocks.

'*Bienvenido*. Welcome,' he said, with overly loud cheerfulness, and Jack noticed he had Monsieur Simon's habit of repeating every word twice as if to enhance its meaning. 'Come in.'

With curiosity, Jack examined the room. It was pleasant, despite being cluttered with both furniture and artworks, evidently a combination of study and studio. The walls were crowded with paintings as well as dozens of line drawings, many appearing incomplete. Jack could not be certain of what he was looking at as he gazed at images of disjointed figures, animal and human, while Andrés and Picasso spoke. Picasso congratulated Andrés on his success at winning the Prado Art Prize and their conversation quickly moved to Málaga, where Picasso himself had been born and spent the first fourteen years of his life before moving to Barcelona. Expressing his fond memories of the town where his artistic passion began, he enquired after Andrés' father and was saddened to hear of his death three years earlier.

While Andrés and Picasso reminisced, Jack quietly moved around the room, fascinated by the variety of objects on display. Picasso's skills were not limited to painting, judging by the three-dimensional sketches and sculptures, both complete and in states of production. With surprise, he found himself gazing at a framed painting of Gertrude Stein bearing Picasso's signature. On closer examination, he realised the collection included many works of other artists, too, some of whose names were familiar to Jack – a range of tropical scenes depicting exotic animals was signed by Henri Rousseau and a series of monochromatic prints by Degas. A small Impressionist landscape with colours of brilliant intensity bore the signature of Gauguin.

Picasso came alongside Jack, breaking his concentration, and said with a smile, 'My friendship wall. Over the years I have exchanged paintings with many of my dear friends. It is good to be able to remember those times we shared together.' Jack made a mental note to ensure that he and Andrés exchanged paintings before he departed for Australia.

'Now, Jack,' Picasso said, 'tell me about yourself. When did you begin painting?'

He listened carefully as Jack described his lifelong habit of drawing, his love for the sweet smell and bold colours of his prep school paint pots – red, yellow, blue and green – which led to his instinct for colour mixing, adding watercolour to ink drawings and, more recently, making a shift to oil painting. He explained how he was drawing on the *Ormonde* when he met Margaret. Picasso laughed when Jack told him about how she had, in turn, introduced him to the Bloomsbury set in London and how it was Margaret's persistence that led to him meeting Roger Fry, coming to Paris and ultimately, to Miss Stein's exhibition.

'Ah yes, bossy women. Found the world over. They either make or break us artists!'

'So. You have had a happy life, Jack?' he asked. 'I can see that in your paintings. I see me in you. I too drew from a very young age. And miraculously, was very good. Who knows why? Jack, your paintings are good. Very good. People will love them, and you will make much money. Yes, be a very rich man! Perhaps even a rich and happy man!' Picasso chuckled. 'But we artists are not about money. Not real artists. A painter may pursue money, but not an artist. We must tell a story, and not all stories are nice. Do you see? Life is not always nice. Art is more than beauty. It is also truth. Not all truth is nice. Your brush, your lines, your colour must expose the truth. Not from here,' he said with a soft tap on Jack's head. 'But from here.' And his hand moved to Jack's chest.

At Jack's puzzled look, Picasso smiled.

'Come, let me show you.' He led Jack over to a heavy wooden shelf crammed with dozens of drawing books of all shapes and sizes, many appearing quite old. Selecting one, Picasso turned through the yellowed pages, and Jack caught glimpses of sketches not unlike those he had recently completed around Montparnasse. Suddenly Picasso opened to a page revealing a sketch of a painting that was familiar to Jack. He recalled the visit to the *Musée du Luxembourg* during his first week at the Academy. The image of the old man and his wife standing in the street had haunted him, an enduring reminder of the contrast between the rich and poor, still evident as he walked the streets of Montparnasse, especially in the very early or very late hours of the day.

'Look at them, Jack. Tell me, what do you see?'

Jack replied that he could see the fall of the man's coat, hanging loosely over drooping shoulders, the long nose, oily thinning hair limply draped across the man's balding forehead. The woman standing beside him, her dress ragged. Thin legs and bare feet told a story of bleakness and poverty.

'Look closer,' instructed Picasso. Jack looked, but did not comprehend what he was being asked to see.

Picasso laughed softly. 'You are too fat... too... well fed. To see these things, sometimes you must be skinny. Hungry.' He beckoned Jack over to the far corner of the room, where a series of four paintings hung together in matching thin rosewood frames. 'These are old now, but the truth is timeless,' said Picasso. 'They call them my blue period.'

Jack could see why, for the paintings were in blue and grey tones.

Picasso laughed again. 'I was very skinny. No fat then.' He tapped his expanded waistline. Suddenly serious, he said, 'I painted these not long after the death of my dear friend, Carlos. He was a wonderful artist. Took his life... just like that! It was terrible. Between that and the death of my beautiful little sister, Conchita, life seemed too sad. I did not think I would ever get over it...' Picasso gazed into the distance, lost in the past. He returned from his memories with a jolt. 'So, Jack, I began to see things that I had not noticed before.' He pointed at the painting before him.

'Look into his eyes, Jack. Look at his shoulders. What do they speak of? Helplessness. Hopelessness. Suffering. Grief. That is his truth. Look at her eyes. Sadness. Loss. Pain. *Désespérés*. Poor people who have lost the light of their life. Their little girl gone, diphtheria, only just buried when I painted this. That is their truth. Hunger, yes. But the loss, the greater pain. Life is not always nice. You must tell these stories with every stroke of your brush, *tu comprends*?' Picasso continued, and Jack listened intently, unable to deny that he had known very little of hunger, grief or loss.

'One day, you will starve a little. One day, you will feel pain. You will learn to tell the story. Then you will say, "Picasso was right. Now I can see it. Now I can draw it. Now I will paint truth. Now I am a great artist. Hey, hey… now I am great like Picasso!"'

Sofia moved restlessly at his side. Jack had not noticed her standing quietly beside him until he sensed her tremble at Picasso's words.

Andrés, who had taken the opportunity to look around the room while Picasso spoke with Jack, returned and Picasso changed the subject. He spoke of alternative ways of expressing reality and showed them some of his experimental works. Picasso's eyes glowed, his hands moving rapidly as he explained his theory of Cubism – the expression of multiple perspectives–and more recently, Surrealism–expressions not just of the rational, but also of the irrational and subconscious mind, ideas which he believed held the power to revolutionise art. Listening, Jack was reminded of Monsieur Simon's passion when he spoke of the various art movements and the way the modern world was using paint to express reality, and it was hard not to be enthralled by Picasso's vision.

The animated explanation suddenly drew to a pause as a young girl entered the room. Pretty, with white blond hair pulled into a high pony-tail, and displaying uncommonly perfect teeth, she smiled broadly at the group as she settled a tray bearing a pot of tea, mugs and a plate of golden-brown gingerbread onto an already cluttered bench. Greeting her with a smacking kiss, Picasso introduced her as Marie-Thérèse. His new model, whom he'd recently discovered standing on the steps of Galeries Lafayette. Jack suspected he now understand the cause of Olga Picasso's dour expression.

As they listened to Picasso expound on his views of art and tech-niques, the room, brightly lit with afternoon sunshine when they'd arrived, became dim as the sun began its fall onto the horizon. Eventu-ally, Andrés, Jack and Sofia prepared to leave. Picasso thanked them for coming to visit him as though they had done him a favour. 'It is wonderful to see such talent. I look forward to celebrating your progress,' he said, and promised to visit their gallery in Málaga next time he ventured to the south of Spain.

~

They left feeling euphoric. How marvellous to spend time with the great artist. And he had been so generous with his advice and treated them as old friends! Jack determined that he would work on Picasso's recommendations to further develop his paintings, going beyond accurate portrayals of the outward expressions of his subjects to imagine their sources of joy, hardship or grief and portray the mysterious depths of human emotion.

Although very tired after the excitement of the weekend, Jack and Andrés' energy was quickly renewed when they received a welcome worthy of celebrities at the academy on Monday morning, many students and masters searching them out to offer congratulations. With obvious delight, Monsieur Simon shared a newspaper article favourably reporting the exhibition, including a small photograph of Miss Stein with Jack and Andrés, as well as a quote from Picasso: 'Wonderful artists. Unique and extraordinarily talented. Young men whose futures should be followed with interest.' Of particular pleasure to the master, the article noted that he and Andrés were currently attending *Academié Julian*, honing their skills under the tutelage of the talented Monsieur Simon.

However, there was to be no time of rest. In the weeks following Miss Stein's exhibition, a wave of nervous energy entered the ancient rooms of the academy as preparations for *Académie Julian's* student exhibition entered full swing. It was a prestigious event for the art school, where the masters were as much in competition as the students, seeking the vicarious glory reflected on the tutors of award-winning artists. With the date set for Friday 15th June, less than two weeks away, Jack and Andrés needed to work long hours to create entries worthy of their newfound celebrity, especially with the best of their works sold at Miss Stein's exhibition. Jack planned to present a series of portrait drawings, as well as two oils.

When he asked Sofia if she would model for him, of course she agreed, and they had a wonderful day wandering along the Seine and around the beautiful Jardin du Luxembourg.

It was mid-morning by the time Jack and Sofia set off, and particularly lovely day. Soft white clouds skipped along the sky, propelled by a faint breeze. There had been a rain shower in the early hours of the morning which had left glistening puddles and the sunlight, filtering through the trees, cast thousands of minuscule diamond-like reflections off moist leaves and petals. The sweet organic smell of damp soil wafted from the manicured lawns. Already, a number of people were about, walking their dogs in the fresh morning air.

Sofia was in a particularly playful mood and they laughed constantly. Everything seemed amusing to them, especially the eccentric old lady walking in the park, her snow-white hair piled high upon her head in a perfect match to no less than five enormous poodles prancing beside her, each with white curls ornately trimmed and matching bejewelled collars and silver chain leads. Sofia entertained Jack by striking silly poses as they walked through the gardens in search of settings for his drawings. Jack found his sketches developed with particular ease, doing what he loved best and with the person he loved most. An astute model, Sofia's knowledge of design gave her an intuitive understanding of how to present herself, her pose further enhanced by the happiness she radiated. It was as though she could see the drawing before Jack had even put charcoal to paper, knowing the emotion she generated would infuse itself into his lines.

Jack kept thinking of Picasso's words, conscious of making every line tell a story, and as his hand moved across the page, he could feel his love for Sofia flow through the charcoal into the smooth lines of her forehead sweeping down to soft cheeks. As he outlined the curves of her full lips, remembering the sweetness of their kisses, a stirring of longing passed through his hand, into the charcoal and onto the page.

It was almost two-thirty when Jack and Sofia finally sat under the brightly striped awning of Angelina Rivoli. They had just ordered croissants and hot chocolate when Jack spied a jewellery shop across the road. Explaining to Sofia that he would only be gone a minute, he crossed the street and entered the store. Pleased that he'd set aside twenty francs for exactly this opportunity when he'd deposited the cheque Miss Stein handed to him only days earlier, Jack wasted no time explaining what he wanted. The shop assistant set out a range of bangles followed by dainty sets of earrings and commenced detailed explanations about carats, light and colours. As soon as Jack saw the pair of jade drops lined with fine diamonds set in nine-carat gold, he knew they were just what he was looking for.

When Jack returned to the table, he passed the tiny package, exquisitely wrapped in silver paper with red ribbon forming a perfect bow, across the table to Sofia.

She gasped with surprise. 'Jack, it looks too perfect. The wrapping is a work of art! I feel guilty tearing it off.' She plucked at the bow carefully and Jack held his breath, waiting for her to extract the small box from within. Finally, opening it, Sofia's eyes lit up with delight as she freed the earrings and held them up. He knew he had made a good choice. Standing, Sofia threw her arms around him and kissed him in appreciation, ignoring the amused smiles of onlookers. Insisting that Jack immediately help her fix them in position, Sofia leaned across him to view her reflection in the café window, before kissing him, again.

They finished the day by returning to Le Grand Colbert for dinner. As on their previous visit, the maître d'hôtel seated them at a window table where they could look onto the Champs-Élysées. Jack mused at the difference between today and that evening, over six weeks earlier. That wondrous evening when he had discovered that Sofia shared the same feelings for him as he did for her. It had been a thrilling time, when just being alone with her caused his heartbeat to race and every minute together was enough in itself.

At that time Jack had ignored the looming complications of the future as he'd basked in the excitement of the present. Learning that Sofia returned the love he felt for her, Jack had felt like the luckiest man in the world – and by default, the happiest. He remembered how everything felt. Light, joyful, funny, beautiful. To look at each other had brought smiles of wonderment. To be alone together was to reach out and touch one another. They had lived in the minute, enjoying every one of them. Dizzy moments borne of simple pleasures: touching hands, sweet kisses and their evenings concluding with passionate embraces. Jack had deferred thoughts of his inevitable separation from Sofia, considering such worries too distant and complicated to consider.

Now, the rapidly approaching date of his departure hung over them like a cloud. In less than a fortnight, he was leaving Paris, returning on the ferry to Dover and catching the train to London. He would have two days with his aunt and uncle and then be back on the *Ormonde* for six long weeks, each day transporting him further away from Sofia, to Melbourne and a future that held no meaning to him. After the richness of his time in Paris, the camaraderie of Andrés and the sweetness of Sofia in his life, the future appeared as a grey void.

Sofia's sober quietness as she sat opposite him reflected the downcast mood that had descended upon him. The atmosphere was strangely inconsistent with the wonderful day they had just shared.

As Jack looked across the table, a sombreness settled over him. This time, her hands were not fidgeting, waiting to be stilled by his. Rather, she reached out and took his hands as soon as they sat down. Saying nothing, she looked into his eyes. Jack returned her look and knew exactly what she was thinking, her thoughts mirroring his own.

He started speaking, grasping at solutions that would see them through the pending months of separation. They would write to each other every week, he suggested. Every day, even. He would work through to Christmas at Goldsbrough Mort & Co and then make his way back to Málaga. They discussed what that could be like, the small house and gallery and the spare room under the stairs that Sofia would prepare for him. Regardless of their plans, they could not erase the palpable emptiness that infused their words. The arrangements they spoke of seemed remote and impractical, as if they were plans for someone else's life. How could they possibly believe that living on the opposite sides of the world would not insidiously erode the memory of

Paris and their love for each other? Surely they were deluding themselves.

Jack did not even consider asking Sofia to leave Spain and her brother. Not having siblings, he could not fully understand the bond, but he knew how much Andrés and Sofia meant to each other.

Somehow, they worked their way through the courses. This time they chose *ratatouille* as an appetizer, followed by beef en daube. The meals arrived quickly and smelled delicious. Today, however, the food seemed tasteless and chewing an effort.

Leaving the restaurant just after ten pm, holding hands, they wandered aimlessly along the Champs-Élysées. Laughter and music drifted through the night as they walked past the Café des Ambassedeurs, on whose floor they'd joyfully frolicked only a few weeks ago. Tonight, the pulsing beat and laughter drifting through the doors seemed to mock them – a confronting reminder of a happier time – and each pretended not to notice.

As silence descended upon them, Jack felt weighed down by sadness. It was as though their separation had already begun as they walked along the streets, absorbed in their thoughts.

Arriving on a quiet corner, Sofia gently tugged on Jack's arm, drawing his attention back to her. 'Jack,' she said quietly. 'Let's go in here.'

He looked at where she was pointing and saw a small hotel with the sign, 'Rooms Available' flashing. As he stood still, not altogether sure of what she was saying, she persisted.

'Come on, Jack. I want to be with you. Together with you.'

In her eyes, he saw resolution. Still, Jack hesitated, torn between the right and honourable way to treat his dear friend's sister and his own desire. His heart raced in anticipation at the enormity of what Sofia was proposing with such determination. She nudged him forward and, in a daze, he held the door open for her to enter, then followed her into a shabby foyer where a small window revealed a reception desk to the left.

CHAPTER 27

'*Bonjour, Monsieur, bonsoir. Puis-je t'aider?*'

'Er... *Bonsoir... Une* room please?' Jack tried to sound confident as he spoke to the small man at the counter, whose badge indicated that his name was Paul and that he was the *réceptionniste*. While Paul's blank-faced initial response to their greeting suggested that he understood little English, there was no confusion about their request. Without so much as a blink, he passed a key with a tag, indicating the second room on level three, across the desk. Then, stepping out through a narrow side door, he beckoned Jack and Sofia to follow him. In single file, they ascended three stone flights of a tiny, narrow stairway, its ceiling so low it threatened to crown Jack on each landing. Their hands clung to the ornately carved handrail. Jack suspected from its smoothly worn glow and the dished-out edge of each step that people had been climbing these stairs for decades, possibly hundreds of years and, as with himself and Sofia, probably not all guests bore the sanction of a wedding band.

Paul led them to the end of the hall, revealing a small, ancient bathroom, copper pipes exposed. He waved his hands to indicate that all four rooms on the third level shared it. Pausing outside a dark oak-panelled door with a shiny brass number two, Paul took the key from

Jack's hand – a relief, as he had felt tremors of nervousness overcome him as they'd ascended the stairs, quickening his breath and weakening his legs. He'd wondered if he would manage the key without fumbling or, worse still, dropping it on the carpet, whose intricate weave told of grand old days when the building was in the hands of wealthier owners than the present.

Opening the door, Paul pointed out the gas lamp on the desk, the small water jug on the dresser, the neatly folded clean towels beside it. Jack tried to avoid looking at the double bed that dominated the room, adorned with a ruffled silk cover and matching pillows - an embarrassing symbol of their illicit presence. Thankfully, Paul soon left, and it was back to himself and Sofia. Not altogether sure what his next move should be, Jack sat down on a small stuffed couch. Sofia, apparently far more composed than he, walked across the room to stand before him.

'Jack,' she said. 'You know I love you.'

Silently, he nodded.

Taking his face in her hands and leaning forward, she kissed him deeply. Jack responded, standing up and wrapping his arms around her to pull her tightly to him. His mouth on hers seemed to find the language required for this moment. Frequently, Jack and Sofia had kissed. Firstly, there had been sweet little pecks, usually in *hola* or *adiós*, Sofia reaching up on tiptoes to plant them on Jack's lips. More recently, their kisses had become warm and lingering, especially as the evenings had drawn to a close. Tonight, however, when they kissed it was like they were communicating urgent feelings that could not be reduced to words. Love. Tenderness. Sorrow. Hope. Farewell. Surrender. All swirled between them as they kissed searchingly, long and deep, and it was as though now that it had started, they were unable to break the contact of their lips. Shuffling towards the bed, Jack leaned forward, using his arm to support Sofia as she lay on her back, his lips remaining firmly fixed to hers.

In his arms, Sofia's narrow shoulders and slender arms felt fragile to him and, by contrast, Jack felt strong and protective. The sense of her vulnerability ignited an exquisite tenderness that was new to him and, leaning up, he looked into her eyes questioningly.

Sofia smiled back at him. 'It is good, Jack. *Si*, it is good,' she said, pulling him down to her. Lying on their sides, they looked at each other in wonderment. Half an hour ago they had been wandering the noisy streets of Paris, jostled by the crowds of fellow pedestrians, and now here they were, cocooned in total privacy in this small room high above the street.

Jack allowed his hands to move across Sofia's neck lingeringly and he marvelled at the soft smoothness of her skin. He ran his fingers lightly, gently, from below her right earlobe along the line of her jaw and dipped down to caress the front of her throat. To his surprise, she groaned. He repeated the motion, slowly moving his fingers now across her throat and down into the crevice at the top of her blouse, where he could feel the rise of her breasts. Jack had no idea what was expected of him and allowed Sofia's reactions to guide him. Their closeness and her relaxed smile assured him all was well and, with trembling fingers, he tugged at the blouse's top buttons, loosening the first but finding the second unwilling to budge.

'Let me, Jack,' Sofia whispered and, standing up, undid the buttons quickly. She leaned close to him, exposing the swell of her breasts encased in the fine lace of her white bra, which shimmered in the light of the street that filtered through their window. Swinging his legs over the side of the bed, Jack sat up. He pulled Sofia close and let his mouth roam, softly searching across her earlobes, throat, and then down into her cleavage. Moving from one breast to the other, first tenderly, then with increasing pressure, he sucked on the velvety soft swell, then burrowed deeply into the lace to expose the hardness of her nipples. He loved their firmness as they responded to the touch of his mouth.

After freeing her blouse until it dropped to the floor, Jack reached around to the clasp of her bra. To make this easier, she turned her back to him, allowing Jack to stroke the curves of her shoulder blades, and then, with trembling fingers, to unclip the tiny hooks that stood between them. Jack could barely believe that he was alone with this beautiful woman, whose lovely curved back was so silky to his touch.

Reaching from behind, he cupped her now freed breasts in his hands, cradling their softness, squeezing them gently and firmly, tugging at the small hard buds at their tips.

Sighing, Sofia turned and faced Jack, and he was overwhelmed by the power of his arousal. Encouraged by her small gasps of pleasure, he pulled her close, his mouth now hungrily sucking at her bare breasts before lowering across her abdomen, where he licked the hollow of her belly button, causing her to giggle softly and push him away.

Pulling at Jack's shirt, Sofia released it from his trousers and tugged it over his head. She drew her hands across his shoulders and down his arms, squeezing the contours of his muscles.

Jack loosened the waistband of the skirt Sofia was wearing and slid both it and her silk undergarments down her slender thighs and then lower, allowing her to step out of them in a single motion. With a quick move, he released the buttons of his trousers and, shaking them off, rendered them both naked. Firmly embracing her in his arms, lips against hers, Jack pulled her onto the bed once again. His lips travelled across her shoulders, breasts and belly. His hands searched between her legs, stroking her curly softness. Sofia sighed deeply, parting her thighs, allowing Jack to burrow further, ultimately finding the place, warm and moist, deep between her legs. He marvelled as she again groaned, her hands gripping his back.

Jack's body seemed to have developed a mind of its own. Suddenly he rolled Sofia flat on the bed before him and raised himself above her, looking into her eyes questioningly. With a small smile, she nodded, and Jack lowered his body against hers, finding her thighs opening still further, the wetness between them a beacon for his entry. Jack moved cautiously at first, for fear that he would hurt her. Matching him, Sofia moved her hips towards him, and they joined in slow, rhythmic thrusts, until Jack felt that he would explode. And that he did, shuddering with the overpowering release, strengthened by the feeling of Sofia trembling breathlessly against him, the muscles in her mysterious depths pulsating their thrilling response.

Afterwards, they lay together, holding each other close. A single beam of filtered light illuminated Sofia's face and Jack was shocked to see tears glistening on her cheek. Wiping them away, she smiled. 'It's okay, Jack. That was beautiful. I am... okay. Just... sad. Just sad,' she said quietly.

Jack pulled her close so her head lay against his shoulder, his chin resting on her forehead. He, too, felt the sadness, and his arms gripped her tightly, as if never to let her go.

'We will be all right, Sofia,' he said huskily, trying to check his emotions. 'I'll be back as soon as I can. I promise.'

Sofia squeezed him in reply. Her lack of words suggested that she was not convinced.

'Sofia,' Jack said with sudden force. 'We can't let these last days together be miserable. I love you. We must look forward to the future. Our future. I will come to Málaga and you will show me the places of your childhood. Andrés and I will paint and you will keep us organised. It will be wonderful,' he insisted.

'You're right, Jack. Now is not a time for sadness. We have found each other and we will be together again soon. We have much to be happy for. I'm sorry, Jack. We'll make these last days full of memories.' She got up, then rolled him onto his back and swung her leg over so that she was sitting above him. Running her hands down the side of his face, gently, she chuckled and said with a low murmur, 'Perhaps we can make another memory right now.'

It was a beautiful night spent together, alternating between being lost in each other's lips, arms and bodies, lightly sleeping and murmuring conversations as they held each other close while darkness slowly gave way to the dawn.

Rising early, they headed down the stairs, dropped the room key into a blue box outside the office door and stepped out onto the street hand in hand. Jack felt like he could burst with happiness. His heart was full of love and pride for the beautiful girl whom he knew returned his love, without reserve. He felt like a new person, a man, with a woman to love and care for, and now with a clearly defined purpose to his life. He marvelled as he thought of the past night, his body tingling with memories of Sofia in his arms.

Making their way across town, they chatted about the days ahead, preparing for the student exhibition the following Friday. Flipping through his sketchbook, Jack showed her the sketches he'd made the previous day. He planned to reproduce these into a small series of drawings – which he would simply call '*Mon amour.*' Already he had commenced work on the two oil paintings for the exhibition. At the last minute, Jack decided to create a third oil, this one of Sofia, portrayed as she had sat before him across the bed this morning, legs crossed in the early light, the sheet drawn up over her breasts, her bare shoulders glowing, the dawn on her face. He did not have a sketch to work from, but every line of her body was imprinted in his mind. He would combine the traditional skills in which he excelled with the modern colour theories and brushwork he had acquired from Monsieur. This painting would be called *Morning Beauty*. Just thinking about it made Jack's fingers itch for his brushes, and Picasso's words rang in his ears. '*Painting must be more than beauty. Painting must be about truth – painted from the heart!*' Jack knew he was about to create his best work ever. His brushwork would not be directed by his eye, but rather guided by his heart, and every single stroke in this portrait would be infused with perfect love.

~

The final week leading up to the academy's exhibition flew by quickly. Jack and Andrés, along with the other students, spent long days preparing their entries. This event was a significant forerunner to Paris' famous *Salon d'Automne*, held in October each year and, although the Academy was only a small art school, its focus on modern art always generated strong media interest. Furthermore, the prize winners gained prestige not only for themselves but also for their masters, and indeed, the repute of the academy itself. It always drew strong crowds. Students' families and friends would arrive, some travelling from as far away as London, Spain or even Italy. Art aficionados from all over Paris would attend, including both discerning and meddlesome critics, whose articles would invariably draw comparisons between the Montparnasse exhibitions and those in Montmartre. Patrons, people like

Miss Stein who bore a deep interest in the arts and liked to support new talent, would be present, as would investors and numerous gallery owners. Emergent artists were exciting finds, and everybody hoped they might purchase intriguing works at bargain prices.

Over the weekend, hundreds of people would traipse through the rooms of the Academy, viewing the students' art. Historically, the exhibition had proved to be a perfect opportunity for not only showcasing student works but also to promote the autumn season of the academy's lessons. To this end, tours around the studios would be offered, and the teachers would be on hand to speak with the public.

Margaret had no intention of missing this special night, so for the third time in six weeks, she undertook the journey from London to Paris, meeting up with Jack, Sofia and Andrés in the afternoon of Friday the fifteenth of June.

CHAPTER 28

*H*igh spirits abounded as, dressed in their best clothes, Jack, Sofia and Andrés approached Le Dôme, where they had arranged to meet Margaret for dinner before the exhibition. Already, the place was jammed–evidently many fellow artists had the same plan.

'Jack, you look wonderful!' Margaret exclaimed, looking at him thoughtfully. After hugging him, she turned to Sofia and Andrés, embracing each of them. She returned her gaze to Sofia and Jack, as if sensing a change in their demeanour, and asked, 'So, how are you two? What have you been up to?'

Andrés replied, 'Occasionally Jack paints and even less occasionally, Sofia cooks – when I can tear them away from each other. I'm nearly fading away!' His words were interrupted by a bout of coughing, reinforcing the tragic picture he'd created, and his attempt to look miserable prompted a shove from Jack and a punch from Sofia in unison, at which they all laughed.

The truth was that Andrés had not seen much of Jack outside their morning lessons, nor of Sofia, as they had been spending almost every minute of their afternoons and evenings together walking the streets of

Paris and sitting in darkened cafés. They alternated between excitedly discussing Jack's return trip to Málaga, planned for early January the following year, and sadly contemplating a separation of six months, twelve thousand miles and numerous oceans between them.

'We have much to talk about,' Jack protested. 'I'm leaving Monday! I won't see Sofia for ages!'

'So, Jack, you are going home in three days… What about your painting? What about…?'

At Jack's reply that he would return to Spain early next year, Margaret shrugged in barely concealed annoyance and, turning away from him, abruptly changed the subject. 'Tell me how about your paintings, Andrés?'

Andrés explained how he had been working nonstop over the past fortnight, arriving early at the atelier and, following a brief lunch with Jack and Sofia, returning in the afternoons. He had submitted three oil paintings, two of which were orders commissioned following Miss Stein's exhibition.

Margaret was amazed to hear about their invitation to visit Picasso's home, and Andrés explained how he'd returned to his studio a second time, seeking advice and support from the older man who'd proved a willing mentor.

Jack was less effusive with Margaret about his own artwork, finding it difficult to admit he had five studies of Sofia. Margaret would think he was mad. However, Monsieur had not commented when Jack had revealed his portfolio of entries, only smiled and nodded. The truth was that Jack's finest skill lay in the portraiture of human subjects, and Monsieur did not seem to see a series based on the beautiful young Spanish woman as a problem.

At six-forty-five, they made their way across town, Margaret linking her arm through Andrés' and leading the way, Jack and Sofia following.

The academy was visible from a distance, strings of electric lights providing a beautiful glow to the entryway. A crowd hovered expectantly, some people in evening dress, others in street clothes. An atmosphere of excitement was in the air as loyal patrons of the academy, including past students and teachers, bustled about, selling programs and offering their services for tours through the rooms. After purchasing a program each, a souvenir of this special event, Jack, Sofia, Margaret and Andrés entered the foyer, now decorated with urns overflowing with geraniums. A series of extraordinary sculptures placed strategically throughout the entrance area and display boards provided information for visitors. They greeted Jacques-Noël. Tonight, the academy's maintenance man was almost unrecognisable, having sacrificed his uniform overalls for a dashing three-piece suit, chequered bow tie and broad smile as he adopted the role of chief usher, directing visitors and answering any questions they had regarding the atelier's classes.

As they entered the main exhibition room, they could not believe its transformation. Hundreds of student artworks were on display in alcoves created from the partitions Jack and Andrés had used only weeks ago. The variety of styles and subjects was astonishing, including cityscapes, scenes from the Seine, nudes, landscapes, still-lifes and abstracts. Watercolours, oils and drawings, traditional and modern works all vied for attention on the walls. Throughout the centre of the room, even more partitions had been used to extend surfaces for artworks to be displayed. A prominent area on the far wall had a smaller number of works carefully showcased. These were the exhibitions major prizes and, led by Sofia, the group walked the length of the room towards them.

She was the first to break the silence as they neared the display with an enthusiastic squeal. 'Andrés! You have won the Academy's Gold Medal! Wonderful! Well done!' She jumped up and down and, throwing her arms around Andrés' neck, she kissed him enthusiastically. Jack and Margaret were equally excited, hugging him and slapping him on the back. Andrés grinned, thrilled to see his painting *Aprés-midi sur la Seine–Afternoon on the Seine*–positioned front and centre of the display, with a large blue ribbon attached to it and the embossed gold-edged ticket identifying it the Gold Medal winner.

Well-wishers gathered around Andrés, keen to congratulate the handsome young Spaniard in the white dress suit. Tonight, he looked every bit the successful artiste with his beaming smile, olive complexion and long black hair tamed and glistening due to the copious application of Murray's Hair Glo that Sofia had purchased that very morning, insisting that both he and Jack smarten up for the exhibition. Jack, Sofia and Margaret hovered, sharing Andrés' excitement, but after a while, they left him to answer questions from journalists eager to submit their articles describing the latest 'emergent artiste' in the French morning newspapers.

They began moving through the rest of the prize-winning works. Jack was surprised to see he had won the Academy prize for portraiture, his painting of Sofia positioned prominently in the centre of the display.

Sofia stared in amazement, her bright eyes expressing a range of emotions from surprise, to pride, to amazement, to feigned annoyance.

'Jack, it is wonderful,' she said, unable to stop looking at the painting of herself so beautifully executed. Jack was relieved to see she was pleased at the scene he had been painting at the atelier in secret. In it, Sofia sat cross-legged, a hint of the large bed in the background, a bare knee visible, her right hand holding a swath of flowing linen across her breasts, her left hand freeing a tangle of gleaming black curls from her bare shoulders. Jack had captured an expression of playful joy as Sofia gazed into the eyes of viewers, her smooth skin glowing with radiant beauty.

'Well!' said Margaret. 'Can't say that you've been wasting your time in Paris!'

Jack beamed at her comment. He, too, believed this was the best work he had ever painted, revealing not only the progression of his and Sofia's relationship but also his growth as an artist. A vast improvement from anything that he'd presented at Charleston four months earlier.

'I can't believe that you're heading back to Melbourne, Jack. You have such an opportunity here! The women would be clamouring for you to paint their portraits. Society women. You could be the most coveted portrait painter in Paris!'

'Jack does not need to be painting French society women,' Sofia retorted half-jokingly, as she placed a possessive arm on his.

'No, of course not. It would be ghastly really, I suppose. But he should be riding the wave of opportunity here! I'd hate to see him sink into obscurity back into Australia.'

'Hey, don't I get a say?' Jack interrupted. 'Firstly, I don't have any problem painting the young women of Paris... and I'm quite sure that Melbourne women would be equally....' A punch in the arm from Sofia, accompanied by her warning look, stifled his words.

'Well, I just hope you know what you are doing! Long-distance relationships can be hard work... and from Spain to Australia...' Margaret shrugged before continuing, 'Once you get back into old routines, the magic of your Parisian affair may very well seem like a distant memory!' She glared at them both warningly and they laughed at her stern face.

'I won't let him forget me, Margaret,' Sofia replied. 'If I don't get a letter every day, I promise you that I will swim the Indian Ocean and bang on his door!'

∽

Just on eight-thirty, Andrés joined Sofia, Jack and Margaret in the foyer for speeches that formally acknowledged the winning artists before the media, special guests, dignitaries, friends and families. Jack and over a dozen other artists received their awards before the prestigious gold medal winner was announced.

They cheered wildly as Andrés was called to the stage and listened with enthusiasm as the director of *Académie Julian* spoke of Andrés' extraordinary talent and the important role the Academy played in exposing new artists. Finally, he presented Andrés with a framed certificate bearing the academy's crest, a cheque for two hundred francs and a semester of free tuition, including accommodation on the school's premises, which he could take at any time over the next three years, followed by a personal exhibition on completion of his residency. It was a wonderful opportunity and the prestigious prize would open doors to Andrés. Furthermore, his success in Paris would be widely reported to enthusiastic Spanish reaction.

Andrés responded with a brief thank-you speech in halting French, acknowledging the wonderful teaching of the Academy and Monsieur Simon and the loving support of his sister, aunt and friends. However, overcome with emotion coupled with yet another bout of coughing, he had to break off, finishing to cheers with a wave of his hand.

$\sim$

At nine-thirty, the foursome left the exhibition for supper at the Carrefour Vavin to celebrate the evening's success. They pushed through the crowded room to find a table at the back. In true Montparnasse style, the voices laughing and calling out over each other were heavily accented. A number of students from the Academy had also arrived from the exhibition and led a round of congratulations for Andrés. He was clapped on the back by everyone in hearing distance, causing one more coughing fit and, this time, Sofia rushed to get him a glass of water. As he drank it, she asked if he wanted to go home for a rest.

'I'm fine, Sofia, it has just been a big day,' Andrés replied. 'A big month, in fact. Tonight, we are here to celebrate. Tomorrow, we can lie down and rest.' Noticing Margaret and Jack's concerned expressions, he continued, 'She thinks she is my mother! Every little sniffle I get and she wants me in bed with lozenges and a vaporiser!'

At that moment they were interrupted by a teary-eyed Spaniard with the paint-splattered garments of a fellow artist who reached out to hug Andrés and kiss him on each cheek.

'Bless you, my brother! Tonight, you are the toast of Spain! You make our country proud! We Spaniards will show the world how great we are, won't we, boy?'

Jack and Sofia openly indulged in their affection for each other, his arm firmly around her shoulder. They interspersed passionate kisses with glasses of wine. She did not have to drag him onto the dance floor tonight, for he was in high spirits and fine form. However, while his confidence had improved in proportion to the alcohol he had consumed, Jack's skills were those of a man with two left feet, provoking hilarity as he tripped around, trying out a few moves of his own as he twirled and wheeled Sofia. They laughed, drank, kissed and danced as if staging their own personal farewell party and intending to enjoy every minute of it. Time for sorrow later.

'I love you, Jack,' Sofia breathed into his ear.

Pulling her close, Jack ran his hands down her back caressingly, oblivious to the crowded room. 'I love you too, Sofia.'

'Aww,' crooned the singer, microphone in hand, catching sight of them from his elevated position on the small stage. 'Seems we have a pair of lovebirds on the floor. How about we sing a special song for them, everyone?'

He opened with the line 'Tell me about love...' and the crowd joined in, rendering a somewhat raucous rendition of Lucienne Boyer's popular tune, 'Parlez-moi d'amour' as Sofia laughed hysterically, doing her best to remain upright as Jack twirled her with so much enthusiasm, she almost landed on her rear. The crowd clapped when they reached the final notes, and Jack and Sofia joined hands and acknowledged their applause with exaggerated bows before leaving the floor and weaving through the crowded tables to the back of the room where Margaret and Andrés were seated.

'What do you think?' said Sofia, glancing meaningfully at Jack. 'Time to go home?'

Andrés and Margaret nodded in agreement and stood up, the movement prompting yet another of his coughing fits. Concern crossed Sofia's face. 'Are you all right, Andrés?' she asked sharply in Spanish. Jack and Margaret watched as he tried to bring his breathing under control, his face pale with a sheen of perspiration across his forehead.

'I'm okay,' he replied. 'Just tired. It has been a long day.'

'No, Andrés. No,' Sofia insisted, 'You are not all right. You must sit down. Immediately.'

'Sofia, don't fuss.' Andrés waved her away, but she refused to be deterred.

'No, sit down. Now!' As she spoke, surprising Jack with the harshness of her directive, Andrés swayed and fell back into his seat. She glanced at Jack as she rushed to Andrés' side. 'It is his heart,' she said with quiet urgency. 'We need an ambulance. *En esto momento.*'

CHAPTER 29

Sobriety rapidly returned to Jack as he watched Andrés' lips and mouth turning blue and his head tilting forward onto the table. 'Ambulance, ambulance,' he shouted with rising panic, pushing through the crowd towards the entrance. Parting before him, others also took up the cry. A French diner sitting nearby leapt into action and followed Jack to the bar. With a quick nod towards Jack, he spoke in rapid French to the bar-man. '*Appelez une ambulance. Immédiatement!*' Without comment, the barman reached for the phone.

Returning to the table, Jack assisted Sofia and Margaret as they pushed chairs aside and eased Andrés onto the floor. He was conscious of a quietness in the room and the faces of shocked onlookers, watching with concern. Two young men, possibly Greek by their accents, assisted by moving tables farther aside to create a clearing around Andrés. 'We thought he'd just drank too much wine,' the taller one said to Jack ruefully. 'Is he going to be okay?'

They watched Sofia, who, with tears running down her face, was on her knees beside Andrés. They listened as she chided both him and herself. 'You were working too hard. I should have been taking better care of you,' she said, while smoothing his forehead. She then loosened his collar and unbuttoned his shirt.

Within minutes, uniformed officers appeared at the entry of the café and were quickly ushered towards the back of the room, where Andrés now lay panting in rapid, shallow breaths, his eyes closed.

Assessing the seriousness of his condition at once, the senior officer spoke to Sofia. 'We must take him to hospital immediately.'

'It's his heart,' Sofia told them. 'He was ill years ago and was left with a bad heart.'

Jack and Margaret were shocked by the sudden turn of events – stunned and confused by the rapid deterioration in their friend. Standing side by side, Margaret gripped Sofia's hand while the officers carefully lifted Andrés onto their stretcher. They followed as the officers wove between the tables, carrying Andrés to the street where the ambulance was parked, and watched helplessly as the stretcher was slid into position. A concerned-looking Frenchman murmured to the ambulance officers and then approached Jack. 'Allow me to take you to the hospital,' he offered. 'My car is just around the corner. We will be there in minutes.'

Gratefully, they accepted his offer, and he led them down a side lane to where his vehicle was parked. The Cabriolet's motor spluttered into life and the Good Samaritan eased his vehicle out, following flashing lights of the ambulance along darkened cobblestone streets to the Hôpital de la Pitié, Paris' largest public hospital.

They were silent as the driver navigated the streets before drawing the vehicle to a standstill before the hospital's main entrance. With a quick 'Thank you, sir – so very much. You are truly a saint,' Sofia leapt out and ran towards the emergency entrance. There, the ambulance that had transported Andrés was visible, its back doors wide open, no sign of the stretcher. Ignoring the 'No entry' sign, she pushed through the swinging doors of the emergency department.

'Thank you so much, I don't know what we would have done,' Jack said as he and Margaret stepped out of the vehicle.

'It was nothing,' he replied, introducing himself as Francois Dumas – Dr Dumas – a psychiatric specialist who worked at the *Salpêtriére*, next door.

'I suggest you go up to the waiting room – just to the left at the top of the stairs. I will find out what is happening and let your friend know where you are, yes?' he offered.

Nodding appreciatively, Jack and Margaret headed up the stairs.

'What's happening, Jack?' Margaret asked him. 'Has Andrés been sick lately?'

Jack shook his head. 'Not really. Just his cough. He's always got that. I barely notice it, really. He's been tired lately, but I guess, with all the preparation for the exhibition... Sofia is always at him to rest. I thought she was just being motherly. You know how she fusses over him!'

They were interrupted by the return of a grave-faced Dr Dumas. He informed them that Andrés was very ill, but in good hands and receiving the best treatment possible. He'd told Sofia that they were in the waiting room, and he expected that she would not be too long.

Expressing his hopes that all went well, Dr Dumas left and Jack and Margaret sat in disbelief. Andrés ill! Gravely ill! Sure, Sofia had mentioned that Andrés had been ill as a child. Jack recalled his antics in the parks and the joy he gained from teasing small children. Sofia had told him those tricks were honed when Andrés was in the hospital for months, bored, and gained amusement from making the sick children smile. But Jack had thought that those days were well in the past.

He and Margaret again commented on the cough – worse tonight for sure, they agreed, but they'd never sensed it was anything serious. More like a winter cough that was slow to go away.

What seemed like hours later, Sofia appeared before them.

'He's going to be all right, thank God!' she said in a wavering voice. 'They have him settled now.' She led them back to Andrés, not wanting to leave him any longer than necessary.

Andrés looked somehow smaller as he lay very still, eyes closed, in the narrow iron bed, its starched sheets pulled up to his shoulders. He looked all the paler, with his black hair and white face startling against the whiteness of the hospital linen. Although the sheen of perspiration remained visible, his breathing had settled into a steady rhythm, the blueness around his mouth had receded and he appeared peaceful.

'What happened?' Margaret asked.

In a subdued voice, Sofia explained that Andrés had caught the Spanish flu when he was fifteen. While he had been a lucky survivor of the terrible plague which had killed over fifty million people, not just in Spain but throughout the world, it had left him with a weak heart. At the time he had been put into isolation where the doctors had tried a range of treatments, including oxygen therapy and bloodletting. Finally, Andrés had been injected with blood taken from recovered patients, which seemed to be the most effective treatment. Sofia and her father did not see him for months, as Andrés had been sent to a sanatorium and then to a small seaside convalescent home in Nerfa to recover. Twice since then, he had been struck down, his heart succumbing to weakness, usually when he was tired. But it had not happened for many years. Up until now, that is. Sofia had been sure Andrés had outgrown the disease's pernicious hold.

Her explanation was interrupted when a tall, thin nurse in a starched uniform and a broad head veil appeared at the door, a look of impatience on her face.

'*Dehors, dehors,*' she said, her hands flapping and leaving no doubts about her demand. 'You mustn't be here. He needs... rest. We will look after him. Come back tomorrow – visiting hours. Ten-thirty. Go.' She ushered them towards the exit.

Sofia, Jack and Margaret retreated as directed, stepping out into the night air. Jack's watch told them it was now almost two-thirty am, the only sound their footsteps echoing on the pavement. It reinforced a surreal atmosphere, fatigue and shock rendering them silent. Margaret's hotel was closest so, after a brief discussion, they decided it would be best to bunk there for the night.

~

The next morning, following a half-hearted attempt to swallow bagels and coffee at Margaret's insistence, they stood at the entrance of the hospital at ten o'clock. Hospital rules were strict, forcing the gathering crowd of visitors to wait – many were foreigners or the poor of Paris, united in their concern for a loved one lying in a hospital bed. In the morning light, the beauty of the building with its grand tree-lined avenue, magnificent domed clock-tower and enormous stone arches stood in conflict with the multitude of dramas unfolding in the lives of those confined within its stone walls. Jack, Sofia and Margaret watched the ticking clock, visible in the foyer, until a loud gong indicated the half hour and the entrance doors swung open.

They half-ran along the shiny linoleum floors of the corridor and turned up the stairs to the second level where they had left Andrés the night before. Sofia gasped in horror when they found curtains drawn around his bed. Andrés lay very still, except for his rapid breathing, a noisy rattle vibrating through his chest on each exhalation.

Gently holding his hand, Sofia did not speak, while Margaret and Jack stood helplessly watching. The same nurse that had been in attendance the previous night appeared, this time with a doctor at her side.

'You are his sister, yes?' he asked, tilting his head and peering at Sofia through pince-nez glasses balanced on his hooked nose. He wore a serious expression on his long, thin face.

Sofia nodded. 'Will he be okay?'

'Let us hope so,' he replied. 'He is very ill. Tell me, what has brought this on?'

He listened, nodding as Sofia described how the lethal flu had swept through Málaga in 1918, with Andrés one of the many people captured in its deadly snare. Since then, she explained, Andrés tended to fatigue easily, and his heart would race, leaving him breathless. She told the doctor how they had come to Paris to attend *Académie Julian* and how hard Andrés had been working, again blaming herself for not caring for him properly.

The doctor took Sofia's hand in his, shaking his head at her words. 'My dearest girl, you cannot blame yourself for an illness like this. It is like blaming yourself for when the snow falls or where the wind blows. Your brother's illness left him with a weak heart. He lived. Thousands died. Sometimes these things just are. We will get him better, and you will take him home, yes. You will look after him. But,' he cautioned quietly, 'this will not be the last time, I am very sad to tell you. This will happen again. Next time may be the last time, I fear. Málaga will be warm. It will be good for him to be home on your beautiful Mediterranean Sea.'

Producing a stethoscope, the doctor placed it on Andrés' chest and moved it from side to side, asking Andrés to hold his breath while he listened carefully. Jack, like Sofia and Margaret, searched his face for an indication of his findings. However, the doctor's features were inscrutable.

Rising suddenly, he told the nurse that they needed to commence serum therapy at once, and he would return that evening to check Andrés' progress. He returned his gaze to Sofia, Jack and Margaret and it became stern.

'Andrés needs rest, lots of rest. We must be very careful that he does not get more infections. These bacteria, they are very nasty. So - one visit for half an hour in the morning, each day. No more, until we get him better. No touching. Masks. Eh?' Returning his eyes to Sofia, his eyes softened. 'Be brave, pray, and, if God wills, you will take your brother home.'

Sofia nodded, though she looked miserable. She clasped her hands together, clearly resisting the urge to touch Andrés'. Jack guessed that she felt exactly as he did, suddenly contagious, a grubby carrier of the worst kinds of bacteria that threatened Andrés' life. As though germs were emitting from their breaths and teeming over their hands. He found himself clenching his fists close to his sides as if to contain them as they left the ward.

~

Descending the hospital's main entrance stairwell, they walked along the tree-lined driveway of the Hôpital de la Pitié in silence. The sun's rays piercing the leafy boughs struck Jack as discordant. His mind raced. Today he was meant to be packing, preparing for his return to London on tomorrow's night ferry, but that was now out of the question. There was no way that he was going to leave Sofia on her own to look after her brother. It could be weeks before Andrés was ready to travel. There could be all manner of setbacks. Heaven forbid, Andrés might even die without ever leaving the hospital walls. Jack was sure Mrs Rix would not mind if he stayed on at her apartment for a while longer. Although perhaps if he got a room nearer to the hospital, it would make things easier for Sofia to visit Andrés. Give her a place to spend the hours between hospital visits. She and Andrés had planned to stay with their aunt for two more weeks while he completed his commissions for Miss Stein's clients. Sofia had planned to follow up on gallery contacts who had requested the right to represent the award-winning artist. She hoped that they might accept Andrés' remaining works rather than leaving the twins to transport them back to Málaga. Jack's too, she'd offered. He'd agreed, laughing at the idea of having an agent representing him in Paris. Today, such plans seemed to belong to another life.

Taking Sofia's hand, he felt her fragility and, although knowing that the fineness of her fingers had no bearing on the strength of her character, he wanted to protect and support her, anyway. 'I am not going to leave you, Sofia. I promise that I will stay here with you until Andrés is ready to go home.'

Sofia smiled and squeezed his hand by way of reply, tears welling. She appeared exhausted, utterly drained, having had no sleep for almost two days and facing the overwhelming emotional toll of first, the plans for Jack's departure, and now, Andrés' illness.

As they turned onto the street, Margaret took command. She steered them towards the familiar striped awning and brightly coloured umbrellas of a café.

'How about we sit and make some plans?'

They settled themselves and, if only to justify their seats, Jack ordered hot chocolate for each of them.

He took the lead. 'I think I'll find a place to stay in the fifth arrondissement. Somewhere near to the hospital. I can start looking this afternoon and then I'll collect my belongings from the Passage Dantzig. Sofia, you are exhausted. You will need to get some sleep.' She did not object.

'How about I take you back to my hotel this afternoon, Sofia?' Margaret offered. 'You can sleep until three and then we can head back to ask how Andrés is. They may not let you see him, but at least we can get a progress report.'

Sofia agreed. 'He'll be much better by then, I'm sure. There is no way that Andrés will miss an opportunity to become Spain's next great artist!'

'Sofia, do you think I should get you a room near the hospital also? Then we'll be able to go back and forth to the hospital more easily.' Without openly saying it, Jack was really thinking that, if Andrés health deteriorated, it would be good for them to be together, as close to the hospital as possible.

'But Jack, I will stay with you,' Sofia replied. 'It is too much money to pay for two rooms. A waste!'

'I will pay, Sofia. I have plenty of savings, plus I have the money from Miss Stein's exhibition.'

'But I want to stay with you, Jack. Save your money,' Sofia persisted, reaching out for his hand.

'Don't worry, in a few months, I will come and freeload on you and Andrés in Málaga. Consider it advance payment,' he said, ignoring the real intent of her words. Although tempted to accept that fate was throwing them together, Jack was not prepared to take advantage of the circumstances. Sofia was not in the right mind to make decisions, especially those that so publicly defied social conventions. While Margaret's family, the eccentric Bloomsburys, might stretch boundaries without a care for the opinion of others, Jack was pretty sure that most people would frown if he and Sofia shared an apartment. Furthermore, Jack was sure that Andrés would agree.

Margaret nodded her agreement to Jack's plan.

'Don't worry, Sofia,' she said with a wry smile. 'Jack will get you a room on the same floor as his. The corridor will be short. It's not what you do that matters. It is what you are seen to do. Same the world over.' She laughed with uncharacteristic bitterness, again making Jack wonder about the shadows that seemed to lurk in Margaret's past.

∾

The Hôtel Lecourbe, an impressive five-storey apartment building whose impressive facade suggested past grandeur, was run by a tiny English lady with snow white hair piled into an intricate bun that sat high on her head. She was used to catering for the relatives of patients and struck the right balance of sympathetic-efficiency as she organised rooms for Jack. Only two blocks from the hospital, an easy five-minute walk, it was a perfect location. After quickly checking the rooms he had booked for the coming week, Jack returned to the street and waved down a taxi. Being Saturday afternoon, the streets of Montparnasse were quiet, although, turning into the Passage Dantzig, Jack was reminded of his first day in Paris. Like then, the street was livening up as sleepy artists emerged to enjoy the sunshine, clustering together, setting up chairs and sharing their bottles of wine. He glanced into the courtyard of La Ruche, marvelling at the dome-shaped building, still cluttered with oddments of furniture and a pile of bicycle parts, and felt a slight pang of regret that he'd never really got to know any of the artists who rented the cheap rooms within. He knew they would have had many interesting stories to share.

Entering the apartment for the last time, Jack looked around. For all of his time in Paris, this apartment had been little more than a bed to him, although in recent weeks, he and Sofia had sought its solitude on more than one occasion. He piled his belongings into his suitcase, loaded the sheets into a laundry basket ready to pass on to Mimi and scribbled a note to Mrs Rix, thanking her for letting him stay. Looking again at the photographs depicting the smiling face of the woman he had never met, Jack added that he hoped they might cross paths at some time in the future and sat the note on the table beside where her original letter to him still lay.

Closing the door, he descended the stairs for the last time and found Mimi waiting in the foyer. She listened to Jack's hurried explanation, expressing sorrow for the trouble that had befallen his friends. She had grown fond of the young Australian who'd always paid his rent on time, lived quietly and avoided the ruckus that befell many of the poor artists who lived in the Passage, where wine and women, in varying combinations, frequently led to the demise of many men. She promised to attend to the bed linen and, when Jack apologised for leaving the bicycle cluttering her storeroom, Mimi waved away his words. Someone would find a use for it, she said.

On the return journey, Jack asked the taxi driver to drop him at a small row of shops just near the Hotel Lecourbe, where he purchased two postcards. As soon as he entered his room, Jack wasted no time scribbling his messages. The first was to his parents, explaining the unexpected crisis that had landed Andrés in hospital and his decision to remain in Paris and support Sofia at this critical time. He would return to Australia when Andrés was well enough to undertake the long journey to Málaga. The second postcard provided the same information to Aunt Elizabeth and Uncle Robert, and Jack wondered if they would receive it prior to his expected arrival on their doorstep in two days' time.

～

Margaret reluctantly left for London on the Sunday afternoon train, and before boarding she made Jack promise to send her postcards with news of Andrés' progress. Without being specific, she also said that if they needed her, she would be on the next ferry across the Channel – all they had to do was ask. With tears in her eyes, she hugged Sofia, with no guarantee when she would see her or Andrés again. Turning to Jack, she reminded him to phone the New Burlington Gallery the minute he was in London. Freddie would give her the message that he'd arrived and she would visit him in Surrey.

After nodding in agreement to Margaret's barrage of instructions, Jack and Sofia stood hand-in-hand, waving as her train vanished into the distance.

Their next stop was to Aunt Christina's apartment. The older woman was still reeling from the news of Andrés' collapse and did not hide her tears. She nodded in agreement that Sofia should move to the Hotel Lecourbe, understanding her desire to be closer to the hospital. Furthermore, Aunt Christina thanked Jack for looking after Sofia. In doing so, she emphasised that Sofia was a 'good girl' repeatedly, and it occurred to Jack that her comments were an appeal for him to guard Sofia's virtue!

The next few days were fraught with emotion for Jack and Sofia, as Andrés' temperature soared and the bloodletting failed to offer any improvement. Each morning they woke with their hearts in their mouth, unsure of how he had passed the night, and only on seeing Andrés did they relax with the knowledge that at least he had not deteriorated further. After their morning visits, Jack and Sofia sat at the Café Eiffel, named for the clear view of the landmark tower it offered, and over lunch they analysed every nuance of Andrés' condition, from his increasing pallor, attributed to the lack of sunshine, to his quiet manner, deemed the consequence of depression, and his thinness, a natural response to the unappetising hospital food nurses attempted to spoon into his dry mouth. Further, they dissected every comment made by the doctor, trying to interpret his ambiguous statements, debating what 'could be' and 'suggests' might actually mean.

After the first week, Andrés was allowed to have afternoon visitors for one hour, and Jack found a deck of cards to help them pass the time. After ten days, Andrés' humour improved, and he kept complaining that Sofia was staring morbidly at him, assessing his weight, colour and heart rate. They finally agreed that Andrés was well on the road to recovery when he began greeting Sofia each morning as 'Matron' and asking for her verdict on whether he might live or die.

～

As Andrés' condition improved, Jack and Sofia ventured out onto the streets of Paris in the evenings, holding hands and wandering without any destination in mind, sitting in one café or another – they had all started to look the same - and leaning into each other in quiet darkened corners. However, Sofia found it difficult to relax, knowing that Andrés was lying in his hospital bed. Furthermore, Andrés' recovery had a bittersweetness for, while they hoped desperately for news that he was ready to be discharged, that news also would mean it was time for them to say goodbye.

It was at the beginning of Andrés' third week that the doctor suggested they could, perhaps, think of discharging him, if his temperature stayed down and his heart rate remained stable for the next week. However, later in the morning, as Jack and Sofia were leaving Andrés, they met his doctor on the stairs. Again, they expressed their gratitude to him for making Andrés well and their pleasure that he would be discharged in a few days.

'Again, I must remind you,' he warned them sternly. 'Andrés' heart, it is bad. Very bad. He will need to be careful. Not too much excitement. Home is the best place for him, that is for certain.' He then looked at Jack warningly. 'No alcohol, no late nights. You must look after your friend.'

The weighty words sent a shiver down Jack's spine and, for some strange reason, he thought of Picasso. The tale he had told about his blue period, and the paintings he'd produced when he was a similar age to Jack, following the death of his friend. He recalled Picasso's words: "Jack, you are too fat... Life is not always nice... One day you will starve a little. One day you will feel pain. You will learn to tell the story... paint truth... Then you will say, now I'm a great artist. Hey, hey... now I am great like Picasso!"

Jack thought to himself with a shudder, *I'd rather never paint again than suffer the loss of Andrés.*

$\sim$

Finally, it was agreed that Andrés could be discharged on Friday, after the doctor's round at ten am. Three days away. This triggered a flurry of planning, as Sofia and Andrés both preferred to set off to Málaga immediately, for his convalescence. Back to the warmth, routine and comfort of Andrés' own home, where they each believed that his health would be quickly restored.

Jack volunteered to go to the railway station and purchase Sofia's and Andrés' tickets for their journey from Paris to Málaga and, with a heaviness of heart, he set off.

Though he was glad for the twins to be returning to their home, the thought of saying goodbye and setting out on his own long journey back to Australia caused an ache in Jack's heart that was hard to ignore. While they occasionally referred to his plan to visit Spain later in the year, Sofia was clearly distracted by thoughts of getting Andrés home. Knowing she was excited about her brother's discharge and focusing her energies on getting him well, all Jack could do was hide his feelings and maintain a positive attitude that he did not feel. He could not deny that he was seriously wondering whether their dreams of a future together were just that: dreams. He loved Sofia, without a doubt, but could not imagine her ever leaving her home or brother, especially with Andrés' failing health. And although he could imagine visiting the twins in Málaga, he could not begin to imagine a life for himself in Spain. He couldn't just paint the days away, as Sofia seemed to think. Nor did it seem right to expect to live at their gallery. He needed a real job. What would he do? Where could he find work? He had no training. He needed to gain some qualifications and earn a good income so he could provide for Sofia. Jack hoped that perhaps his few months of experience with Goldsbrough Mort & Co would count for something when he returned. Everything was so uncertain and just thinking about it depressed him.

After booking two tickets to Málaga via Barcelona and Madrid for Saturday afternoon, with a heavy heart, Jack booked his own ticket to London. While he was dealing with business, he sent brief postcards:

Dear Aunt Elizabeth,

I will be leaving Paris for London this week. Hope you don't mind a surprise guest for a week or so while I organise a passage home. Looking forward to seeing you both. Should be sometime on Tuesday.

As an afterthought, he added,

Uncle Robert, you might like to warm up the cards and prepare yourself for a thrashing!

Love,

Jack

· · ·

The postcard to his parents was more difficult, as Jack could not begin to pretend he was looking forward to the trip home.

Dear Mum and Dad,

Andrés has made a good recovery, thankfully, and is being discharged from hospital on Friday. He and Sofia will commence their journey home to Spain on Saturday afternoon. I have booked my trip to London, and will organise my passage home from there.

Love,

Jack

Posting the cards through the slot, Jack was overwhelmed with a sense of finality. Business done. Their respective futures, at least for the present, determined. All there was left to do now was to pack.

He smiled wryly at Sofia as he placed the train tickets on the table in what had been her room for the last three weeks. She reached out to him and held him in a long embrace. 'I know, Jack. It is hard. It is hard for me also,' she whispered softly as she pulled him onto her bed.

~

Dusk was settling over Paris as they lay together and discussed the day's events. As if to prevent any further conversation about their approaching separation, Sofia gave Jack a detailed description of her morning. She'd visited the two galleries that had shown the most interest in their work, and both had been happy to accept Jack and Andrés' paintings on consignment. Jack was surprised when he heard that Sofia had told the galleries she and Andrés would return to Paris the following summer. It seemed to him that she was refusing to accept the precarious nature of Andrés' health, but like her, he was very pleased for Andrés to know his work would be displayed in Paris.

They considered whether to go out on the town for a last evening, but neither had the heart for bright lights. Instead they dined at the small café near the hospital, enjoying its good food and familiar presence, before returning to the hotel to spend a final night together.

∾

It was hard to know who was most excited when they arrived at the hospital the next morning. Andrés sat in the chair beside his bed, looking strange in street clothes rather than the pinstriped pyjamas he had been wearing for the past four weeks. The clothing Sofia had provided yesterday hung loosely across his shoulders and his wrists looked pale and thin, highlighting the significant weight he'd lost. His face lit up immediately on seeing them.

'Thank goodness you are here!' cried the morning nurse, and Jack was pleased to see it was Carla, their favourite, whose bright mood and quick humour always made them laugh. Today, she was briskly cleaning the wooden chest by Andrés' bed. 'I swear he was going to walk right out of here if you had not arrived in another minute. I threatened I would be getting the manacles and strapping him to the chair if he didn't calm down.'

In turn, Sofia's joy that Andrés was finally healthy enough to take home overflowed in nonstop chatter about every detail of the planned journey to the Costa del Sol, even though he had heard it all the previous day.

Carla was clearly sorry to see Andrés discharged, and jokingly offered her services to transport him to southern Spain anytime–all he needed to do was say the word and she would be at the station. She'd even wear her nurse's uniform if it pleased him.

Their laughter led to a spasm of coughing, which Andrés brought under control with a sip of the water a frowning Sofia handed to him.

'Don't look at me like that! I am fine... Come on, let's get out of here.' And to prove his point, Andrés grabbed at his bag, which was quickly retrieved by Jack, and stood, ready to leave.

'Take me away, Matron, and I warn you, if you are half as cranky as the nurse here,' – he winked cheekily at Carla – 'I will be throwing myself over the castle wall into the Mediterranean Sea.'

Despite his bravado, even Andrés was surprised at just how tired he felt after walking down the long corridors of the hospital, dealing with the particulars required to enable him to sign out at the discharge desk and riding the taxi two blocks to the Hotel Lecourbe. After a cup of tea and some sweet biscuits, they left him, tucked in Jack's bed, where he slept through most of the afternoon. He woke for a few hours for a light supper and, pleading fatigue, he looked relieved to escape back to his bed to get a good night's rest before the next day's journey.

CHAPTER 30

*I*t seemed incredible to Jack that everything about the Gare du Nord felt so normal the next day, as if they were meeting Margaret or catching the Métro on one of their afternoon adventures. Instead, today they were lugging three heavy cases and lining up on the station's platform. Departure time had arrived for Sofia and Andrés, and the carriage before them, its engine slowly rumbling, would take them via the Pyrenees to Madrid, where they would arrive late tomorrow afternoon. Following an overnight rest, Sofia and Andrés would then continue the journey to the southern Andalusian region, arriving at Málaga on Monday afternoon. Just thinking about it - the enormous distance about to come between himself and Sofia-caused a tightening in Jack's chest.

Andrés, despite his weakened state, was the only one who appeared anywhere near normal, as Sofia and Jack had long lapsed into a silence so heavy that it hovered like a thunderous cloud over the three of them.

Jack's mind filled with a buzzing that drowned out his thoughts and, subsequently, no words would come.

'Are you right, mate?' he'd managed, directed to Andrés a couple of times when his cough returned, or 'Let me take that,' to Sofia as she wrestled her suitcase through the turnstile at the train's platform.

Sofia just looked stony and glum. Nothing about this farewell matched anything Jack had imagined. Teary romantic embraces. Passionate lovers' kisses. Joyful plans for their reunion in January. Perhaps they had exhausted words. *January is not that far away. Time will fly. We'll be together before we know it.* Rah–rah–rah. Perhaps they just did not believe those words anymore amid the starkness of the cold, hard walls of the station on the cooling afternoon.

'What was that seat's number?' Andrés asked Sofia and, turning to Jack, he extended his hand. 'Thanks, Jack. Mate,' he added with a tired smile as he grasped Jack's hand and shook it firmly. His expression bore a tinge of sadness at the separation from this friend of whom he had grown so fond. 'Thanks for everything. I look forward to seeing you in January. You have a safe trip, too.'

Andrés turned and stepped onto the train with a final wave.

Left alone amid dozens of fellow commuters, who bustled around them, jostling suitcases onto the carriage and calling out final farewells, Jack gazed at Sofia. Then he pulled her tightly to his chest, kissing her face, hair and mouth, wondering if the unfamiliar salty taste on his lips was coming from his own tears or hers.

'You take care on this trip. Look after Andrés. And look after yourself. I will be there as soon as I can,' he whispered. He inhaled deeply as if committing the sweet, familiar aroma of her shiny hair to his memory, and then his hands gripped the sides of her face and he looked deeply into her eyes. 'I love you, Sofia. I'll write every day! And you must write back. Tell me everything!'

Sofia nodded a silent reply, tears raining down her cheeks, as the porter's whistle blew to announce the train's imminent departure. 'I love you too, Jack. Yes, I will write!'

She boarded the train, her hand still held firm in his as the train started to move along the track, slowly at first and gradually picking up speed.

'Step back, behind the line,' a stationmaster called in a singsong voice as Jack's pace increased alongside the open door of the train. Still, his hand refused to release its hold on Sofia.

A deafening blast emitted from the train's horn as the engine accelerated yet again and Jack started jogging to keep up. Glancing ahead, he could see the blackness of the tunnel. The platform end was looming closer. For a split second, he looked into Sofia's eyes, as if to ask a question, but her only reply was a look of terror. With a jolt, Jack realised that she might well feel at risk of being pulled through the open doorway, onto the hard surface of the platform, so tight was his grip.

Thinking no more, Jack executed a determined launch, landing inside the carriage. He clutched at Sofia, who gasped with surprise, as she tried to regain her balance.

'Jack, what are you doing?' she asked, her eyes wide.

'Yes, young man… What do you think you are doing?' came the stern voice of the carriage conductor, although the smile in his eyes indicated that the couple's embrace had already answered his question. 'I suppose you have a ticket–yes?'

Looking at him ruefully, Jack shrugged, not quite sure what his best response would be.

'I'll see you in Madrid and we will get your ticket sorted,' the conductor said and turned on his heel, leaving them alone.

His arms around her, Jack grinned wryly. 'Looks like I am coming to Spain!'

Again, Sofia's tears flowed as she clung to him, holding his face in her hands, kissing him over and over.

Then grasping his hand, she led him through the carriage to where Andrés leaned back in his seat. He turned his head towards them as they approached him.

Smiling, without any sign of surprise at all, he adopted Jack's Australian expression. 'Mate! So good of you to come and visit us. Didn't expect you'd take long.' He cleared his bag off the seat beside him to make a space for Jack.

'Might have to borrow a brush or two. And a shirt. And some

pants,' Jack replied happily. In his spontaneity, everything he owned was sitting on the platform in a neat pile.

'Not a worry. I am sure the Matron here will have us both sorted out in no time.'

Jack took a deep breath as he returned his gaze to Sofia, her face a picture of sheer joy.

His parents' gift, the ticket to London, had offered the promise of a thrilling adventure. Never had he imagined the worlds that would be revealed to him. The Bloomsburys with their eccentric ways, life as an art student in Paris, his deep friendship with Andrés and now, the woman of his dreams who sat beside him. To think that he was here; seated on a creaking, rattling train that was transporting him south to the Costa del Sol and the world of Andrés and Sofia. A world he knew nothing about. Jack could barely contain his excitement.

The End of Book One

CONTINUE THE SERIES HERE!

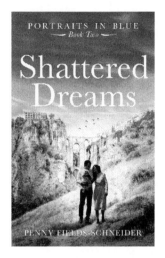

Shattered Dreams

Would you like to continue reading the Portraits in Blue series?

Book Two: Shattered Dreams takes you into the world of the twins finca in Malaga, Spain. In this idyllic setting, Jack experiences the pleasures of a simple life as an artist, and is captivated by the charming traditions of Spanish life. All is not perfect, however, and miscommunication sends Jack into despair as the love he and Sofia share is threatened.

Circumstances force Jack to bring Sofia to Australia, and they are drawn into the complex world of Montsalvat, an artists enclave led by the charismatic but overbearing Justus Jorgensen. Here, Jack and Sofia find a life that they love, but neither are prepared for the shocking events that threaten their very existence.

Shattered Dreams **brings alive the factual events of the modern art world of the early twentieth century entwined with a story of friendship, love and loss.**

'...Truly a great story, bringing me right into the rooms where the stories take place. The story is well wrought and fascinating...'

'The author's attention to detail, and her research are to be commended.

This is a very emotional read, and I can't recommend highly enough!'

READ NOW!

Portraits in Blue: Book Two
Shattered Dreams

DID YOU ENJOY BOOK ONE: THE SUN ROSE IN PARIS?

DID YOU ENJOY BOOK ONE: THE SUN ROSE IN PARIS?

If so, perhaps you might consider leaving a review at your favourite online bookstore, and helping others to find it!

I would be so appreciative if you would, because reviews
really … really … matter!

A PARTING NOTE FROM THE AUTHOR

When the idea for the *Portraits in Blue Series* came upon me, I had a few simple thoughts in mind.

My central character would be a Melbourne boy - Victoria being the state that I grew up in and Melbourne, a place that I love-increasingly more so as I return as an adult, wandering through the lively lanes buzzing with coffee shops, gourmet restaurants and wonderful stores all set amid the historical buildings of the city. If you've never been, I encourage you to go!

My story would set in England and Paris as well as Spain, somewhat satisfying my desire to know more about these places, all of which I have been fortunate enough to visit.

Montsalvat (Eltham, Victoria), would be pivotal. Although not revealed until Book Two, *Montsalvat* captured my imagination when I learned of it from my father when I was a young child. I had never forgotten his enthusiasm for this artists' enclave; however, I remembered little more of his comments beyond the name. My research revealed a location with a rich history and it was thrilling to find that it still functions as an artists' retreat as well as a tourist attraction and function centre. It is a fine testament to Justus Jorgensen's dream back in the 1930s, when he embarked on his ambitious, alternative building project, assisted by his cohorts of art students, some of whom remained with him for decades.

Unquestionably, I knew that art would be pivotal to the theme of my story in order to satisfy a desire to deepen my knowledge of the art world. From technical skills to history to famous paintings to the intriguing lives of artists, I wanted to know it all. I chose the 1930s as a period of interest that combined many of the events I wished to embrace. I have loved every minute of research and my thirst to learn more remains strong.

I intended my story to be underpinned by themes of relationships and love. These aspects of the story evolved organically as Jack became his own person and forged his own friendships, while I merely recorded the words of his emotional journey. I hope that you enjoy his friendships and romance as much as I enjoyed writing about them!

From the outset, I also decided that my story would serve as a memorial for a terrible tragedy that occurred in our family, over fifty years ago. Shocking as it was, I was determined to resurrect a fictitious version of events and honour a life that holds precious memories.

With these simple thoughts in mind, I laid out timelines and investigated art movements, individuals and historical events which aligned to give my story both authenticity and accuracy.

Finally, when as a first-time author, I embarked on writing this tale of a fictitious man's life wandering through the streets of 1930s Bohemia, interacting with lives both well and badly lived, I was oblivious to the potential legalities or otherwise of such a venture. I will say that I have made every effort to portray those real-life characters with respect and, where irresistible opportunities to include intriguing scandal and unpleasant behaviour arose, I have ensured that such events are on the public record and used eye-witness accounts as reference points to inform my writing. I have attempted to keep my imagined dialogue within the realms of the perceived nature of such characters. Hopefully, a modern account of these past events may serve to increase public interest in the lively art movements of the 1930s to new generations.

Penny Fields-Schneider

PENNY FIELDS-SCHNEIDER worked as a Registered Nurse before completing a Bachelor of Arts and Diploma of Education and henceforth, redesigning her life as a secondary teacher. An avid reader from a very young age, Penny has always aspired to be an author. In recent years, she became seduced by the world of art, dabbling with paint and brushes, attending art courses and visiting galleries. Penny aspires to create works of historical fiction that leave readers with a deeper understanding of the art world as well as taking them on emotional journeys into the joy and heartbreak that comes with family, friendship and love.

When Penny is not writing, she enjoys helping her husband on their cattle farm in northern NSW, loving every minute she can spend with their children, grandchildren, friends and family.

Penny would love to hear from her readers and you can join her newsletter or contact her through the following channels

Email PennyFieldsSchneider@gmail.com
Website
http://www.pennyfields-author.com

facebook.com/PennyFields-Schneider
instagram.com/pennyfieldsschneider

Let's Talk about Reading and Writing

I would love you to become a part of my writing journey. Subscribe to my monthly newsletter to learn more about the settings and characters in the Portraits in Blue series. Additionally, you will receive freebies including short stories and articles of interest and you will be the first to know when my books are available at discounted prices.

To join, drop me a message at pennyfieldsschneider@gmail.com

Acknowledgements

Thanks to the many people who have read and critiqued various drafts of the *Portraits in Blue* series. Cassie, Rosemary, Pauline and Jany - your collective feedback forced me to dig deeper to polish my manuscript.

Special thanks to Jacques-Noël Gouat for your unfaltering enthusiasm for The *Sun Rose in Paris*. The time you gave reviewing drafts to ensure the French components of the story were correct is hugely appreciated. If any inaccuracies remain, they are my own!

Thanks to the wonderful Tarkenberg, who patiently bore the grunt work of editing *The Sun Rose in Paris*. I appreciate your patience and many lessons along the way, as you've attempted to turn a very green, first-time writer into an author and a rough draft into a somewhat publishable manuscript. I am constantly in awe of your attention to detail and amused by your gentle humour!

To my husband and children, my enormous thanks for sharing in my all-consuming creative endeavours. Your support, encouragement and time spent reading drafts and listening patiently as I bounce the multitude of thoughts I have off your well-worn ears are much appreciated!

Made in the USA
Middletown, DE
29 July 2023